Maid For Your Master

Afipia Felis

Editor: Emily Paige
Cover Design: Eve A. Hard
Cover Photography: Mr. B. Felis

Publisher's Cataloging-in-Publication data

Names: Felis, Afipia, author.
Title: Maid for your master : Gravelorne Manor series , book one / Afipia Felis.
Series: Gravelorne Manor
Description: Cleveland, OH: Rosen-Hart Press, 2022.
Identifiers: LCCN: 2022906576 | ISBN: 979-8-9860924-0-9 (paperback) | 979-8-9860924-1-6 (ebook)
Subjects: LCSH Murder--Fiction. | Horror fiction. | Mystery fiction. | BISAC FICTION / Gothic | FICTION / Horror | FICTION / Fantasy / Dark Fantasy
Classification: LCC PS3606.E55 M35 2022 | DDC 813.6--dc23

A word of caution to unwitting readers:

This story is a **horror** story with dark romance elements in which "you" (the reader) play as the main character. The relationship portrayed in the book is, at best, unhealthy and more often, horrifying.

You are guaranteed that, by the end of book two, you'll get your man in a monogamous relationship. However, if the author has done her job properly, you will question whether or not that classic ending is really what you want.

If you ever watched a horror movie and said: "I would totally shag and bag the monster if I could be guaranteed to not die, be maimed, be permanently injured, or be physically tortured", this story is for you.

If that statement made you so much as raise an eyebrow, you should throw this book across the room and light it on fire.

Alternatively, if you believe forwarded is forearmed, please go to afipiafelis.com/tw for a list of the darker happenings in this story (may contain spoilers).

Author's Dedication:

To the sick kittens for whom that warning brought more anticipation than alarm: I wrote this for me, but you can read it if you want.

An Excerpt From:

"INAUGURAL LECTURE ON THE ORIGINS OF MANKIND"

—His Grace, Creipus the Pious
Head Cleric of the Holy Temple of Coriland

"When the flora and fauna of the world grew monotonous, the gods crafted two creations who could provide entertainment. The elder gods made the fae, beings of beauty and magic who shared their creator's likeness and longevity. The younger gods made mankind, beings of passion and dedication who shared their creator's hearts and spirit.

No one is certain when the fae realized their power over mankind. All that is known is that, like their makers, the fae eventually turned to humans for entertainment. However, unlike our benevolent creators who use suffering to strengthen the soul, the fae saw human agony as their personal pastime.

As the malice of the fae became too much to bear, the gods crafted a great golden tree deep in the bosom of the world. There, they trapped the eternal souls of the fae, thus saving mankind.

Then, our creators each gave a piece of their heart to create a new god: the keeper of the Fae Tree, who we call the Dark One. Together with his Shadowhounds, he guards the souls of the fae to this day.

Woe betide the human who inflicts cruelty upon his fellow man, for in death, his soul will be placed in bondage with the fae."

Chapter One

Rain Season – Day 57 of 92, 47th Year of Creipus the Pious

The three struggled to carry the professor's coffin to the grave.

Townsend, the elderly butler, was sallow and sweaty as he tried to keep the left side even with the short, portly funeral director. At the back, using his only good arm, the professor's son, Mr. Campbell, bore the weight without complaint. As he passed the mourners, the wet winds ripped at his military dress uniform jacket, revealing the gaping nothing below his bandaged shoulder.

From behind you, the harsh whispers began.

"Why is she here?"

Ah… Mrs. Beaker. You recognized her big mouth anywhere. A shame she got over her laryngitis. Losing her voice had been a service to the world.

"She was the professor's maid. Both of the servants are at his funeral," replied a second woman.

"Maid?" There was a scoffing chuckle. "What kind of maid is called to her master's chambers every night?"

"His son says she was just reading for him," the second woman whispered back.

"Then why didn't he hire a proper secretary? Really, Clara, do you honestly believe no one ever lied to preserve a family's reputation?"

"Don't say such things! The professor was nearly fifty years her senior!" Clara protested.

"So? Probably thought she could charm the inheritance away from his child." You felt Mrs. Beaker's burning gaze on your neck. Her words were becoming louder. "Bet she hoped the gunfire had gotten more than just his arm."

"Hush now, you two. This is hardly the place," a third voice pointed out.

You straightened your back and kept your eyes forward. With a deep breath, you willed the fist at your side to loosen. Hot blood filled the cold fingertips. The ache in your elbow burned long after the prickling in your knuckles subsided.

The pallbearers lowered the coffin onto the planks while the grave keeper threw his body behind the thick rope. One by one, they left their positions on the handles and took up the loose hemp behind him. Then, hand by hand, the casket found its way deep into the ground. The only sounds were the protest of the pulleys and the rumble of thunder in the distance.

The small gathering formed a line. Each took a pinch of dried spices and cast it into the deep soil. Not even the clerics knew when the tradition began. It was pagan, but they allowed it. It would not do well to tell the grieving that the dead are beyond aid.

When you tossed your pinch, your heart nearly went with it.

Walking away from the man who made you was as cruel as forbidding a loyal guide dog from sitting at her master's side. There would be no more raspy admonishments about your pronunciation. No more jeering compliments on the improvement of your penmanship. No more nightly adventures to faraway places hidden between moleskin covers. You would not require the troubles of fantastical lands anymore. Dark times already had settled upon you.

In your pocket, the letter the professor wrote remained under his pressed boar's head seal. Between the grief and the gossips' blows to your ego, you could not find the courage to open it. With a tight chest and a deep sigh, you resolved to take it to your best friend, Rebecca. She was fearless. With any luck, she would open it for you and tell you how silly you were being.

You took your place at the far end of the line, waiting for the ceremony's closing. The people around you were like ghouls. Their teeth seemed fanged and their features a nebulous miasma. Only Townsend was willing to stand beside you. You glanced at him and noticed his eyes were misty. It was the first time you saw the man cry.

A soft crunching called your attention away from dark thoughts. At the far end of the cemetery, beyond the wrought iron fence, a long-hooded automobile rolled up the gravel drive. The sleek machine was pitch colored with lines slippery as cream. The wheels were cupped by teardrop-shaped casings that sloped like cresting waves. You paused only to hear the whispers start again.

"Who shows up late to a funeral?" Mrs. Beaker muttered.

"My husband might be tardy to his own if I don't mind him," teased Clara.

"Don't make me laugh. It isn't proper!" the third woman whispered.

When the door opened, the driver rose to his feet with the grace of a jungle cat. His skin was stark pale against his black suit, like fine linen splashed with ink. Tall cheekbones looked carved, as if one of the old masters sculpted him from marble. Age gave him shadows that accented their shape. The hardest feature to ignore was the deep scar running down the right side of his scalp. Stretching from the top of his head to his eyebrow, it looked like a trench dug between his silver locks.

He strolled to the graveside, one hand in his pocket. When he reached the back of the line, he tugged off his tinted glasses and placed them in his coat. The wrinkled bags under his blue eyes were dark as bruises against his fair complexion. From the other pocket, he produced a filigree encrusted silver watch. Its hands lay as still as your master.

When at last it was his turn, he took no spice between his fingers. Instead, one hand still in his coat, he tossed the watch into the grave. It clattered on the wood, leaving a dent in the smooth varnish before sliding into the muddy ground. You were close enough to hear his hoarse voice swell with amusement.

"Sorry to be late, Professor. Your watch stopped working three days ago."

Ignoring the scowls of the procession, he took his place beside the professor's son. All eyes fell to the two men. Lightning flashed at the edge of the horizon and a growl echoed from the sky. Then, a snort of laughter escaped the son's lips.

"I'm glad you could come."

"I would not miss it if there were wild dogs," replied the odd man. He glanced to the empty space beside the host. "Where is your wife?"

"She said she and father never got on in life and she doubted he would wish her near in his death," Mr. Campbell explained.

The stranger grinned. "Given his temperament, she's probably not wrong."

"It was hardly an inconvenience for her to come across town but it was not worth the fight," the son said with a long-suffering sigh. "Speaking of travel, weren't you in Gamoid this week?"

"I was."

The son whistled. "How fast did you drive to get here?"

The pale foreigner leaned back to smirk at the clouds. "Faster than The Dark One could claim me."

"Even then, it's a three-day drive." Mr. Campbell paused and raised a brow. "Did you sleep?"

"Do we ever?"

Tired eyes fell back to the grave. "No, I suppose not."

When the cleric finished his prayer, the stranger elbowed the son and cocked his head towards the car. The host tossed a worried glance at the hole in the ground. Below the well-pressed uniform, he began to shake. He sniffed and tilted his head to the storm clouds gathering in the sky. A grin crossed his tear-streaked face.

"Father would be proud," he murmured. "I'm not much in the mood for drinks."

"Cake then."

Mr. Campbell's ringing laughter caused people to stop and stare. Mrs. Beaker began her mutterings again. You noted her voice was far softer than when she criticized you.

The son ignored the gossip and shook his head. "Ten minutes. I need to thank the guests."

The scarred man's eyes crinkled at the edges as a sharp smile tugged at his hollow cheeks. Turning on the balls of his feet, he ambled his way back to the car. As he passed you, your gazes met. Ice blue eyes felt like they pierced your very soul. Your heart jumped as primordial alarm flooded your veins. His grin stretched one tooth wider. You hurried to look away.

Even as the son received them, some of the procession peaked over his shoulder like curious owls. Finally, Mrs. Beaker failed to contain herself any longer.

"Who was that man just now?"

The boy shrugged. "An old friend of my father's. They used to travel together."

Mrs. Beaker's gaze caught your own. In an instant, her brow hardened. She crossed her arms and cupped her elbows. Her eyes narrowed as she looked you up and down like a housekeeper inspecting an overloaded waste bin.

You turned your cheek and walked away from the grave.

Later that evening, you dragged what little was left of your pride to the factory district. Two streets over from the largest steam plant in the city of Illestrad, The Worn Elbow Pub was a quiet place with late hours that catered to the working class. Rebecca Baylord, the wife of the proprietor, took one look at your sullen expression before forcing you to sit at a table. First, she read Professor Campbell's letter aloud. Then, loaded with a pint of ale and strong opinions, she demanded a full account of the funeral. As you summarized the events, her grip on her glass grew tighter and tighter. By the time you paraphrased the gossip's snide remarks, your best friend was thirsty for blood.

"Snooty old dingbats! Every last one of them sinning through their lives to sing on the Holy Day like they 'taint done nothing never!" Rebecca's hard finger stabbed the old, scratched tabletop. "Mark my words, it's that foul daughter-in-law setting the Beaker and her ilk upon you." Your friend shook her head until a few milky brown locks spilled from her ponytail. "Why do they hate you so much anyways?"

You sighed. "The professor left me and Townsend money. Ever since Mrs. Campbell found out, she insisted on replacing us. She said he was too old to work and then looked at me like I clawed my way up her leg."

"Ah… so here comes the new mistress of the house only to find out that the servants were given pie before she even got home." Rebecca's grin was smooth as she leaned into her slender arm. "You ought to take her man, just for show."

Your nose wrinkled in disgust. "He is a toddler."

"That's war. 'Tits all toddlers and grave fodder what's left. Lucky my husband's bad heart kept him from the draft or I'd be a widow too."

She waved the back of her hand at the room. Most of the congregation was full of working girls on lunch, still wearing canvas jumpsuits from the factory. Of the few men, the only one not missing a piece of his body or soul was her husband. Bad heart and all, he chuckled while serving drinks at the bar.

"There are so few men left after the war," Rebecca grumbled. "Even a decent man cannot get a decent burial!"

You nodded, letting your head slip into the palm of your hand. "Thank heavens the professor was not alive to see the pallbearers. You know how he was about symmetry."

The brunette eyed your wrinkleless travel frock and starched neckline. "Aye, but not as well as you, I'd venture." Her finger swirled into the peeling varnish, short nails picking at a loose patch. She flicked it across the room and sighed again. "I cannot believe you're going to stay in service after living with that man all those years!"

Your voice was soft with a hoarse rasp. "You read the note. He gave me a personal recommendation. I can hardly let it go to waste."

Rebecca sneered. "You ought to send a copy to the mistress and let her steam her head off."

You laughed. "Perhaps I could ask her to write an addendum in which she calls me fifteen variations of 'trollop'. I am sure that will clinch the job."

Rebecca began ticking off her long fingers. "Slut. Cunt. Whore. Night girl. Bed warmer. Tramp. Floozy. Hussy. Pussywillow. Harlot. Tart. Streetwalker—"

You elbowed her in the ribs. The warmth of her laugh filled your stomach like a hot cocoa on a cold day.

"'Her Highness the Queenie is opening more and more of her Steamworks by the day." Rebecca tipped her glass before taking a large sip. "Take unemployment like the rest of us girls and get yourself a living wage when one of Her Majesty's jobs opens up."

You shook your head. "Factory work is too monotonous for me. All day at one machine until you become one yourself? Sounds like a nightmare!" You shivered. "Besides, the professor spent a decade molding my habits to be fitting for a lady's maid or housekeeper."

"Molded indeed! Thanks to him you can't even use a contraction without having a heart spasm!" Rebecca said, rolling her eyes.

"Be that as it may, these manners and this voice..." Your hands balled into your thighs. When you looked up, the edges of your swollen eyes were kissed with more tears. "It was his gift to me. I do not want his efforts to be wasted."

Rebecca pursed her lips until her nose wrinkled to one side. "You don't owe them rich toffs."

She nodded to a corkboard on the far wall. The messages were littered with advertisements for employment agencies seeking servant labor for wealthy households. Every listing was the same:

No experience required! Room and board! Positions available immediately! Apply today!

The bottoms were neatly trimmed so any potential applicant could tear a slip of the office's contact information with ease. Each and every one of the paper tabs were untouched.

"The mess they got themselves in is their own fault, isn't it?" Rebecca loosed a bitter snort. "Should have paid us better and not worked us into the ground. Now with all the menfolk dead all they've got left is us that they sneered at— and we've got other options! Oooooh to see the day when the grass eats the cow!" She licked her lips and raised her glass. "A reckoning like the clerics promised."

You shook your head and smiled at her. "I appreciate what you are trying to do for me, but I will find my own way."

"All right, all right! Do whatever pleases you." Rebecca wrinkled her nose and sneered at you. "But wherever you end up, you'd better send me your address. Us factory girls only have proper ten-hour shifts and a break every fortnight by the benevolent order of Her Royal Majesty herself. None of that fifteen hours, six days a week nonsense them fancy 'ladies' try to sell." She clutched her hands to her chest and squealed. "Four days in a row! I shall scarcely know what to do with myself with all that time!"

"I shall look forward to your letters with keen anticipation."

Rebecca cocked an eyebrow and winked at you. "Oh, you'd better. 'Twill be the highlight of your week to be sure!"

Despite the horrid day, you smiled.

Twenty days later, you were learning that the difference between an oddity and a conspiracy was merely a matter of numbers.

The conversation with Rebecca felt like centuries ago. Nearly a month into your job hunt, you found yourself a connoisseur of every type of polite rejection the big city could offer. Sitting inside the last employment office on the farthest side of town, your understanding patience was morphing into tight-lipped doubt. Even worse, you were quickly becoming convinced that this trip was going down the same road as all the others. Watching the employment agent scan your reference letter made your stomach turn. Waiting for her to reach the bottom was torture.

Sure enough, when the beak-nosed woman's attention settled upon your name, her body hardened like she had encountered a skunk in her bedchambers. She hummed with concern before shaking her head.

"Miss- ah… Missus…" The word hung in the air like loud flatulence. The woman's lips pulled tight enough to blanche. "How do you pronounce your name?"

You kept the "employee of the year" smile plastered on your face and said it for her. It was neither the first, nor would it be the last time your late husband's name did not fit in 'polite' society. Townsend and Rebecca both suggested you take up your maiden name for the job hunt, but you had not the heart to do so.

"Ah... Well... Missus—" She coughed, making a foul sound that refused to even approximate your name. "I'm afraid we simply don't have any openings right now. With the men back from the war and all..." She trailed off.

Your gaze flicked to the massive stack of papers on the left side of her desk. In neat cursive writing, the one on the top said:

Position: Lady's Maid.

Details: Position will involve dressing the employer. Women only.

She followed your attention. A bead of sweat crawled down her brow. Poorly faking a stretch, she laid her elbow over the employer's name.

The muscles in your temple spasmed. Your smile never faltered. "It need not be a lofty position. I was a maid-of-all-work. I am capable of performing any task put to me."

The woman's eyes dashed away with all the haste of a person fleeing a stampede. "Yes, so I gathered."

You frowned. "Madam, have I done something to offend you?"

If she looked any further to the left her eyes might roll out of her head. "What would cause you to think that?"

"You seem tense."

"Tense?" Her voice squeaked. She fanned herself. "No. No, not at all. I'm quite well. Yes. Quite."

You stared at her with a raised brow.

She coughed. "Well... let me get you a list of other agencies in our ar—"

Her words died as she watched your eyes drift to the left side of her desk. Folded at the top was a copy of this morning's City Press. In bold text it proclaimed:

LORD DANKWORTH CONFRONTS UNEMPLOYMENT ABUSES

With fiery rhetoric, His Lordship John Dankworth pronounced today that the Queen's new unemployment benefits had turned former servant girls to a life of idle frivolity.

Dankworth proclaimed: "Unemployment was meant for women who were displaced by our brave soldiers to ease back into careers more suitable for them. Now these same females refuse to "lower" themselves to any industry which does not suit their slothful tendencies. It is well known that service is an old, noble, and necessary profession. Mark my words, if these layabout "ladies" do not return to the country manors, we shall see more than dusty halls! Without workers, the landowners will be forced to pull day laborers from the farms! There will be starvation as the crops of the great estates rot in the fields!"

When asked why men could not pursue traditional roles in service while the women remained in the factory (as they have been for the past seven years), he replied:

"What an absurd question! Our men need the higher paying factory jobs! How else will they support their families?"

The woman feigned a cough and shoved the paper into the trashcan beside her desk. With a crooked ankle, she dragged her waste bin towards her. The metal can scraped the tile floors. The room paused. Onlookers craned their necks to find the source of the offensive screech. The woman froze and then retracted her leg. Nervous hands tugged at her collar.

"So, about that list—"

You snapped open the satchel in your lap and extracted fourteen copies of paper. Each contained a list of the addresses of employment agencies in the city. All were written in different hands. A single, neat line crossed out all the items on the lists save for one: the name of the agency in which you currently sat.

"I do not suppose you are hiring a messenger?" you joked. "I am acquiring great skill at traversing the city and I am growing less attached to the particulars of my profession with each day."

The woman slumped into the chair. Her deep breaths rattled in her ribcage. You tucked the papers back into your bag and folded your hands in your lap. Your tongue tapped the back of your teeth three times. In the protracted silence, you swallowed to loosen your throat. When you finally spoke, it was with a tone of empathy.

"I do not blame you. After all, a maid can hardly fault a woman for following orders." Your gut growled. You brought your hand to your mouth to cover a weary laugh. "Though, since I have no living family who need care, my unemployment application was turned down as well..."

The woman's face contorted in pain. Her hand came to rest on her belly. She licked her lips. "Well... there is one place that might hire you, but I make no guarantees."

Your stomach rumbled again.

She winced. "If you're quite serious about the job, I will call and let them know you'll be by tomorrow afternoon."

You flashed her an apologetic smile. "If it is not a brothel, I promise to be most obliging."

CHAPTER TWO

Snow Season – Day 14 of 90, 47th Year of Creipus the Pious

"Ma'am." There was a soft touch on your arm, like a cat pawing at a dead vole. "Ma'am, you alive there?"

You inhaled, letting the smell of horse and winter's chill fill your senses. Head swirling with the weight of exhaustion, you swallowed thick saliva and licked your dry lips. The old cart rattled up the half-frozen road as the farmer dodged slush-filled potholes. His wind-worn face peered at you from the driver's seat.

"Oh!" You startled to your senses. "Please forgive me. I seem to have dozed off."

The farmer looked into the back of the cart. You were propped against the wooden edge, curled under a blanket to fend off the cold. His young daughter was fast asleep, leaning on your arm. He smiled through the deep wrinkles in his leathery skin.

"Ought to be able to see Gravelorne around this here bend."

"Thank you for waking me."

You glanced at the cherubic girl and brushed a loose curl from her face. When you moved, the blanket shifted low around her waist. You shuddered in the frosty air and placed it back over her shoulders. She sighed and snuggled into the warmth of your body. It took everything you had not to coo.

"Were you a nurse in the war?"

You shook your head. "No. Why do you ask?"

"Ever since that foreign feller took Gravelorne Manor, I ain't seen nothing but old soldiers and curious folk go there. You seem like the rich ones he has for dinner, but you ain't come with your car and your ego." He snorted at the same time as his horse. "Figured you might've been one of them war nurses come to stay with those that left more on the battlefield than bullets and body. Ya know? Someone who understands what it was like to be there and all."

"No, I am just a simple maid in need of work."

He looked you up and down before frowning. "You're sure you cannot find another place?"

You laughed into your hand. "It would seem not. Apparently, the whole world did not require my services."

He sighed. "Don't seem right leaving a woman at the gate. It's a bit of a hike to the house on foot." The farmer paused before a gap-tooth grin broke on his face. He winked at you. "I just recollected that the cook owes me a bit of coin. What say you if I drop you around the servant's side?"

"I would be very grateful for your kindness, sir."

"River's up ahead. You can see the manor from there." He sniffed back a ball of snot. "Up in that hillside."

Calling the pale rock that jutted upward like an explosion a "hillside" was like calling a dead body a speed bump. The rigid peaks before you climbed high enough to scrape the clouds on stormy days. Below the mountain was a small gap in the trees. From there, you could see the third story of a grey bricked manor. The front was flanked by twin peaks capped in pointed gables. Between them, recessed walls surrounded a limestone encrusted entryway. The symmetry would have made the professor weep. You covered your mouth to conceal the drop of your jaw.

"Aye, it is a pretty house. Staffed with ghouls, though."

"Ghouls?"

The man turned back to the reins. "You'll see. Bodies might be there, but it doesn't mean the souls are in them."

A shiver rippled down your skin. You pulled the blanket a little higher up your neck.

Over the short stone walls of the bridge was the muddy, grey river flowing east towards the coastline. The water rushed over the great slate slabs below the surface, churning into white foam at every dip of the bed. Dark woods on either side of the shore whisked away all sound under bristled bowers. It was as if the gods bid the lowland be hushed.

Past the bridge rose a towering stone wall better fit for a battlement than a border. It stretched across the forest edge, farther than the eye could see. The top of the brickwork cascaded into a series of perforated arcs. A wrought iron gate hung on heavy hinges between twin stone columns with recessed niches. You raised a brow at two translucent, white statues seated deep in the cavities. One was a rendering of Mirtha, the Goddess of Fate, weaving the life threads of all mortals into the tapestry of destiny. The other was Haltor, the God of Justice, holding his sword of judgment high.

"Is that... bone china?" you questioned.

The old farmer threw his head back and laughed. "Sure is! The statues contain the ash from the original manor."

"Original manor?"

"The Gravelornes who built the estate all died in a great house fire before the new master bought the place. They were running outta money and most folk 'round here believe they set the fire themselves for the insurance." The farmer grinned. "Rather poetic, isn't it?"

Who exactly was the ghoul in this area?

The farmer continued on: "When the new owner first arrived, he hosted a huge party. Told all of us in the village he wanted to commission statues in their honor and asked for ideas."

You forced a polite smile over gritted teeth. "Why justice and fate though? Choosing those two almost sounds like..."

"Oh, it's *exactly* what it sounds like, ma'am." The farmer snorted. "All of the villagers *hated* them idiot nobles. They'd let their dogs run free, biting people and killing livestock. Not a one of us was sorry to see them gone. Mr. Estrova has been a much better land steward."

You stared at the delicate piles of curls atop both the deities' heads. "Are they not rather fragile for outdoors? Why not marble?"

The farmer chuckled. "The gardener's wife used to be Royal Master Ceramist for the Queen herself. The pair of them wouldn't be parted, so Mr. Estrova hired them both. Mr. Norton's got a huge glasshouse garden to run, so the master likes to give Mrs. Norton lots of projects to stay busy. Happy wife, happy life, I suppose."

The old farmer coaxed the horse to a stop and hopped from his cart. On stiff legs, he huffed over to the wall. Muttering to himself, he began to palm his way down the mortar lines.

"Can never even find that stupid butto—Oh! There it is!"

As his thumb pressed a hidden switch, the great archway groaned open. The little girl on your arm mumbled in her sleep and nuzzled into the wool of your cape. Her father returned to the cart, hoisting himself up into the driver's seat with a groan and several loud pops.

"The gearboxes on the backside are ugly as sin, but 'tis nice not to have to drag the stupid thing open."

As you passed through the opening, you could see two black metal canisters clinging to the masonry like bats to a cave wall.

"Are those electric?" you asked.

"Nah. Steam. Can't run wires this far up. What electric they got comes from the steam generator at the back of the house. Stupid thing makes a monstrous racket when it's running. All burbles and gurgles like it's got a belly ache." He rolled his eyes. "The Queen's energy might be better for your lungs, but if you want my opinion: old coal fire's crackle 'tis a lot kinder on your ears."

The cart's wheels started to whine as the dirt road gave way to a sleek asphalt drive. Like a great black serpent, it wound through five full switchbacks before it reached the top. Looking up it made your knees ache.

"I really must thank you for taking me up to the house," you insisted.

The old man tipped his hat. "It's not any trouble, ma'am."

Gravelorne Manor was even more imposing up close. A full fifteen sets of windows, each much larger than a grown man, winked in the afternoon sun. Traditional white marble carvings, like those of the old masters, flanked the entrance. On the left, a statue of a woman with bat's wings clutched a drawing to her chest. To the right, her lover stood above a blank scroll, a pen held tight in his fingertips. Each reached out a hand to the other—destined to never touch. You recognized the story from the professor's book of legends: "The Nightmuse and the Seventh Son". It was a tragic tale of love at first sight.

A dubious snort flew from your nose. "Love at first sight," you muttered to yourself with an eye roll. "As if that really happens."

Below the central eaves was a small circular carving. Eight spindly legs joined at a plump thorax. On the long, pelican-like head, four pairs of eyes, cast in bronze, glittered in the sun.

"Is the family crest a spider?" you asked.

"Don't know that them foreigners have family crests like we do. I think he just put it up there to frighten off folks that's not welcome. Far as I know, the man has a thing for cats." Your escort sniffed and pointed to the east wall of the manor. "See up there?"

At the top of the brick partition that divided the house from the garage, licking its paw, was a fine feline with plush white fur. It flicked its ear and looked down on you with glowing green-yellow eyes. Then, with a swish of its tail, it slinked off in the direction of the roof.

The back of the home was hidden by a well-groomed hedgerow and a gated archway. Behind them, the servant's entrance sat in a small muddy yard off the asphalt drive. Jutting from the rear of the main house was a long corridor with squat windows. Amongst the stonework were tiny vents that loosed the occasional puff of steam.

The old man stopped the cart and reached over the side to shake his daughter's shoulder. "Time to get up, princess. The lady has to go to her interview."

With a squeaky yawn, the child wiggled her nose and wobbled into a sitting position. One tiny fist came up to rub her eye. Tucking the blanket around her, you took the old man's hand and descended from the cart. Your tingling legs were unsteady, but tapping your toes on the road helped some.

"Doorbell is on the right side," the farmer instructed before jerking his head towards the back of the building. "I'll head over to the kitchen to harass Cook."

You bowed your head. "Thank you again."

He waved his hand before climbing into the cart. The little girl fluttered her fingers from the back. All too soon, they disappeared around the rear wing of the house.

Turning to face your fate, you took a deep breath, hitched your travel satchel up, and climbed the ramp to the door. You bit your lip. A trembling hand reached for the bell.

"Look out below!"

Whump, clang!

Whipping around to find the source of the noise, you widened your eyes. There, laying on the pathway behind you, was… a leg?

You stared at the disembodied limb. It was shin high and constructed from a series of pistons, springs, and corrugated conduits. The foot piece was a curved blade that arched into a brace near the calf. At the top, a smooth leather cup tapered down into a small metal valve.

"Sorry! You alright down there!?"

You looked up at the voice only to see a bright-eyed redhead waving at you from the second-floor window.

His pale face was splattered with freckles and his brown jumpsuit with oil. He grinned and scratched the back of his neck.

Before you could reply, the door swung open to reveal a dark, coily haired man with a wide nose and a stubble beard. His silk vest was delicately embossed with iridescent coppertone paisleys. Each of the buttons on his waistcoat was custom-molded with the same spider seen on the front of the home.

"Oh! My apologies, ma'am!" He bowed at the waist. "I didn't hear the bell ring."

You glanced from him to the leg and back. Your hand was still extended, a mere flick from the button. You squatted to collect the escaped limb and presented it to the man at the door.

"Ah, looks like Lyle's still fiddling with it," he said, taking the leg from you. His apologetic grin was dazzling. "I'm Garrick Reeves, the footman. I guess you are the maid we've been expecting?"

Fiddling? Stars above, his language was so casual. Still, as you scanned his handsome face, you knew he was not lying. Footmen were notoriously hired for "the look" and this deep brown beauty certainly had that.

"Have I… come at a bad time?" you asked in a halting voice.

Reeves fixed the window above with a hard glare. "No. I'm ashamed to say that this is not wholly out of the norm at this house. Please ignore him. We do."

The redhead cringed. "Oh sure, like it's my fault the light in here is so bad I gotta use the window sill to work!"

"You are more than capable of changing your own light bulbs!" Reeves's eye twitched. "And don't you have a pressing apology to make?"

Lyle turned to face you with a crimson flush from neck to ear tip. "Sorry about the scare, ma'am! Hope you weren't hurt or nothin'."

"No, no. I am well," you called back, nodding to the open air behind you with an uneasy laugh. "As luck would have it, you seem to have missed me."

Reeves rubbed his temple and rolled one hand at the young man in the window. "Your name?"

The redhead's spine went straight as a board. He took off his goggles and gallantly swept them in front of himself. "Lyle Watts, ma'am, at your service." He beamed and thumbed his chest. "I'm the house's mechanic."

"Yes, I gathered as much." With a bow of your head, you added: "It's a pleasure to meet you. My name is—"

All at once, a primordial sense of alarm sent the hairs on the back of your neck straight up. With a nervous gulp, Reeves turned back to the hall behind him. There, looming in the shadows, stood a stern-faced elderly man in a black tailcoat. His dark grey vest was engraved with the same paisley pattern as the footman, but in the shade of milky silver. His dark face pulled taut with controlled fury.

"Mr. Watts." The butler's voice was deep and carried like a battle horn. "While the master tolerates an insufferable amount of your antics, I *will not* have you injuring our visitors."

The young man looked about four years old. With the haste of a rabbit, he ducked his head back through the window and bolted the sash shut.

Behind round-framed glasses, the butler's brown eyes flashed in your direction. "Mr. Reeves, you will put on your coat and escort this woman to the back parlor. Bring her some tea and I will be along after I deal with this"—he glared up the stairwell— "unacceptable buffoonery."

Reeves snapped to attention and clicked his heels. "Yes, sir."

"I'm sorry, Mr. Ellsworth," Lyle babbled from out of sight. "Really, I am! It was just—"

"Silence." Despite his cold countenance, the butler's eyes blazed like the pits of the lower world. He stalked up the steps, eliciting a whine of terror from the younger servant. "Words are meaningless. You are a grown man, and your actions will reflect that or so help me, I will—"

As the butler vanished out of sight, you could hear the apologetic rambling of the mechanic bouncing off the walls. The low growl of the butler's admonishments reverberated down through the servant's quarters like the grumblings of a dragon on a distant peak. You exhaled the breath you did not know you were holding.

The footman hurried to a nearby rack and snatched up his tailcoat before thrusting both arms down the sleeves. With two sharp tugs of his lapels, he turned back to you. "Please follow me, ma'am."

At the end of the servant's hall was a wide, heavy door. When Reeves opened it, you clenched your teeth to keep your jaw from dropping.

The main passages of the home were unusually wide, with walls papered in a fashionable damask of ivory and gold. Richly stained, dark walnut floors looked like ink below your feet. Every door you passed was embossed with ribbon-like carvings trimmed in aluminum leaf. China vases filled with fresh flowers dotted the hall tables. While most nobles favored the stuffed heads of woodland creatures for decor, Gravelorne's walls were dressed in oil paintings in dreamy pastels.

"Just in here, ma'am," Reeves instructed, ushering you into a room at the end of the hall.

The parlor itself was no less splendid than the preceding decorations had promised. Mint green wallpaper with subtle tessellations of flower petals matched the pristine jade and marble fireplace. Wide windows looked out onto a well-groomed hedge maze. In the right corner, a glass and silver grandfather clock ticked away.

This was the *back* parlor!?

"Please have a seat," Reeves instructed.

You stiffened at the thought of a maid taking tea in such a fine room. "I do not wish to—"

The door clicked shut.

"—impose," you murmured to no one.

Alone in the room, your eyes fell upon the delicate porcelain figurines in the white cabinets. The fired lace dresses worn by the women were as fluffy as pastries. The men were clothed in elegant tailcoats with powdered wigs and ruffled cravats. Even one of those statues was apt to be years of a maid's salary. You scooted away from the cases and took a seat on the edge of the sofa. As you focused on keeping your muddy boots off the cream rug, one thought ran through your head: Touch *nothing*.

When Mr. Reeves returned, your nausea only deepened. On an embossed silver tray was a coral and white bone china tea set with scalloped stripes. He set the finery upon the coffee table and poured your drink. The scent of mint filled the room. As he handed you the cup, he said: "I hope you like the blend. We grow the mint in the conservatory."

Your hands clenched in your lap. "Will the lady of the house not miss her tea set?"

"Lady?" There was a snort followed by a toothy chuckle. "Forgive me, ma'am. The master is just fond of florals. There is no woman in this house, save yourself."

Your fingers picked at the darning on the edge of your glove. "But surely this set is far too nice for..."

"For a servant?"

You nodded.

Reeves sighed and scratched the back of his neck. "Now I see what Ellsworth is on about."

"What do you mean?"

"Oh!" Reeves waved his hand. "Just some self-deprecation, ma'am. Most of us were not brought up as servants, as I'm sure you've gathered from our manners. Mr. Ellsworth is training us, but..."

He stuffed his hands in his pockets and examined your straight posture and neat hair. Compared to his fine uniform, your dark, utilitarian clothes made you look like a puddle of shadow which could disappear under a chair at anyone's convenience.

"Anyway"—he continued with a cough—"in this home, you will find that there isn't a lesser set of anything. Our patron only bothers with the best. Consider it a habit of his."

"Of course," you replied. "Please, forgive my protests and any inconvenience they may have caused you."

Reeves's smile was as warm as the tea. He held the saucer out to you. "You were just being polite. That's easily forgiven."

Nervous hands gripped the handle like the cup might flee at any moment. You stared through the liquid, admiring the fanciful peony blooms glazed to the bottom of the china. When you looked up, Reeves's brown eyes were upon you. As your gaze met his, he glanced away.

You smiled at him. "Thank you for your kindness."

"Just following orders," he replied, rubbing the back of his neck. Taking up the tray, he strolled to the door. "Enjoy your tea."

When the latch clicked shut, you took another sip. This time, it did not feel like you would choke on it.

In the hall, a bitter laugh escaped Reeves's throat. With a guilt-riddled smile, he repeated, "We're all just following orders."

Chapter Three

When the grandfather clock chimed a quarter to the hour, a knock sounded at the door. You placed your tea on the table and rose to your feet.

"Mr. Ellsworth, is that you?"

With a face as placid as a frozen lake, the butler entered the parlor and strode to the sofa. He snapped his polished heels together and bowed his head. "I am sorry to keep you waiting."

As the sun filtered through the gauzy curtains, wide eyes noticed something they missed in the shadows of the hall.

The man had no outer ears.

Behind a coiled silver beard, both sides of Ellsworth's head bore a jagged set of raised scars. The hole for the ear was still there, but only a piece of uneven tissue implied that the shell once existed. A taunt braided cord held the wire frame of his circular bifocals in place.

"I must apologize again for Mr. Watts." Dark eyes flashed as Ellsworth said the name. "He is talented, but his manners can be reprehensible."

You raised a placating hand. "It is fine. No harm came of it."

Ellsworth gestured to the sofa. "Will you please sit down, madam?"

Stiff as a board, you resumed your perch on the edge of the couch. His ever inspecting gaze measured the distance between your clothing and the back of the seat. You stayed still, like a baby rabbit in the grass. When Ellsworth closed his eyes, you felt like you could breathe again.

"By now, I am sure that one such as yourself has noted the peculiarities of this particular home."

You nodded.

"When I was brought on, it was with the general guidance that our employer had a preference for staff who possessed talent. It did not matter if they lacked the polished manners that other more reputable households would find palatable." He coughed. "In addition, I was summarily informed that unmarried female staff would serve as a distraction and were not to be considered."

Your stomach clenched at his words.

"However, Professor Campbell was a dear friend of my employer."

Dear friend? You were with the professor over a decade and a half and never heard of Gravelorne Manor before yesterday.

"In addition," Ellsworth continued, "my master surmised that, as an older widow, you are less inclined to flights of fancy. This made you an acceptable exception."

Older widow? Wonderful. Pity the poor old thing, my loves. How she ever keeps both feet out of the grave, we shall never know.

Or... you could fail this interview and be a brothel girl catering to drunken sailors too tipsy to notice your pain.

Old hag sounded lovely.

You forced a smile. "I am grateful for your consideration."

He closed his eyes and rubbed his temples in tight circles. "Before hiring you, it behooves me to explain the nature of this household. The entire manor and grounds are managed by a staff of six. Myself, our footman, our cook and undercook, our groundskeeper, and Mr. Watts are all we require to keep the entire manor in the style as lays before you."

Your eyes bulged as you scanned the magnificent room. Every piece of it was flawless and free of dust. In addition to those six positions, an estate this size should require at least five maids to manage the cleaning and another two to three to assist the cook. Besides that, even if the household raised no animals or crops, there was no way one groundskeeper could possibly manage the lawns and gardens by himself.

"You are wondering how this is possible, I presume?"

Unable to trust your own voice, you nodded again.

"Look under the sofa."

With eyebrows raised, you bent over and peeked into the shadows. There, under the sofa, was a flat, circular machine. The top of it contained a large gear that ticked exactly one tooth per second. Around this was a circular piece of brass with round bolts positioned like a clock face. As a stately chime rang the hour, an orange bulb glowed in the center of the gear. The mechanical wonder crawled out from its hiding place. You jumped to your feet.

"W-what is that?"

"Mr. Watts calls it a 'dust-mouse.' I thought it best to show you one of the little hellions before you stumbled across it in the dark. These smaller ones siphon the floors for debris before their larger counterparts steam clean the halls and rugs."

"Surely someone must do the dusting?"

"There is a hovering version, but I do not trust it with the paintings or china. It is tolerable on the cabinets, tables, books, and ceilings." Ellsworth tapped the floorboards with his shoe. "The house is heated by steam conduits, so the ash we generate is minimal. Electric lights mean we need not trim the candles. That limits our dust to a very manageable level. At present, Mr. Reeves cycles through the house every fortnight doing the polishing and fine dusting."

The buzzing from the little robot sounded like the call of locusts feasting upon your livelihood.

"Who empties the machines?" you inquired, battling the strain in your voice.

"When they are full, they return to the mudroom at the back of the servants' quarters. Organic debris is composted while inorganic materials are sorted and compacted. Mr. Watts takes what he cannot reuse to the village garbage once a week."

Your soul was leaving your body. "What about the laundry?"

"A chute and conveyor belt system transports it to the washroom where machines sort it by texture. The automatic washer-dryer handles everyday pieces while fine fabrics are bagged for Miss Jasmine at the village laundry service."

"The shoes?"

"We put them through the auto-polisher."

"The waste bins?"

He pointed to the dust-mouse.

"The dishes?"

"There are two steam dishwashers: one for the finery and one for the kitchenware. Cook's machine sorts his equipment into specific slots so he can find what he needs. I hand-sort the good china."

Your head spun as Ellsworth continued on.

"Mr. Norton, the groundskeeper, uses the ride-on cutter to handle the lawns. He also has some horrid buzzing blade for the hedges." Ellsworth sniffed. "It makes a filthy racket in my opinion."

Your eyes glazed over as you squeaked out, "The whole house cleans itself?"

"Once a year, we do have to scrub the windows. Fortunately, the mechanical lift basket makes that easier."

You tried to stifle the bubbling sensation sweeping up your throat, but a small huff danced past your fingertips. Your shoulders began to shake. Your eyes squeezed shut. Finally, you gave in and let the laughter fly.

"Oh, Mr. Ellsworth, sir, I am sorry," you explained between gasping breaths. "I understand now. These things—" As the dust-mouse scurried across the room, another giggle rippled from your throat. "It would seem my position is rather obsolete."

Ellsworth nodded. "I would say that the *traditional* role of a maid is unnecessary at Gravelorne. However, since you now understand, would you be willing to hear the proposed position?"

What did he want you to say to that? You came all this way as a last resort only to find out you were replaceable with some sort of dirt-eating mechanical mouse.

With a well-practiced false smile, you replied, "Yes, I would be open to it."

"As I have mentioned, Mr. Reeves is caring for the duties that the dust-mice can not. While there are significantly fewer tasks to complete than in a traditional house, it consumes hours of his day. Therefore, our employer suggested that this work could be left to you. This, in turn, frees up Mr. Reeves for a proper education in manners and estate management for when I retire." Ellsworth's tone darkened. "I expect it will take several years, so the sooner it can start, the better."

"Yes, sir."

Ellsworth sighed and pinched the bridge of his nose. "In addition, our employer keeps late hours which I am rapidly growing too old to accommodate. Therefore, your hours would be set to match his." Sharp brown eyes watched your reaction. "You would work from one in the afternoon through one in the morning on weekdays. There would be a thirty-minute meal break at four and another hour and a half break for dinner around eight o'clock. A short nap at that time would be advisable."

Your heart was fluttering in your chest. At your first place of employment, your day started at seven sharp and ended no earlier than ten in the evening. If you spent more than one hour of that time eating three hot meals, your meager pay was severely docked. The professor had been a bit more generous, giving you a start time of nine in the morning and two hours' rest in the afternoon. However, this was in exchange for keeping you up early into the morning reading his books. If Ellsworth was truthful, this position was even better still. In particular, there was one part of his statement that captivated you.

"Weekdays, sir?" You fought to keep the excitement out of your voice. "Do you mean—"

"You would have the weekends off, of course."

Grasping hands cupped your mouth. Your heartbeat thumped in romantic couplets like the backbeat of a song. The melody was the triumphant crowing of a woman gone mad with excitement.

Every. Weekend. Off.

A tremble wracked your body.

Oooooh! Say it again.

Every. Weekend. Off.

"Madam? Are you listening to me?"

You snapped to attention. "Yes, sir. Sorry, sir. Afternoon into the early morning with a lunch and dinner break, sir." Clasping your fingers together was the only way to keep them from vibrating. "To clarify, you said it would be"—you swallowed, trying not to let him see the fanatical furor pulsing through your blood—"*every* weekend off?"

Ellsworth raised a feathered eyebrow. "Yes? Will that be a problem?"

"No, sir!" You blurted the words. A furious heat filled your cheeks. "No, sir. I am willing to accommodate most schedules."

Ellsworth looked you up and down, taking in your sparkling eyes and ravenous interest in his words. "Room and board are included, of course. You will stay in the servants' quarters with the rest of the house staff. Our gardener and his wife live in a separate cottage on the grounds."

"Of course," you agreed. "I am accustomed to a live-in arrangement."

"As for your pay, we can offer you seventy drossler a year. I hope this will be acceptable."

Your bones felt like they were made of lead. "Sorry, sir. Could you repeat that?"

"Seventy drossler. It will be dispensed in dividend payments over fifty-two weeks, payable every fortnight."

Seventy drossler *per annum!?* That was over double the average salary for a parlor maid! It was more than what a butler should make! Perhaps a noblewoman might scoff at it, but it was on par with the highest-paid factory workers. Stars above! It was…

…too good to be true.

As the accusations from the funeral flew through your thoughts, your eyes narrowed. "That salary is rather suspicious."

"Is it?"

"I do not know what reputation has preceded me, but I suspect a gross misrepresentation of my character was made." You clasped your bag in your fist and rose to your feet. Head tilted back, you fixed the man with a glare sharper than any blade. "I may no longer be some doe-eyed maiden, but I am unwilling to be some sort of sexual play toy for hire. I will see myself out."

As you stormed to the door, a small smile flashed onto Ellsworth's face. "Madam, before you go, I must apologize to you."

You paused, fingers coiled tight around the door handle. "Oh?"

He gestured to the sofa. "Please, sit down. I will explain."

Gritting your teeth, you acquiesced to the request but placed yourself at the edge of your seat.

Ellsworth walked to the window, folding his arms behind his back. "My employer holds no formal title, only a fortune built-in merchant's trade. However, thanks to his talents, his holdings have long outstripped even the nobility of Coriland. It is my job to ensure applicants with ulterior motives do not trouble him."

You clenched your teeth. "I am no fortune hunter, and my recommendation letter is genuine."

"I find actions are the bearer of character, not pen and paper."

"A fair assessment, I suppose," you agreed, crossing your arms.

Ellsworth turned to face you. "I admit, when I heard the rumors associated with your name, I had my own doubts about your character. However, it would seem that these reports were inaccurate." He swept into a low bow. "Please forgive an old man for testing you in this manner."

You observed the gesture with a frown unchanged.

When your companion lifted his head, he touched the scar on the side of his greying temple. "I owe Mr. Sicarius a great debt. Therefore, I do what I can to serve him."

Your chest tightened as a flurry of images flashed through your memories. Your husband's grave. The stone steps of a great library. The smell of wet cement and sticky mud. A sore throat and an empty belly. The professor's umbrella and his unkind words.

"Crying in the rain? Well, I suppose some might call it romantic, but I think it is a tedious way to waste a life. If you have no more need for yourself, then at least allow me to make something useful out of you. What do you say, girl?"

You glanced at the long scars, eyes moist and throat burning hot.

"Let us begin again." Ivory teeth peaked from between tawny lips. "Knowing everything I have told you, would you be willing to work at this estate?"

You mustered a coy smile. "Yes, Mr. Ellsworth."

Two hours later, as Mr. Reeves walked the new maid out to the garage, Ellsworth watched from the rear parlor window. The light in the hills was fading fast into golden hour. Reeves had straightened his back, but not his manner. His arms flapped about. By comparison, the maid's hands stayed folded, so they were not tempted to run away with themselves. Slowly, as their conversation continued, Reeves began to adopt the same posture. Ellsworth let the curtains droop shut.

Walking to the hall, Ellsworth spun the dial on the rotary phone. An operator connected him to the network in Illestrad.

"Grand Vision Hotel. How may I help you?"

"The terrace suite, please."

"May I ask who is calling?"

"Walter Ellsworth. I am Mr. Estrova's butler."

"One moment."

Static crackled in the speaker. The line rang once. The line rang twice. The line rang—

With a click, a smooth baritone poured through the phone. "How did it go, Ellsworth?"

"I had to lower the pay, sir."

There was a pause. "Lower it? Whatever for?"

Ellsworth pinched the bridge of his nose. "One hundred and forty drossler per annum was a staggering amount of money. I judged that it may alarm her, so I offered seventy instead."

"And?"

"Still alarmed, but not enough to bolt."

"Ellsworth, your skills with negotiation near the occult." The man on the other end chuckled. "Did you know that Lady Eiden wishes to steal you away from me?"

"With all due respect, sir, Lady Eiden is a twit."

"So she is, Ellsworth. It is lucky for me that you have no more use for pathetic employers."

"It is not luck that draws people to you, sir. It is wit, wealth, and will."

The voice on the phone hummed. "How do you like the professor's pet?"

"She is skittish, but her manner is tolerable and unobtrusive."

"A high compliment indeed, coming from the man who is never impressed."

Ellsworth snorted. "Reeves has taken her to her room at the Portly Porcine for the evening. I have sent for her things and expect them to arrive the day after tomorrow."

"Excellent. I will be along after I have closed the last of the doors."

Though Ellsworth's expression never changed, he swallowed thick saliva before he could speak.

"Very well, Master Sicarius."

Chapter Four

Snow Season – Day 17 of 90

As you entered your new quarters, your travel satchel hit the floor with a thud. The room was double the size of the space you shared as a maid at Fulston Manor, your very first place of employment. Turning back to your escort, you fixed him with a frown. "This cannot be a servant's room," you protested, jabbing a finger at the hand-carved, blonde wood headboard on the twin bed.

In the doorway, Reeves scratched the back of his neck. "Would you believe me if I showed you mine?"

You shook your head at the champagne-colored dressing table with its curvaceous legs and matching velvet seat. "No, I doubt I would." As you opened the doors of a standing closet fit for a princess, you noted no indication of a roommate. "I truly am the only woman living in the servants' wing?"

"Yes, but during the reconstruction, Mr. Sicarius saw that we all have private rooms." The brunette rolled his eyes. "Probably a wise choice. Lyle keeps his in a frightful state, and Alex hardly says two words together that aren't dipped in annoyance. If they had to share, there might be a murder."

"Alex?" you asked.

"Alex Slater, our undercook." He raised a lecturing finger. "And don't let him catch you pilfering the larder, or the boy will give you an earful that makes a cleric's scolding sound like a sweet song."

You raised a dubious brow. "What kind of servant would pilfer the larder?"

Reeves winced. "Ah. I forgot. Proper maid. Ignore what I just said."

You nodded, examining knobs on the drawers. There was a distinct pearlescence to them that simple porcelain could not possess. More bone china, then? One would think over fifty vases was enough. You pinched the bridge of your nose. "This is ridiculous," you muttered.

"Not up to your standards, Your Highness?"

Your glare sent Reeves into a chorus of hearty laughter. He bent over, grabbing the door for support. "Stars above! You look like my old quartermaster. Can't you take a joke?"

You turned away and walked to the window. A short gap of grassy turf separated your room from the side of the ten-car garage. "Well, at least the view is appropriate for a servant." You smirked at him. " Even if nothing else here is."

Reeves grinned. "So you *do* have some wit under the propriety."

You wrapped your arms behind your back and stood up straight. "I do not know to what you refer."

"Right," he teased, scanning up and down your wardrobe again. "Onto our next subject, are all your clothes like that?"

Your hands fell to your skirt. It was a bit old, but in good condition. You glanced back to the man in the door. "What do you mean?"

He clicked his tongue. "They're just...*plain*, aren't they?"

"What did you expect? I am a maid, not some diva of the opera house."

Reeves rolled his eyes and muttered something under his breath. He walked across the room and handed you a squat key on a leather cord. "This is the skeleton key. Most of us wear them on our pocket chains, but I confess I don't know where a woman keeps—"

You took the key and placed it around your neck.

"Right..." A nervous chuckle slipped through gritted teeth. "Well, I suppose it's out of sight but *do not* let Mr. Sicarius see you do that."

"Why not?"

Reeves shrugged again and gestured for you to follow him out into the hall. He shook his head when you locked the door and tucked the key down the collar of your dress. As you followed him down the wide corridor, he pointed out the sights.

"The bathroom is there on the left. You'll share with Alex. We banished Lyle to the wash in the garage, so you needn't worry about him leaving oil stains everywhere."

"Am I to assume that indoor plumbing was installed during the reconstruction?" you asked, hurrying to keep pace with his long strides.

"Yes. The water is flash heated by the steam system, so you needn't worry about running out. You can bathe every night if you wish. We encourage Lyle to do so."

A warm bath every night? Incredible.

"Do you have any hobbies?" Reeves asked.

"Cleaning?" you replied, voice dripping with sarcasm.

"I meant any non-work related hobbies."

You stared at him. "With fifteen hour days six days a week, what hobbies does one develop?"

Reeves cringed. "You can't be that boring. No one is."

"I enjoy reading," you replied. "Though, at my last employer, I never had the opportunity to choose the books."

"Mr. Sicarius will probably let you borrow some if you ask."

A servant? Allowed to borrow the master's books for herself? That was doubtful.

Reeves chuckled at your dubious expression. "Moving on, breakfast is served at eight for servants, though I doubt you'll want to wake that early. Luncheon is about quarter to one. Once you eat, you'll see to the dusting and polish work." He dug in his pocket and extracted a crumpled paper. "I wrote down some tips. You can read, right?"

"I am literate," you replied, taking the list. The hand was sloppy. Your lip twitched as you kept the snide remark inside.

Reeves scratched his cheek. "I know, I know! It's awful, isn't it? Ellsworth said I won't make a proper valet until I improve, but the practice is rather dull."

You hummed and kept your mouth shut.

Your companion sighed. "You know, the head maid and footman are on the same level. You needn't be so formal with me."

"First, one can hardly be called a *head* maid when there is only one maid." With a sad smile, you added, "Second, as a male servant, your rank is higher than mine, even if we are on a similar level."

He frowned. "You will find that this household has much easier manners than most."

"So I have noticed," you replied with a grimace. "However, please do me the favor of allowing me to keep to the manners with which I am most comfortable, Mr. Reeves."

Reeves shrugged. "All right, have it your way."

"Thank you."

As you crossed the threshold into the main house, he began to tick away on his fingers. "We've seen the front hall, the dining room, the servants' area, both parlors, the formal hall, the office, the billiard room, the sunroom, the wine cellar, and the conservatory." An uneasy grin crossed his face. "It'd be best to tour the kitchen after dinner. Both Cook and Alex get fussy when there's work to be done."

You smiled. Cooks were notoriously protective over their domain. Given Reeves's earlier comment about the larder, you suspected this was well warranted.

Down the elegant halls, you followed your companion until you came upon two dark doors with imposing bronze handles. Without pause, Reeves pushed forward. Your heart leapt at the sight.

To call the room a library was to call a masterwork a painting. Polished white marble floors glowed under sunbeams from the two-story windows on the west side. There were weighty shelves, black as pitch on both levels. Each was heavily laden with countless titles. Upon an ornate wool rug, an overstuffed lounge chair and massive leather sofa surrounded a claw-foot coffee table. Above all these luxuries, a crystal chandelier made of rectangular shards hung from the coffered ceiling. Glittering glass sent sparkling light scattering across the bronze foiled recesses.

You grabbed hold of the rolling ladder to keep from falling over. "Stars above," you murmured.

"Yes, I know." Reeves winced. "Thank the gods for the dust-mice. All those books to clean. Makes you want to sneeze just thinking about it, right?"

Dumbstruck, you walked past him. The vast forest of leather and linen swallowed all sounds, leaving only a peaceful silence. A tentative hand reached for the spines on the nearest row. Bound in kidskin, their beveled edges were smooth and pleasant to grasp.

You shook your head. "To just *be* in such a place as this…"

A decade-old memory of the professor's study crept into your mind. Clear as the day it was made, you still felt the warmth of the lazy afternoon sun on your skin. A younger version of yourself picked your way through the first lines of a story, word by word. Your tongue was slow and halting, shaping the syllables like a child learning to walk. When you reached the end of the page, you realized he had not corrected you. You looked up. There was a proud smile upon his thin lips.

He would have loved this room.

"Are you all right?"

Your hand retracted from the books as if their spines belonged to a quill fish. "Forgive my impertinence, but I must disagree with you, Mr. Reeves." You lifted your head and smiled like a little girl. "I would dust a million books just to see this room."

"A million, you say? That would be an impressive collection," a smooth voice said from above.

Both you and Reeves lifted your eyes to the second floor. Standing at the railing was a tall man with tall cheekbones and a long scar slicing through his silver hair. A form-fitting, double-breasted vest of elegant charcoal grey accented broad shoulders and a tapered waist. Ice blue eyes never left yours as he walked to the spiral stairs with all the grace of a cat.

"Si-Mr. Sicarius! When did you arrive?" Reeves stammered.

The pale foreigner held up his hand. "Shortly before dawn. If it mattered, I would have told you."

"O-of course." Reeves tugged his jacket straight. "Would you like me to bring you breakfast, sir?"

Your eyes flickered to the chime clock hanging below one of the wall sconces. Breakfast? At two?

The man above traced your gaze. His lips twitched into a wry grin. "Reeves, is this my new maid?"

"Ah, yes, sir. I was giving her the tour and reviewing her duties." Reeves turned to you. "This is the owner of Gravelorne Manor, Mister Sicarius Estrova."

You took the hem of your dress in hand and bowed at the waist. "It is a pleasure to meet you, Master Estrova."

The hairs on the back of your neck prickled. There was a great pause, as if all the air had left the room. You lifted your head only to see your employer's shoulders shake. His wrinkled eyes were crinkled with delight. He brought his large hand to cover his mouth. Your face fell as a short snicker escaped his fingers. When you turned around, Reeves's gaze failed to meet yours. A cunning grin split his lips.

In a tone ill-fitted for a lecture, your new employer said: "Reeves, you cannot tease *every* new hire."

You looked back and forth between the two men. "Have I done something out of order?"

"Nothing as would offend," the scarred man assured you. "However, when in my own home, I prefer to be called by my first name." He drank in your stiff spine and tight frown. "I know it is against etiquette to call an employer by their given name, but I insist upon it."

You closed your eyes. "I understand, Master Sicarius."

Reeves's puffed cheeks looked like a balloon about to pop. "P-please excuse me for a moment," he stammered, pointing at the door. "I-I'll go fetch you s-something to eat."

Your employer nodded.

As a man with food poisoning hurries to the bathroom, Reeves rushed out of the study. Muffled by the heavy wood door, you could still hear gales of raucous laughter echoing down the hall. A dread heat bloomed in your cheeks.

"Please ignore him," the master instructed. "My relationship with Reeves began on equal footing. Given our history, the formalities between us are very minimal."

"I see," you murmured.

Your employer took a seat in the lounge chair. "I am surprised he held out this long calling me *Mr.* Sicarius. I can only assume your use of the word 'master' tipped him over the edge." Sicarius propped his elbow on the soft leather arm and rested his chin on his long fingers. The other hand gestured to you and then the couch.

First, the overly casual footman treats a maid as a guest, and now the nonchalant owner invites a servant to sit? What was wrong with this house!?

Unsure what else to do, you bowed to the master's whim and took the seat he indicated. Perched on the very edge of the sofa, you folded your hands in your lap. As you bristled with agitation, an amused smile broke across his lips. You swallowed to clear the stone in your throat before speaking again.

"Should I refrain from calling you that, sir?"

His eyes were mesmerizing and cold, like some great ice sculpture at the frost festival. Up and down your body they swept, never pausing until they met your gaze again. Goose pimples ran along your arm.

"No, in fact, I rather like it. Please continue to do so."

The down-filled cushions made it difficult to keep your posture. With as much decorum as you could manage while being swallowed by the sofa, you replied, "I understand, Master Sicarius."

"Now then, has your trunk been sent for?"

"Yes. Mr. Ellsworth called for it after I accepted the position."

Sicarius frowned. "Are those clothes generally representative of your wardrobe?"

You looked down at your dress. It was a simple black column silhouette with a drop waist and a long skirt. The linen fabric was tolerant to wear and washable without the fuss required of a fine lady's filmy nets.

"Yes, Master?"

Sicarius wrinkled his nose. "I must go into town myself in three days. Reeves and I will accompany you to my seamstress." He nodded to your travel frock. "Burn that and anything of similar appearance when your new wardrobe arrives."

"E-excuse me? Wardrobe? You can not mean—"

The master leaned back in his chair and held his hands out, waving at the entire room. "I am sure you have realized this by now, but I only bother to keep fine, useful, and beautiful things around me. The result is as you see: a restful home filled with the best." He sneered at your dress. "If my servants mill about in drab attire, it detracts from the aesthetic."

You pursed your lips. A seamstress sounded expensive.

"Of course, all the clothing will be from my wallet as it is my folly," he explained with a wave of his hand.

You bowed your head, trying to hide your stunned expression. "If that is your wish."

"It is."

You winced at the sharp finality of his statement.

"Now... about your nightly duties..."

Your heart pounded at his words. Always the same implication. Why could no one take the truth at face value? Why could no one believe that you just—

"I understand that you used to read my friend to sleep."

Lifting your head, you scanned the pale man's face. There was no derisive sneer, and no insinuation of impropriety in his tone. His features were placid and smooth, like someone commenting on the weather.

"Yes!" In your excitement, you blurted the word. With another cough to hide your embarrassment, you steadied yourself. "The professor had difficulty sleeping. As his vision failed, I read to him to quiet his nerves." Your voice was weak as specters of all the gossip-mongers haunted your thoughts.

Slut.

Fortune hunter.

Maid-of-the-night.

You shook your head to dispel their slander. Stinging eyes lowered to your lap. "I just read to him. Nothing more."

"Yes? That is what your letter said, is it not?"

Your skirt wrinkled in your grip. "Not everyone believes it."

The master scoffed. "Not everyone knew him. Anyone that did knew that man was irrevocably blunt. Why lie when he found such great entertainment in ruffling people with the truth?"

You lifted your gaze. The sparkle in Sicarius's eyes was as impetuous as a schoolboy recounting his summer adventures. You covered your mouth to hide the relieved giggle that fluttered from your lips.

"Very true," you agreed.

Sicarius ran his fingers through his silver hair. "One time, a fellow classmate tried to claim a death in the family as an excuse for missing a deadline. The professor told my classmate that his grades were already so low they could be placed in the coffin alongside the dead man."

Was this man *trying* to break your composure? You clamped your teeth, sides splitting from holding in the laughter.

"Worse yet, when the headmaster demanded to know if Professor Campbell really said it, he doubled down!" Sicarius sat up straight. With a pompous huff, he pantomimed pushing a pair of glasses up his nose. His voice drifted into a tenor tone that perfectly mimicked your previous employer. "The boy's brain should go along with them both as it may yet gain more use than in its current employment," Sicarius quoted.

A few whiney noises blew between your fingers, but you managed to control the worst of it.

Your companion folded his hands in front of his smile. "I am glad you stayed. Ellsworth told me that the salary almost ran you off."

Recalling the terse conversation, you scratched your cheek. "Knowing what I know now, I feel awful assuming the position was just a ruse for—"

Sicarius raised a single finger. "But the position *was* a ruse."

You blinked at him. He grinned at you. Cold sweat beaded down your neck. As the man stared at you, there was a dark fire in his eyes that made your stomach flop. His lips curled into a menacing grin.

"To be blunt, I was not looking for a maid. I only ever wanted you."

"E-excuse me?"

All at once the tension snapped as Sicarius descended into a round of cackles. "You look like a startled cat! It was just because of the professor's complimentary letter. That's all I meant."

"O-of course. The letter. How silly of me."

"You must understand, when a man like Professor Campbell makes a recommendation, I always take it." The master nodded to the books behind him. Then, he crossed his arms and lifted his chin like a man at a lectern. In that same flawless mimic of your old employer, Sicarius droned out: "West facing windows, my friend. A well thought out library must maximize the evening light to reduce strain on the eyes."

Sicarius clearly knew the professor *very* well. The west-facing windows were located in the professor's private parlor. No one was allowed in there who was not a close personal friend.

The first time you were permitted in the study was a disaster. Wanting to impress the professor, you stayed up past four in the morning practicing your letters. By midday, you were so dizzy that he forced you to sit. The sun was warm. The overstuffed arms of the club chair were comfortable. When you awoke, the old man was staring at you from his desk. You blubbered out apologies, but Professor Campbell just scoffed.

"Does one commonly apologize for following instructions? I told you to rest before you fell over, and you did so. Now silence your sniffling, girl. I wish to finish this letter in some semblance of peace."

As the memory faded, the grim sense of something forgotten crept up into your gut. You cocked a brow, still trying to recall the man before you. Professor Campbell suffered few guests. Yet, no matter how hard you tried, you could not recall one instance where you saw this man in the professor's townhouse.

"Is there something on my face?"

Your cheeks burned. Stars! How long had you been staring!?

"Forgive me, Master," you apologized, bowing your head. "You clearly knew him well, but I cannot seem to recall—"

"Seeing me at his home?"

Hot with shame, you nodded.

Sicarius shrugged. "My job kept me away more often than not. I should have visited more, but in my mind, he was like an ancient tower. He had stood on his own for ages before I met him, and in my foolishness, I assumed he would be here long after me."

As your master scanned over all the finery and knowledge in the room, there was a cold melancholy in his gaze. When his eyes became unfixed and distant, you recognized the look. It was one you often saw on Professor Campbell's face when his insomnia was most acute: hot and muggy evenings after a heavy summer rain.

"The professor was the only one who truly understood me." Sicarius swallowed, like the words choked him. "The deprivation of his companionship will be my greatest regret."

Your heart skipped.

Sicarius sat forward, putting his elbows on his knees, observing you over folded fingers. "Did he ever tell you about his work as my translator?"

You shook your head.

"Perhaps that is wise." Sicarius's gaze turned to the window. "It was not always pleasant."

In the pale light of a winter afternoon, your master's expression seemed as ragged as wet paper. Dark shadows and deep creases spoke of restless nights staring vainly at blank ceilings as if they would yield some great truth beyond the pain. His eyes glazed with icy grief that seemed no more likely to thaw than your own. He simultaneously looked childlike and weighted down by too much life.

Your chest squeezed. "Thank you, Master."

"Whatever for?"

One hand coiled to your breast. "Somehow, hearing you speak so fondly of him, I…" Your voice trailed off.

"I understand." A pensive smile played upon Sicarius's lips. "There is a certain comfort in shared pain."

"Yes," you agreed. "Forgive me."

He chuckled and shook his head. "There is nothing to forgive."

Sicarius rose to his feet and strolled to the shelf nearest the staircase. His large hands traced the bindings like a boy dragging a stick along an iron fence. "Reference texts," he declared.

Puzzled, you repeated, "Reference texts?"

Long, powerful legs reached the wall by the window in less than fifteen strides. He rapped on a few large tomes with his knuckles. "Philosophy, religion, social sciences, languages, and customs are here."

"Ah!" You snapped to attention. "Of course!"

He pointed to each set of shelves in turn. "The natural and applied sciences are near the door. On the other side, geography and history." He turned to you with a twinkle in his eyes. "Do you follow so far?"

"Yes, Master," you replied.

He folded his hands behind his back and turned his gaze upward. The gesture stretched the fabric of his shirt over his toned chest. "The upper south and east walls are entirely fiction from horror to romance. To the north, art and architecture are paired as I consider them much the same."

As he reviewed his collection, Sicarius's posture was open and cordial. Standing amongst his fine belongings, he held all the bearing of gentry without the presumption of class. Your stomach twisted in knots. In a normal home, with status and roles sharply delineated, it was easy to predict what was expected of you. However, Sicarius Estrova and his "easy manners" were like a fog over your mind. He commanded you like a servant but treated you like a guest. It made your head ache to puzzle over your place. Reeves could keep his "easy manners." You would take clear expectations over this nebulous role any day.

"Biographies are there." Sicarius thrust a finger toward a small section near the window's edge. "I confess my temperament makes me poorly inclined to hear men prattle on about their own greatness. However, I do prefer learning from the mistakes of others to living them myself."

You nodded along.

"Every evening, after your dinner, you are to report to my study. If I have selected a title, it will await you on the desk. If not, there will be a sheet of paper with the general genre I wish to hear." He flicked a finger over his shoulder. "I trust you will be able to find something of interest?" he teased.

You bowed your head. "I will endeavor to always please you, Master."

An eerie smirk stretched his cheeks. "I shall hold you to that promise."

CHAPTER FIVE

Snow Season – Day 20 of 90

"Do you have something..." You clenched your teeth, trying to find the right words. "...with fabric on it?"

The bubbly blonde before you raised a thin, blue brow and pouted her painted lips. "This style is very popular!" She swept her hands along her thighs. "It accentuates the legs."

Your eyes raked up and down the bustle skirt. The damask taffeta was pearlescent emerald green and of exquisite quality. Plump tufted gatherings gave it volume, but without cumbersome width. You had no doubt it was the latest couture, direct from Kestania's winter fashion shows. The trouble was that delicate copper chains in the front hitched it so high, people could comment on the lace trim of your undergarments.

"The straps are adjustable." She tugged the front panel down. It was only a hand's length lower. "See! Now, what do you think?"

"Are they removable?" you muttered.

If she cocked her head any further, her ridiculous, sky-high wig was going to tumble right off her scalp. "Why would you want to remove them?" She shuffled her skirt, drowning her legs in a tidal wave of frills. Her bubbly wink set your teeth on edge. "How will you show off your assets?"

Your jaw started to ache as terrified eyes searched the room for aid. Your employer was no help. With a sadist's satisfaction, he smirked at you over his long fingers. Reeves was even more useless. He was bent over in the corner, shoulders shaking from holding in his laughter. You hoped he suffocated from all his efforts.

The blonde bounced to another satin mannequin with the glee of a yappy dog nipping at its mistress's guests. "Perhaps this will be better?"

Upon the figure was a monstrous mound of lace, layered like an over-frosted cupcake beneath a knee-high, pink velvet bell skirt. While the droopy sleeves reminded you of a butterfly's wings, there was a certain horror in imagining a poor creature being ripped apart to create… this. Splattered with polka dot bows and trimmed in fur, the brightly colored nightmare looked like something a four-year-old would force upon her doll for the unicorn princess's tea party.

"This has much more length, yes?"

You glanced at the door. With a wave of his hand, the master put the choking Reeves between you and the exit. As you were contemplating the virtues of death by self-immolation, Sicarius's smooth baritone called out to your torturer.

"Georgette, I am ever pleased with the *wide* array of options you offer. However, our maid is a widower, and the social circles she was brought up in were"—he raised the back of his hand to his mouth and lowered his voice to a gossip's hush—"very traditional."

The blonde looked at your dowdy clothing with a pity-filled frown. "Oh, yes… Of course. Of course."

Your master continued his insinuations, "Though she has passed her mourning period, we all know that the heart does not heal quickly. Perhaps, after such a long seclusion, something of a simpler style would suit her better?"

The blonde took your hands in hers, coiling her painted claws around your wrists. "But you mustn't, dearest!" she begged, tears in her eyes. "You still have your looks. You cannot give up hope."

If you cringed any further, your head would disappear into your collar.

Sicarius's smile was as charming as a devious fae bidding a lost soul to come into the night. "Then what would you suggest?"

At once, the silliness in her expression was gone. She drew herself up and took a deep inhale. Crimson talons tightened their hold. "Come, darling. Georgette knows what to do."

When you emerged from the dressing room, Georgette guided you to a raised pedestal between four scalloped mirrors. With tightly restrained hope, you looked up from your feet. Despite yourself, a gasp escaped your lips.

"Oh Georgette, my little muffin, I knew I could count on you!" Reeves cooed, pinching his wife's cheek.

The tea frock was jacquard cotton in ivory cream. Its V-shaped neckline plunged to your navel around a high collared panel of modest smocking. Trimmed with small ruffles, it coyly suggested femininity without the garishness of youth. Embroidered ribbon accents were a burgundy overlaid with delicately tatted chains of picots and rings. A simple silk sash tucked the dress tightly to your waist. The flounced petticoat was impossibly light thanks to the fine chiffon construction.

Sicarius hummed. "It is missing something."

With a click of her tongue, Georgette shook her finger at the image in the looking glass. "Pearl teardrop earrings."

You whipped around in horror. "Oh no, Master, no! You can not!"

"They make it more mature." Georgette snapped her fingers. "It must be done."

Sicarius's hand curled over his chin to stifle the snort. "You heard the woman." He mimicked her snap. "It must be done." The sadist turned to his manservant. "Reeves, talk to VosKart and Bronsk. Get something conservative in ivory. Nothing gaudy like those awful cufflinks they showed me last month."

Reeves extracted a paper pad and pen from his pocket. He jotted down the note with a snotty grin.

Your master turned back to the seamstress. "Now, as to the uniform…"

"Ah!" Georgette clasped her hands by her cheek. "I thought of it as soon as you sent her measurements! You will be pleased! Dainty, but with grace. Tasteful, but ornate. It will make for excellent scenery."

"Show me," Sicarius commanded.

Georgette rounded on you with quivering fingers and a predatory grin. A cold sweat trickled down your neck. You took a step back. With both hands, she seized your arm and tugged you down the stairs. A bouncing push sent you spiraling into the dressing room.

When you emerged from Georgette's lair, your face was slack in sullen defeat. She paraded you onto your perch and twirled her finger. Like a well-trained stage monkey, you turned in a tight circle.

Your calf-length black dress had puffed gigot sleeves that tapered at the upper arm. The skirt, neckline, and cuffs were stark white with a scalloped hem. An underbust apron was trimmed with bobbin lace below four bronze buttons. Each of these was pressed with Sicarius's spider seal. You frowned at the delicate details. It would be impossible to keep clean.

Georgette grinned as she held a matching, but plainer, drape aloft. "One for the housework and one for the serving."

You sighed with relief.

She turned you to face your master and pointed to the ruffled jabot tie. "It wants a brooch."

"Bronze like the buttons?"

"All bronze? Too masculine." She paused and tapped her chin. "Though, with a mother of pearl core…"

Reeves hastily scribbled down the note.

"For the headpiece, would you like a bun, a cap, a headband, or a headdress?"

The master stared at your hair with the intensity of a society widow eyeing a prospective suitor for her child. "A headband seems the most practical for all lengths. However, I do want better than a simple ruffle."

"An accent ribbon. I will weave it in the crochet, so it is not so childish." Georgette set her hands around your head to indicate the distance. Her long nails scraped the edges of your scalp. "This wide?"

Sicarius clicked his tongue. "Perfect."

She grinned. "I will have them complete in a few days."

Your master thumbed his chin. His eyes rolled to your old dress, hanging like a sad sack from the dressing room hooks. "I do not suppose you have anything ready-made?"

Georgette's smile was coy. "Do you think me one of your little machines, Mr. Estrova? A simple seamstress cannot just"—she popped her lips— "make dresses fall out of the sky."

The silver-haired man tilted his jaw back until the shadows filled the crevices below smooth cheekbones. "No, I do not believe you to be a machine, but neither are you a *simple* seamstress."

The sly way she raised her painted brows tightened the knot in your stomach.

"Perhaps I have something that may work." Georgette peered over her shoulder at Reeves. "If my husband could have the night off?"

Sicarius groped deep into his pocket. With a frown, he turned to the footman. "Reeves? Do you have the time?"

"Half-past noon."

Sicarius nodded. "If you can complete the task by three, you would have plenty of time to make my standing reservation at Riverside Bistro."

Georgette flapped her hands towards the door. "Off with you boys, then. We shall work faster without you."

Your master turned his back and strolled to the exit. Reeves blew a kiss to the blonde before tugging the door shut. As the lock clicked, your hackles rose. An oppressive aura of desperation oozed from your captor's every pore.

You took a step back. "Mrs. Reeves, I am sure you must be rather excited about your date, but I—"

A soft finger pressed itself to your lips. "Do not worry." The frenzy in her blue eyes made you feel like a toy in the hands of a rambunctious child. "Georgette knows what to do."

Two hours later, you sat on the velvet cushion stool as the furious churning of the sewing machine filled the room. Georgette's fingers flew across the navy skirt, tacking the hem into submission. When at last she reached the end of her task, she nipped the thread with a flourish and stuffed the dress into your hands. A flick of her wrist was enough to send you skittering into the changing drapes. When you stepped out again, one thing was clear: Georgette did, in fact, know what to do.

The dress itself was a simple princess cut bodice attached to a long, pleated skirt. Flowing sleeves were easy to move in but tapered to an elegant cuff. A rounded flat collar and pintuck yoke displayed modest professionalism befitting of a governess. The detail that set it apart from such an occupation was the copper colored tie around your neck. Too rich for a traditional servant's wardrobe, its fine paisley fabric mirrored Reeves's waistcoat.

"He likes his collections to match," Georgette explained as she evened the knot.

"Is that why you forced this ridiculous girdle set upon me?" you demanded.

"It's called a *garter* set. Less restrictive than the corset or the girdle but it still tucks the waist." Georgette winked at you. "Besides, pretty underthings are the pride of every woman."

"Pretty as they may be, these briefs are riding up my backside!"

"It is called a cheeky cut for a reason."

You sighed in defeat.

As Georgette dipped to secure the hemline, a general feeling of constrictive unease engulfed your gut. Your eyes fell to the window, examining the ice on the single pane glass. Beyond the boundaries of Georgette's shop, the city of Marinar was bursting with activity from the Frost Festival. The burbling purr of steam-ore engines was interspersed with the nickering of horses and the clop of carts in the lane.

"Mrs. Reeves, how long have you known my master?"

The blonde smoothed the last pleat and stepped back to take in her work. "Six years. He came for a suit. When I saw the delectable man he brought in tow, I knew I must keep him as a customer."

"Have you noticed anything… odd about him?"

She raised a thinly penciled brow. "Darling, all the rich are odd. You must be more specific."

Memories of a charming smile and witty banter fluttered across your thoughts. You shook your head like a dog throwing off mud. "He speaks to his servants in a very different tone than that to which I am accustomed."

The seamstress plucked a loose thread from your shoulder. "He does not look down upon someone because they lack *noble* connections." She scoffed and draped her arms one over the other. "They treat us like dirt, but he is a man who judges talent over breeding."

"I can hardly find fault with that," you agreed, biting your lip. Your new kidskin boots toed the floor. "…but does not his manner seem *too* at ease with his employees for a man of his standing?"

The woman stared at you with narrowed eyes and pursed lips.

A burning itch crawled up your neck. "Please forgive me. I spoke out of turn."

Georgette sighed and shook her head. "Dearest, you are in a new place. That would make anyone feel uncomfortable." She patted your cheek. "Life brings so many troubles. Do not bring your own."

The clock on her wall chimed three times. Turning to face the looking glass, you fanned your skirt. The woman in the mirror was unfamiliar, but as you swung your new dress from side to side, you resolved to become accustomed to her.

All at once, there was a cheerful voice in the hall and a jaunty series of raps on the door. Reeves swaggered into the room with a hoard of shopping bags swinging from his wrists. In his hands he held a long leather box bearing an embossed lyre and a brass tag labeled "Froskwick's Fine Instruments." He pecked his wife on the cheek and peeled the packaging off his sore arms. From a monogrammed silver sack, he extracted a charcoal grey cloak.

"Sicarius awaits you downstairs," he instructed, handing you the mantle.

You took the garment in your hands. The wool was finely crimped and soft to the touch. Once you closed the clasp, Reeves hung the bags from your outstretched arms. He opened the door and shooed you out into the stairwell. You staggered as each of the purchases rocked in a different direction. Toddling down the steps with the grace of an overladen pack mule, you planted one foot on each tread before easing onto the next. When at last you reached the bottom, you sighed with relief.

The city of Marinar was an ocean town and Coriland's largest port. On winter days, sea breezes choked travelers' throats with salty cold. Digging through a paper bag from Sanderson's Sweet Emporium, Sicarius seemed unaffected by the winds. He popped a crunchy toffee into his mouth and closed his eyes. The orgasmic expression on his face was enough for one mother to usher her children to the other side of the street. You lowered your head to hide your smile.

"I am sorry to have kept you waiting, Master."

The scarred man licked his lips and tugged black calf-skin gloves back over his fingers. He then eyed the parade of packages digging into your arms with an amused snort. Beckoning you with one finger, he strolled down the sidewalk.

"Lyle will be arriving in about half an hour to take you home in the Benson. Reeves and I will stay at the townhouse and return tomorrow morning."

You dodged around a group of cackling middle-aged women. "I understand."

Sicarius pointed to a paper bag with twine handles. "Be sure Cook gets his spices as soon as you get home. For my stomach's sake, I strive to keep him happy."

"Of course," you replied, scurrying to keep pace with his stride.

"You will want to use the lap harness when riding with Lyle. He obtained his lessons from a man that used to import wine and spirits into Antellas."

You raised a brow. "I thought the Holy Nation of Antellas was a dry country?"

"It is." Sicarius smirked. "It makes his driving rather more exciting."

Your stomach flopped. "Thank you for the warning, Master."

When you neared the intersection, you came to a halt two steps behind your employer. Tired arms ached from the weight of the luggage. With a deep breath, you rolled back your shoulders and lifted your head. There were five blocks yet to go. You could tough it out.

When the traffic police tweeted for you to cross, your master strode out into the lane as if he owned everything down to the core of the world. You frowned at expensive labels on his purchases. Perhaps he did.

Though the streets were too frozen to be muddy, it was odd that one who could afford such luxuries did not bother to hail a taxi. Then again, as you watched him savor another toffee with pleasure too sinful for temple approval, you thought back to Georgette's words.

She was correct; all the rich were odd.

On your right side, there arose a chorus of shrieks and a horrific clatter. You looked up from your thoughts only to see a carriage with no driver a few strides away. The lissome beast who pulled it was wild with fright. Panicked eyes bulged from his skull as he stampeded towards the crossway in a hurricane of hooves and hysteria. All the sounds of the world dropped away until only the pounding of your heart throbbed in your ears. All at once, your vision went pitch black.

It took four ragged breaths before you realized the inky dark was not the bowels of the lower world, but the lapels of an elegant wool coat.

Shaking from head to toe, you looked up into an exquisitely carved jaw and teasing blue eyes. Two strong arms wrapped around your waist, pulling you tight into a firm chest. The smell of burnt sugar was sweet on his breath.

"While I do appreciate a woman who would die for me, I am accustomed to my new hires living longer than five days in my employ."

With each shallow pant, the surrounding sounds returned to your ears. Above the roar of the crowd, a policeman was screaming for everyone to stand back. You turned and wished you had not. The splintered carriage lay on its side. A lamppost on the corner was bent to the ground. Between them, the poor creature flailed three of its legs. The fourth was pointing the wrong way.

"Come." Sicarius set you back on your feet, his arm never leaving your waist. "The authorities will handle it."

Cold and trembling, you nodded.

As he led you away from the scene, that same smile from the funeral stretched across his face. Staring into his strange expression, the hackles on the back of your neck rose. With a deep breath, you swallowed down your unease. Far be it from you to criticize your savior for having an eerie face.

CHAPTER SIX

Snow Season – Day 21 of 90

The difference between affluence and opulence was the decor of Gravelorne manor.

Stepping onto the black floors of the great hall, the click of your heels was as sharp as a snare drum. The inky marble's white veins coiled around your dark reflection like smoke in still air. Two stories above, the vaulted plaster was embossed with water lily motifs as fine as wedding lace. When the morning sun filtered through the great windows, the ceiling's aluminum leaf backdrop glowed like starlight.

In the center of the hall, more ostentatious than the luminous ceiling, was a massive gnarled tree rendered in tendrils of gold. Perched on a bed of opalescent river stones, it stretched taller than the second-story banisters. Smooth crystal glass pooled around tumbling roots like water on a windless night. Jade lily pads, seating on wire stalks, dotted the surface of the artificial pond. Their tiered blossoms were rendered in capiz so fine you feared your breath might shatter them. Every child in Coriland would recognize the design. It was printed on the front of the Holy Text, guarded by the Dark One and his Shadowhounds.

"I still can not believe he has a scale model of the Fae Tree," you groaned.

Still, as you examined the problem before you, the tree's beautiful appearance belied what legend told you lived beneath the golden bark.

You put your hands on your hips, staring into the tall branches. "Pretty as you may be, how am I supposed to clean you?"

The lovely tree did not bother to answer the question.

With a sigh, you retreated to the closet below the grand staircase. Inside the spacious cupboard were ample cleaning supplies. There were buckets and broomsticks enough for fourteen maids. Rows upon rows of sponges and rags were neatly stacked on labeled shelves. A veritable army of polish and powder blue sat in bottles near a small sink. On the left of the chemicals, there was a flask of gin. The alcohol had a large label which read: *For cleaning, not consumption* in tidy scrawl. You extracted Reeves's list from your pocket, and compared the two. Clearly, the note on the gin had been written by someone else. One could actually understand it.

Deciphering Reeves's handwriting was an exercise in patience. Disheveled words blurred together like one long scribble. The letters were tiny, bearing neither depth nor contrast. What little punctuation he used was smudged. You had spent easier days translating Olde Tronkish with the professor than reading this "note" from the footman. Still, squinting your eyes, you managed to decode it as follows:

1. Aside from the master's bed and bath, nothing needs tidied every day. Just divide up the work into days of the week and do the best you can.

2. Use Lyle's gear cart to bring any laundry up when you clean the bedroom.

3. Only Ellsworth answers the front door. Do not deprive him of his fun.

4. If you see Norton the gardener in the glasshouse: yes, he is always like that.

5. By order of Ellsworth: do not help Lyle with the laundry room.

6. Do not touch the kitchen or the larder. Punishment exceeds death.

You sighed. Somehow, it felt like Reeves's note gave you more questions than answers.

Collecting a stepladder, you made your way to the grand portraits on the wall.

On the right, a teasing ethereal beauty with powder-white skin sat on her pedestal. Clothed in a low shouldered gown of cream silk, she hid a coquettish smile behind a folded fan. Golden butterflies trimmed in ivory pearls adored waves of hair as pale as moonbeams. Half-lidded eyes of aquamarine sparkled with saucy delight. Below her painting was a nameplate which read: *Mrs. Estella Hedgecoth.*

On the left, the twin painting contained a pale man, not older than twenty-five. Wearing a black tuxedo and a coy smirk, he leaned into his index finger and thumb. Though the slick quiff was longer than the taper cut he wore nowadays, there was no mistaking the teasing gaze of haunting blue. As smug as the slinky feline in his lap, your master stood for all time staring out on his handcrafted domain.

While you dusted the gilded frames, all three pairs of painted eyes seemed to follow every flick of your wrist. Despite the warmth of the afternoon sun, goose pimples crawled up your arm.

"Did he trap their souls in the oil?" you murmured with a shudder.

As your silent audience looked on, you turned your attention to the various furnishings of the hall. Thanks to your mechanical replacements, the mirrored facets of the deco sideboard were already immaculate. A simple cleansing with warm water removed the dust from the soapstone top. You wiped the rotary phone down with gin before turning to your next task: a pair of feathered glass vases near the door. While the curvaceous outsides were clean, you were appalled to find a layer of dust hiding within.

"How shoddy." You unbuttoned your cuffs and rolled up your sleeves. "We shall fix that."

Strapping on your cleaning gloves, you returned to battle armed with a bottle, brush, lukewarm water, and a determined sneer. Thirty minutes later, your elbow burned, but the twin jars were a flawless luster gloss. With a satisfied nod, you rolled your shoulders and faced the problem child of the hall.

Looming above you, the gleaming golden menace reached out to the ends of the room. You stalked around the sculpture three times, looking for weaknesses. It was no use. The upper branches were too high.

"Do not think you have escaped that easily, my friend," you told the tree with a shake of your finger. "Once I find a taller ladder, I shall return."

As the clock struck half-past two, you pushed your way through the etched wooden door into the master's office. You chuckled at the monochrome mosaic on the floor. Asymmetrical triangles trimmed with brass? How "new money" of him.

"Less of a study and more of a party," you joked to yourself.

When you drew back the heavy grey curtains, sunlight spilled across a tufted wingback chair and dark pedestal desk. You frowned at the empty bone china utensil cup. Clearly, your new master had an unhealthy love of the material.

Under the chair, you spotted a flash of gold. With a snort, you retrieved the fountain pen and tucked it back in its proper place. The convex brass shade of the enamel lamp attracted fingerprints like liquor attracted sots. A rag and sharp polishing put an end to that. Once the desk was in order, you turned your attention to the built-in fixtures.

The bookshelves were an ebony walnut, much like the desk. You ran your finger over their edges. It came back clean and smelling of lemon oil.

The alabaster fireplace had tiered columns of round molding, which were already dust free. As you inspected the triangular inlays of obsidian and brass, a sigh escaped your lips. The mechanical mice had handled this too! You checked the crevices of the scallop-backed guest chairs. There was neither crum nor hair to be found. It seemed that your robotic replacements could vacuum even the deepest parts of the furniture. That was convenient to see but not a comfort to know.

By the time the hall clock chimed three, you were back to your list.

"Gear… cart?" You set your bucket down in the stairwell closet. "What is a gear cart?"

"Would you like me to show you?"

With a startled hiss, you whipped around, clutching your pounding chest. Leaning on the door frame, wearing the same smirk as his portrait, was your master.

"My… I did not intend to surprise you that much."

Willing your breath to even, you bowed your head. "It is not a problem. How may I assist you?"

"I came by to check your progress." Sicarius turned his gaze to the gleaming glass vases by his front door. He raised a wry brow. "It seems I am getting my money's worth."

"I merely washed them. It is hardly worth praise."

"Reeves has been terrified to do so since I brought them home from Lustras."

"L-Lustras?" you squeaked. "Those are *real* Lustras glass?"

Sicarius's lips curled in a grin. "Were you expecting imitation?"

Two Lustras glass vases. Your old mistress would have shrieked with jealousy. The famous Gamoid glassmaker had a three year waitlist for paperweights, let alone vases *plural.*

Oh stars above, and you *touched* them!

"I-I see." Inhaling to stave off the dizziness, you faked a polite chuckle. It sounded pinched. "Well, I am glad you are satisfied."

The master hummed and strolled over to the stairs. Anchored to the wall was a long brass track. Sicarius depressed a small button. From above, the click of metal teeth grew louder and louder. Around the bend, a strange apparatus made of strong steel construction descended the stairs. When it reached the bottom, your master unfolded the device to reveal three heavy prongs.

"You will find the gear carts in the laundry. Once their pegs are sealed into the magnetic bolts, you can use the hand lever to move them up the track."

Your eyes traced the long path up to the second story. "Mr. Watts made this?"

Sicarius leaned against the wall and tucked his hands in his pockets. "He said it was more fun than an elevator."

"Your house is incredible, Master."

"I try." Wearing a wolf's smile, he nodded to the list in your hand. "What other questions have you come across?"

Swallowing your pride, you pointed to the tree. "With sincerest apologies, how does one clean that?"

"The sculpture?"

You nodded.

Sicarius chuckled. "Statistically speaking, with my butler's tears."

Leaving you flat-lipped and alarmed, the silver-haired sadist strolled to his office. You glanced up at the golden nightmare one last time. Its winding branches felt like they were wrapped around your neck. The study door snapped shut. Your trance broke. Slapping your cheeks, you set off for the laundry.

"Get yourself together, woman. You are a professional."

The office floor you might forgive, but the master's bed was just folly.

Standing beside the blonde four-post, you pursed your lips. Ivory silk sheets seemed to sneer at you. As you reached out, the threatening prickle of static charge rolled up your arm. With a grimace, you clutched your hand back to your chest.

"Who in the world actually sleeps on these things?"

With a sigh, you lifted the heavy damask comforter from the floor and folded it over the smooth satinwood hope chest. Your nose tickled when you sniffed the navy velvet bed curtains.

"Honestly! When did they last wash these!? The whole staff is so complacent from their little toys that they manage a half job at best!"

After bundling the dusty drapes down the laundry chute, you turned towards the bathroom door. The lights snapped on, revealing a tile floor with tessellations of creamy blue shells that matched the scallop-shaped sink. There were no walls around the shower, only a rainfall spout above a drain. Near the window, a bone china soaking tub was mounted on clawed feet. When weary eyes settled upon the dark, tarnished faucets, you nearly threw a clot.

"*Silver!?*" you squawked. "What madman puts silver in a *bathroom!?*"

Your vision blurred as phantom pain burned up your elbows. There was only one rational thing to do: turn off the light and come back later.

Once the bed was made, you proceeded with your inspection. The tulipwood waterfall vanity was already polished to a glowing sheen. Dusty window drapes were dragged off to the bowels of the laundry. Yet again, the carved marble fireplace looked unused. Good. That was one less headache to deal with. You ticked off the last items with a bouncing finger. Oversized down pillows? Fluffed. Custom-tailored clothing? Hung. Water lily bed lamp? Dusted. Gaudy silk boxers? Folded.

Throughout your cleaning fit, your attention was hopelessly drawn back to the evils which you could not unsee. Your wild eyes stared into the great black maw leading to the bath. You cracked your wrists.

"Let the gods have mercy upon you, for I shall not."

At nine twenty-nine that evening, you rapped on the study entrance.

"Enter," your master called.

Using your hip, you pushed through the heavy doors. Spread across his workspace were stacks of papers in a whirlwind of chaos. The waste bin was filled with crumpled envelopes and shredded letters. You placed the tisane service at the corner of the desk. The smell of apricot scones and grassy chamomile filled the room.

"Good evening, Master. Would you like me to light the fire?"

Sicarius slumped into his palm, rubbing his temple in firm, tight circles. "No, I hope to be done with this nonsense before eleven." He waved at the book sitting on the velvet guest chair. "When you have finished with the bathrooms, return here. My mind is a jumble tonight."

Amber liquid filled the squat teacup. "I have completed that task."

Sicarius glanced at the clock. "I meant all the bathrooms."

You buttered the scone. "As did I."

"All seven?"

"Twenty, sir."

"What?"

You placed his plate beside his right elbow. "There are twenty bathrooms in your estate. Four in the halls, one in the garage, twelve for the guests, the master suite, and the two in the servants' quarters." Your eyes glowed brighter than his lamp. "With the dust-mice handling the floors, the work was much speedier than I expected. I finished changing the linens as well."

The fountain pen hit the desk. "You cleaned Lyle's bathroom?"

You shook your head. "No, I taught him to clean it."

Sicarius turned his chair to face you. "You expect me to believe that you completed twenty bedrooms and bathrooms, washed the vases, dusted all statues and paintings in the main hall, tidied my study, polished the metalwork, and hung my laundry by yourself in"—he glanced at his mantle clock—"eight hours?"

"Six hours," you replied, turning the handle of the cup to face him. "Two half-hour meals, and after dinner, Mr. Ellsworth instructed me to take a nap. I can stay up past two, should you require it."

Sicarius regarded you with baffled amusement. "I assume you encountered the infamous *Black Faucets of Gravelorne* during your journey?"

"Those *silver* faucets of yours are heinous but nothing beyond salvation." You held the saucer out to him. "Would you like sugar?"

Sicarius burst out laughing. With a shaking hand, he took the clattering cup. Fearing for his papers, you hastily surrounded the china with a cloth napkin. As he banged his free hand on the desk, you lifted the drink out of his grasp and set it upon the tray. When you turned back to him, his grin stretched wide as a skeleton's.

"What force have I unleashed upon my home?"

For the next few hours, you sat in the guest chair, flipping through *Gemstones and Jewelry: From Historical*

Pieces to Modern Design. Representations of antique rings, pearl hairpins, and ancient beadwork filled the first ten chapters. However, your area of focus was the nearly hundred pages on gemstone properties and practical applications. At the master's request, you bookmarked options which were both pretty and pragmatic for daily wear.

As the chime cried quarter to eleven, your master dripped golden wax onto the last envelope. Removing his signet ring, he stamped the spider seal onto the letter. Bloodshot eyes stared at the overloaded outgoing correspondence pile. The only sound was the ticking of the mantle clock. Holding his breath, Sicarius eased the letter on top of the tower. The stack swayed to the left. Both your heads followed the lean in synchrony. When it stopped, there were two quiet sighs of relief. The master pressed his index finger to his lips and motioned you to your feet. Sicarius edged his way around the desk as you grasped the weighty tome to your chest. Once both of you were in the hall, you drew the office door closed behind you.

Like ghosts in the night, you climbed the long stairs in uneasy silence. The dark bronze banister felt cold in your hand. By the time you reached the second floor, your heartbeat quickened from more than the ascent. Overlooking the northern hills, past the dim wall sconces and wide windows, was the entrance to the master suite.

Sicarius strolled into his bedroom and made for the nightstand. With the flick of his thumb, the water-lily lamp glowed to life. He motioned for the book. You uncoiled your arms and handed it to him. As he set it upon the dressing table, the hairs on the back of your neck stood.

"The blue pajama set if you please."

"Of course, Master," you replied, hurrying to the wardrobe. Cold hands thumbed through the fabrics until you located an azure satin with white trim. You hung them on the door hook and unbuttoned the front. The room air was dry and static crackled along your forearm. You frowned at the garish sheets but said nothing. If the man wanted to be electrocuted, that was his business.

When you turned back around, Sicarius had his arms spread open. Wide eyes flitted between his face and the clothing. It felt like you had swallowed an icicle.

"Is something the matter?" he asked with a coy smirk.

Stars above, why did you not think of this problem before!?

You glanced at the clock. Nearly midnight now. No doubt the other servants would be tucked away in their beds. Your eyes met his. There was nothing there but amusement.

"No, Master," you answered, reaching for his striped tie. When you touched the shell knot, you forced yourself to breathe. "I simply did not want to overstep my bounds."

"Boundaries are often blurry in the dark."

You nodded to the nightstand. "Then I am grateful for the light."

Sicarius chuckled as you pulled his jacket off, sleeve by sleeve. After you hung it in the closet, he was still standing in the same position. You cursed under your breath. Was he oblivious, shameless, or simply teasing you?

"You've forgotten some things," he stated, pointing to his chest. There, at the edge of his mouth, you caught the upward twitch of a smile.

With new information in hand, it did not take long to formulate a plan. After all, you were far closer in age to an implacable dowager than a blushing virgin. This should not ruffle you.

You approached him with all the passion of a limestone block. Sharp fingers plucked the buttons down to his belt line. The hem pulled from his pants with an abrupt tug. Musky sweat threatened to distract you. You bit your tongue hard, forcing any bashful impulses into painful submission. With the flick of a wrist, you tore the warm fabric from his pale skin.

He whistled. "Cold."

As you stuffed his shirt down the chute, your smile was as frigid as dry ice. "I had not noticed, Master."

Your hand hit his belt buckle. He refused to yield. There was a loud jingle and a rush of fabric. With an unflinching nerve, you squatted down, keeping your gaze on his. As wool pants began to slip down thick, unshaven legs, his eyes seemed to spark like static.

"Tell me, did you always need to be in control or was that a habit you learned to survive?"

"Discipline is expected in the face of duty."

Dressed in only socks and underwear, Sicarius hummed and stroked his chin. "So it is *not* your natural temperament?"

"What is the difference between one's 'natural temperament' and the pattern of behavior one consistently displays?" you asked, peeling off his socks.

"Quite a bit, really."

Folding his pants over your arm, you replied: "Behaving however one wishes is the purview of children, the senile, and those that can afford it."

"I cannot tell if you are a cynic or a pragmatist."

You nodded to his dresser. "What color drawers would you like this evening, Master?"

There was a deep chuckle. "The ones with the papyrus."

You lifted the garments with both hands, presenting them like a street seller hocking a cheap pan. "These?"

"Yes."

"The bathroom is clean." You flipped his wrist over and pressed his underwear into his palm. "I shall turn down your covers while you wash your face."

With a snort, the master closed his eyes and chuckled. "Very well then."

As you gave him your back, he strolled to the closet and claimed his satin pants. The bathroom door closed and the unmistakable sound of water on tile filtered through the wood. With a firm slap to your own cheeks, you set about re-fluffing the pillows until you practically coughed feathers.

Ten minutes later, when the shower flipped off, you were prepared for the next wave of attack. A plush robe hung over your shoulder. You held the pajama shirt aloft, long sleeves at the ready. Loins girded, you clenched your teeth.

The door opened. Steam tumbled through the frame. Shuffling a towel over his short locks, the silver-haired hellion strolled into the room, bare-chested and brazen. A stray bead of water trickled down the center of his rolling pectorals. Your traitorous eyes trailed it along smooth abs. By the time it reached his navel, your mouth was dry. It was too late to conceal the stare.

With a calculating smile, he held his arms aloft. "If you would be so kind."

Burning with frustration of all kinds, you slipped him into the smooth satin. Your eyes remained fixed on his buttons until every last one was in place.

He nodded to the robe. "I appreciate the effort, but I do intend to sleep at some point this evening."

The master walked to his bed and slithered beneath the covers. He wrapped lean arms behind his head. As you tucked him in, blazing blue eyes never left your face.

You turned away and folded his dressing gown onto the nightstand.

He patted the side of the bed. "Pull up a chair. I am rather restless tonight."

"Yes, Master."

Retrieving a heavy sitting stool, you took up your usual position on the edge of your seat. The weighty tome unfolded in your lap. Using your page markers, you turned to the gem section. The first images were of sparkling clear stones scattered over white chantilly lace.

"Not diamonds." He waved his hand. "The Gause family has a stranglehold on the mines. Those rocks are far less rare than they would have you believe."

"Ah." You flipped forward a few pages before stopping on images of glowing blue stones. "Would you like to hear about sapphires?"

"Are they good for daily wear?

On the next page was an image of a woman's engagement band. The stone was a brilliant marquise cut surrounded by tulip-shaped filigree. Seeing it made your stomach flip. Without thinking, your right hand coiled around your empty left ring finger. When you realized what you were doing, you jerked the two apart.

"Y-yes." You cleared your throat. "Are you designing a new pocket watch?"

"Something like that."

You scanned the text for an acceptable topic. "They score a nine out of ten on the hardness scale."

"And the blue would complement my eyes."

Your hand paused mid page turn. "I suppose it would."

With a grin, his lids drifted shut. "Read to me," your master commanded.

Chapter Seven

Snow Season – Day 22 of 90

The next day, as you walked the servant's corridor, your thoughts about your master were still a jumble.

This was not the only time you were the target of an employer's interest. Your first position was chambermaid to the second son of Fulston Manor, the noble bred Hunter Highton. Unlike Gravelorne, the relationship between maid and master at Fulston was simple. You cleaned the beds, and Hunter treated you the same way he treated dust bunnies: only a problem if seen. However, on the night of his eighteenth birthday, Hunter met Evangeline Calcraft, the heiress to the Calcraft Firearms fortune. Second sons may inherit names, but they do not inherit money or titles. Hunter was an idiot, but not a fool. He ponied around like the prince from a fairytale all night. Evangeline fell for Hunter's chiseled jaw and painted personality. Mr. and Mrs.

Calcraft, both of commoner background, fell for the noble Highton name. All of society agreed it was a match well made.

However, that very evening, Hunter's drunken frustration about the situation became your problem.

"She is pretty enough for me, right?"

"Ms. Calcraft is very pretty, Master," you had agreed.

"Maybe a bit too much, though. I bet she's not a virgin anymore." Hunter's nose had wrinkled in a vile disgust. *"Probably got taken by some uncle already. That's what you females do, right? Play pretty and dumb so old men like you."*

Your heart clenched tight when he said those words. It was not a conversation anyone wanted to hear, let alone a servant girl. When his hand clamped around your wrist, it felt like your lungs were filled with cement.

"Well, I won't let her laugh at me for being one."

Only two things saved you that night: Hunter's alcohol-induced erectile dysfunction and ugly sobbing. His slap had sent you reeling to the floor. A kick to your leg left you limping for two days.

"You're going to pretend you're so pure? Lying dog. Just get out."

When you rushed for the door, Hunter waved your torn panties at you. Shadows engulfed his handsome face.

"Breathe a word of this to anyone, and this will be the only character reference you get."

Perhaps it was the word he used. Maybe it was divine guidance. Either way, when you finally realized where you had fled, you found yourself hiding amongst the hunting spaniels. There in the kennel, sharing rowdy spirits with the eldest son of the house, was your late husband, Piotr. One look at your broken lip sent both men straight to Hunter's bedroom for a "chat." From that day forward, all the dogs at Fulston manor growled whenever the boy walked by.

This time, however, there was no big, strong gamekeeper to "talk" the problem away. You were on your own.

As you neared the servant's entrance, a voice yelled:

"Watch out!"

You slammed back against the wall. A silver blur of metal and steam swept past you and out the door. It chugged down the ramp before bursting into the muddy courtyard with a whistling screech. Wild steel hands flailed in the air, flinging laundry everywhere. Wide eyes watched as clean undergarments fluttered into the muck.

Lyle came to a halt in the door frame, grabbing his red curls with both hands. With a horrified stare, he watched the mechanical nightmare charging straight through the opening of the north hedge maze.

"Oh shi—" He paused mid-word, casting a panicked look behind him. With a nervous chuckle, he swiftly corrected himself. "S-shipping routes! Oh! Shipping routes!"

You hid your laugh behind a cough. "Mr. Ellsworth has been upstairs all morning. I doubt he can hear you."

Lyle shook his head and pointed to the side of his skull. "He reads your thoughts!" he hissed.

"Right…" You patted the young man's shoulder. "Perhaps you should refrain from taste testing Cook's dandelion wine."

Whirrrrrrr, crunch!

Turning to the maze, you both saw a stream of steam and leaves churning into the air.

"Ohhhh!" Lyle moaned in panic. "Norton's gonna use me as fertilizer!" As if the gardener himself were on Lyle's heels, he dashed off towards the shrubs.

When he rounded the corner of the maze, you could not hold the laughter in. Chest burning, you bent over and sputtered into your hand. Once your body stopped heaving, you started to collect the runaway laundry from the muddy yard. "I suppose progress cannot exist without failure," you mused.

As a neat pile began to form, there was a great clunking noise. From the hedges, hopping behind the demon machine, came Lyle. His prosthetic leg was draped across the top of the casing. Next to it was a small metal box with loose wires. He waved at you. "Had to disconnect the friggen power source, but I got it contained!"

You frowned. "What happened to your leg?"

Lyle rolled the mechanical monster to the bottom of the ramp. "Got caught in the mud, and the suction broke. I think the valve seal cracked." He slapped the washer. "Give me a hand?"

With a short grunt and a mighty push, the two of you managed to shove the hellacious creation back inside. Lyle sighed and grabbed his metal leg. Plopping down on the cement, he pointed the attachment into the sun and frowned at it.

You squatted down beside him. "Is the damage very severe?"

He shrugged, turning the limb this way and that. After twisting a loose screw back into place, his hand depressed the vacuum seal. A rush of air burst from the valve.

"Not too bad," Lyle scratched his cheek. "I think."

You patted his shoulder. "Take the time you need. I will collect the undergarments."

Lyle hummed in response, still searching for defects.

You clutched your hem to your thigh as your leather boots squished in the half-melted mess. Step by step, you picked your way through the driest parts of the yard. Cold fingers plucked a deep purple V-string from the ground.

Lyle grinned. "That belongs to Reeves. Georgette bought it for him."

Just what every woman wanted: a rundown of her coworker's underwear selections and who purchased them. Apparently, Lyle had yet to learn about boundaries.

"Boundaries are often blurry in the dark."

Your face burned hot. "May we talk about something else?"

"Like what?"

Your eyes rolled to the bulky apparatus inside the doorway. "How did you become a mechanic?"

"Family business. I'm the first son, so I was supposed to take over." He patted his leg. "The shop got hit during the bombings five years ago. I made it out but dad didn't."

Your frozen hand hovered over the next pair of underpants. "I am sorry."

Lyle shook his head. "It's not all bad, you know. Losing my leg kept me from being drafted." With a forlorn smile, he stared at the cloudy sky. "My little brother never came home from the war. Dunno what mom would have done if she lost both of us."

You closed your eyes and folded your hands in front of you. "I am not happy you were hurt, but I am glad that we met."

Lyle's grin glowed like a warm ember. "Me too. It's nice being here. Peaceful. All the yelling at home got old."

"Yelling?" you asked in shock. "Did your mother yell at you?"

Lyle waved his hands. "Oh no, not her! Customers. People get all weird when you're in a wheelchair. They'd talk real slow and yell at me, like: How! Are! You! To-day!? Same way a lot of them talk to foreigners." Lyle snorted and pursed his lips to one side. "They always pucker-up like a fish when they do it too."

You stifled a snicker behind your hand. "I see."

"Sicarius came in one day because he was having trouble with the steam pressure in the Lacrima. He was the only one of them who treated me like… well…" Lyle pointed to his freckled nose. "Like me."

At the words "treated me like me," a moment long-cherished shoved its way to the front of your mind. The smell of hay and animal dander filled the air. As real as the night you first met, Piotr's massive hand reached out to you from your memories.

"Come now. This is a place for the dogs to sleep, and you are not a dog."

Hot tears seared your eyes. Before the red-head could see, you tilted your head back and swallowed down the salty pain.

"He's weird, but he's the only toff I can really respect, ya know?" Lyle continued with a stretch. "He treats people like people because of who they are, not what happened to them."

"I understand that you used to read my friend to sleep."

"Yes," you agreed, dabbing your face with the cuff of your sleeve. "Yes, he does." With a deep breath, you leaned over and plucked a pair of silk-black boxers from the ground. The tooth of your dry fingers snagged on the fine material.

"Those fancy things have *got* to belong to Sicarius!" Lyle laughed. "He has gaudy gold-trimmed ones too."

"Indeed," you muttered. "I have encountered them before."

Lyle cocked a saucy brow at you. "Oh really?"

The back of your neck burned as you realized your mistake. With a stately cough, you replied, "Handling clothing is in the normal course of my duties."

Lyle snickered. *"Right…"*

Your eyes narrowed. "I do not appreciate that tone, young man."

The mechanic threw his head back and cackled. "You can be such a stick in the mud."

You snatched a pair of teddy bear embroidered boxers from the ground. A wiggling finger poked through a hole in the seam. "My goodness! Are these not your favorite pair?"

The mechanic gulped.

A cold smile curled on your lips. "I shall call that charming young lady at the laundry straight away! Her darning work is excellent." You tapped your chin and faked confusion. "What was her name? Josephine? Jessica? Jada?"

Her name was Jasmine. Lyle said it fifteen times a day.

Eyes as wide as saucers, the young man scrambled to the edge of the ramp. "It was a joke, ma'am! A joke!"

"A joke?" Your face was placid as a porcelain doll. "Whatever are you talking about? I thought you *wanted* to discuss underwear?"

Lyle hung his head. "Reeves was right. Under all those manners, you're a fiend."

You strolled over to him and tossed the adorable undergarments into his lap. With two firm pats to his shoulder, you replied, "As long as we have an understanding, I shall return these to your care."

"Boundaries are often blurry in the dark."

As evening fell, Sicarius's comment repeated more often in your mind. While Gravelorne's electric bulbs burned brighter than candles, the extra light only deepened the shadows at the edge of the wide passages. The black windows of the front hall looked like an open chasm to the below world. You turned your back on the night and knocked on the study door. Goose pimples prickled down your arms.

"Enter."

Sicarius leaned back in his leather chair, balancing his pen upon his upper lip. As you closed the door, a wide grin knocked the writing utensil from his face. He snatched it from midair and set it in the cup. "So you found it then?" he asked.

You held the thick book of legends tales aloft. "You put it under C for Coriland, not F for Fables."

"I really should create a more exact filing system," he murmured, rising to his feet.

You glanced at the large stack of papers and then the mantle clock. It was only half-past ten. "Are you done for the evening, Master?"

"More than done, I am afraid." The desk lamp clicked off. "The work will keep. My attention span will not."

Sicarius strode to the door, holding it wide open. As you walked through the threshold, blue eyes stared at your bare neck. When you slipped past him out into the hall, it felt like the shadows licked at your heels.

"Boundaries are often blurry in the dark."

Your fingers curled around the leather binding.

"I hear that Lyle's new invention created quite a spectacle today," a low voice said in your ear.

Your heart slammed against your ribs as you jolted to the side. When you turned to face him, the master was standing tall, hands in his pockets.

That was odd. You swore he was right next to—

You shook your head to clear the thought. "Y-yes. There was some damage to the hedge maze. Mr. Watts has been avoiding Mr. Norton since this afternoon."

Sicarius's grin looked fanged. "A wise choice."

As you climbed the stairs, the darkness around you pressed in from all corners. You glanced back at the Fae Tree. Rising from a pool of shadows, the golden branches looked like groping hands reaching for your body.

"Are you all right?"

Your head snapped back around. "I am fine, Master."

Despite his long legs, he kept pace at your side. "You seem on edge."

"It is nothing."

Sicarius hummed. "That makes it sound like it *is* something."

His elbow brushed your sleeve. You clenched your arm tight to your side.

"Are you scared of the dark?"

"I am a grown woman."

Sicarius's taunting smile did nothing to ease your worries. As his eyes rolled from your gritted teeth to your tight shoulders, it felt like you were being stroked with flames.

Your master's chuckle was low and deep. "Yes, I suppose you are."

When you reached the second floor, Sicarius swaggered into the shadows, never turning on the lights. You froze at the top of the stairs. He looked at you and raised his brow. You swallowed and followed after him. Upon reaching the end of the long hall, Sicarius strolled straight into his lair. Pausing in the threshold, you buried your chin in the top of the tome. The bedside lily lamp flickered to life with a soft glow. His teasing smile was tempered by the calm courtesy in his voice.

"Better?"

You nodded, slinking into the room.

"You are as skittish as a kitten tonight," he remarked, eyes flashing in the lamplight. "Are you *sure* nothing is the matter?"

Ignoring the question, you placed the book on the velvet-trimmed seat. Tight shoulders burned with tension. A breath of cold air filled your lungs. Try as you might, the heavy furniture was awkward to lift. One rosewood leg scraped the floor. You cringed. All at once, the weight disappeared from your grasp. Startled eyes looked up. With as little effort as lifting a feather, Sicarius carried the stool to his bedside. He patted the leather-bound collection and smirked at you.

"I know my maid cannot be perfect in all ways." He faked a pained sigh. "I will have to settle for most."

Shaking hands clenched in front of your stomach as you begged the pounding of your heart to be silent. Fighting your nerves, you looked him dead in the face. "Will you require me to help you undress?"

His eyes sparkled with amusement. "Would you like to undress me?"

Your smile creaked. "I would like to perform my prescribed duties to your satisfaction, Master."

He ran a hand through his hair and smirked at you. "My, this room got chilly."

You turned on your heel and strode to the wardrobe. "I shall fetch your long underwear."

As you sifted through the clothing, his gaze burned your throat. Quiet steps crept to the closet. A long arm reached past your shoulder. He leaned over you, watching the selections drift in and out of your fingertips. You stiffened but said nothing. Acknowledging it would only cause him to tease you more. Best to wait for him t—

All at once, you felt the bristle of a man's whiskers brush against your neck. You whipped around, pressing yourself flat against the closet.

Sicarius laughed and held up both hands. "Easy now. I was just checking what colors I owned." He pointed to the bathroom door and rotated his shoulder. "Would you go draw a bath for me? My arm is rather tense from all that writing."

You frowned at him. "Master, please refrain fro—"

He turned his back to you. The clink of metal set your pulse pounding. His belt hit the floor with a thud. "Are you still here?" Wicked blue eyes peered over his shoulder. "Is watching me undress one of your prescribed duties?"

As you clenched your teeth and hustled to the bathroom, only one thought occupied your mind: Maybe if you filled the tub deep enough, he would drown in it.

Sitting in the bedroom waiting for your master to return, you were convinced that Sicarius loved his ridiculous bone china tub more than most men love their wives. Every time he sat in that basin, he hummed cheerful marches better suited for victory ceremonies than an evening wash. Honestly, how long could one man bask in a bath? The water had to have gone cold by now!

When you finally heard the sound of the drain, bloodshot eyes glanced at the clock. Eleven seventeen. You snapped the book shut, picked up his plush dressing gown, and rose to your feet. As you waited by the door, the smell of roses and salt hung in the air. You rolled your eyes. Great. Now the silver would tarnish all over again. Honestly, did this the man ever think for one sec—

The door pulled open. Flower-scented steam rushed into the room. You held out the dressing gown, eyes averted. Terry cloth slipped from your fingers. He chuckled at your efforts.

"You need not look away. I put on all my clothing before coming out."

Did he really expect you to praise him for that? How old was he? Six?

Stomach squeezing tight, you plastered on an apathetic façade and turned to face him. Towel tousled hair? Check. Ruddy cheeks? Check. Saucy smile? Check. Clothing?

You steeled yourself and lowered your eyes.

Check…ish?

While the satin pajamas were in place, the loose lapel dived into a tight V, ending in the middle of his navel. On the left side of his chest, between the third and fourth ribs, was a wide, gnarled scar. Trying not to stare, you flicked your gaze lower. The chiseled divot between alabaster abs held your attention longer than you were proud to admit. When you looked up, Sicarius was smirking at you. You clamped your teeth around your tongue until you tasted copper.

"I will turn down your sheets, Master."

As you reached for the bedspread, Sicarius loomed behind you. A prickling heat spiraled down the inside of your legs. Though the calf-length uniform did not expose anything, nervous fingers still tugged the skirt down. Bursts of static light danced across the silk sheets. The hairs on your arms stood on end as his hand caught your wrist.

"On second thought, the robe is warm. I'll lay on top." He nodded to the stool. "Have a seat."

While you took your place, Sicarius brushed past you. As he settled on the covers, long legs clipped the lacey hem of your dress. His toe hoisted the fabric into the air, depositing the edge above your knee. Without thinking, you snatched up the twill and threw it back into place. Sicarius curled onto his side, his half-lidded eyes glowing in the dark.

"What are my options tonight?" he asked, leaning over to look at the book. The smooth fabric of his open pajamas dipped low to expose his pert nipple and broad chest.

Oh, he was going to play that game, was he? Fine. If he wanted to act like an attention-seeking child, you would treat him like one.

In an instant, you snapped into full-service mode. An impersonal smile and neutral tone became the hard wall between maid and master. Perched on the edge of the seat, you flipped open the cover and ignored the distraction.

"Shall I read you the table of contents?"

He huffed and flopped onto his back. "Please do."

Your finger scrolled down the page. "The Cookie Cabin and the Witch of the Forest?"

"Something a little less gory."

"The Cat Who Lived Thirteen Lives?"

He waved his hand. "I have that one memorized."

Of course he did.

You flipped the page. "The Sour Apple and the Fiendish Fox?"

"A bit childish."

Your lips stretched into a painfully tight smile. "It is a book of legends, Master," you pointed out.

Sicarius hummed and dragged the cover down with his pointer. "How about a love story?" The long finger tapped on one specific name.

"The Nightmuse and the Seventh Son?"

"Yes." Sicarius closed his eyes and flopped onto his fluffy pillow.

You supposed that was no great surprise considering the front of the house. Holding back an annoyed sigh, you flipped to your least favorite fable.

THE NIGHTMUSE AND THE SEVENTH SON

Long ago, there existed many creatures who preyed upon mortal souls. Amongst these fiends, the most cunning and beautiful of all was the nightmuse. Crafted from shadow and starlight, she sought out the hearts of lonely men. In exchange for sweet inspiration, she took from them a meal of vitality and vigor. Untouchable as dawn, she flitted from home to home, leaving nothing but smiling corpses in her wake. Because of the life she stole, neither age nor decay could tarnish her beauty.

For all her success, the nightmuse was cursed by her own kind. Fae have no lost love for humanity. By partaking in their souls, the nightmuse defiled her own. The realm of the flowers closed to her from her very first bite. Still, with a heart of ice, she took and took without regretting what she lost in exchange.

One summer's eve, the nightmuse drifted through the open window of a small cottage. The humble home was owned by a simple farmer, too poor for a wife and too lowly to be missed. She hovered by his bedside and scoffed at his plain face. Every trait of the farmer was unremarkable, save one thing: as the seventh son of a seventh son, he was blessed with fae sight.

When the nightmuse leaned over her prey, his eyes opened wide. She froze, her hand cupped around his cheek. His tears spilled across her fingers. Only one word fell from his lips:

"Beautiful."

Startled by his voice, the nightmuse stopped her feeding and fled into the morning light. The farmer ran after her, but she was long gone. With no other choice, he returned to his bed and etched her lovely face into his mind.

As days turned to weeks and summer turned to fall, the nightmuse returned each evening to spy on the farmer. Though she did not feast upon him, the curse of her touch lingered on his heart. Like a man possessed, he spent each day at his desk, ruining scroll after scroll. The fields matured and rotted. Strong muscles withered. His dreams faded. A once lively spirit soured in baggy flesh.

As the nightmuse watched, her stomach twisted in knots. All she had to do was touch him once more, and his soul would fill her belly. Despite the cries of her stomach, she could not. Boundless hunger turned to pained nausea. She tried to find another man, but every time she reached out to inspire them, she saw the farmer frantically sketching at his desk.

So it was that, as he starved, so did she.

On the final night of his life, as he lay prone at his desk, the nightmuse pushed open the latch on the window pane. Like a spring breeze, she fluttered to his side. Dull eyes filled with tears as she stood beside him. With the last of his strength, he reached out a shaking hand. On the paper, rendered in charcoal and devotion, was a mirror image of her beautiful face.

"I love you," he whispered.

Until the day she faded into the shadows, the nightmuse never ate again.

The last words fell from frowning lips into tepid silence.

Sicarius's left eye cracked open. He studied your dull, distant expression. "Is something the matter?" he asked.

"It is nothing," you replied flatly. "What story would you like to hear next?"

"You look like you drank sour wine," he mused, wagging his finger. "Tell me what the trouble is."

"The trouble is over. Let us move along."

He clicked his tongue and grinned. "So it *was* the story then?"

A neutral stare was his only response.

"You do not enjoy hearing a story about a woman taking a man's life?" He rolled onto his back. "Somehow, with the way you looked at me earlier, I thought you might."

Your shoulders stiffened. "If you insist upon continuing this topic, you may take solace that a woman murdering a man is not the part I find unrealistic."

"You are looking for realism in fables?"

Refusing to rise to the taunt, you continued: "Love at first sight is a pathetic trope to begin with, but a love for which a woman would starve herself to death from one word of praise?" You closed your eyes and lifted your chin. "It is beyond any reasonable bounds of relatability."

Sicarius's eyebrows climbed halfway up his forehead. "Reasonable bounds? For love?" His body shook as he snickered into the back of his hand. "Are you too jaded to feel, or is your heart is left cold by anything less than pure romance?"

You gritted your teeth.

The scarred man pointed at his nose. "Do you want to know what I think?"

The book snapped shut. "I am at your disposal for the evening, Master."

Sicarius climbed to his elbows, leaning into the space between your bodies. Like the fae flames that once tempted travelers into the night, azure eyes danced with a hypnotic spell. You sat, transfixed by the sight. As he held your gaze, the fire inside his words burned you to your very core:

"I think we are all waiting for the right person to consume our soul."

Chapter Eight

Snow Season: Day 62 of 92

My dear Rebecca,

I am overjoyed to hear that little Lillith will make a full recovery from her influenza. I suppose there must be some drawbacks to the daycare the factory provides, but I suspect the pre-school socialization will be better for her than the bar patrons' manners. As to Jace's troubles with grammar, tell him I would be happy to tutor him when I am next in Illestrad.

My employer's freeness with the servants continues to be, at best, eccentric and, at worst, wholly improper. However, I cannot deny that the general frivolity in this home has a certain chaotic charm, which you would enjoy. Aside from the ever-serious butler, Mr. Ellsworth, and our prickly undercook, Mr. Slater, I fear I am in the company of clowns.

Mr. Watts's "automated laundry folder" is now contained, but his workshop bursts into smoke twice a week. Mr. Reeves spends more of his time telling jokes than learning his duties as an under-butler. Cook is a jolly gossip. I fear by the time I meet his wife, I will know more about her than she does about herself. As to the master of Gravelorne, I must conclude that the only way he can sleep at night is by exhausting himself taunting me.

While I do my best to rise above the nonsense, I confess to what I suspect will be your delight, that the "easy manners" around me have made my own slip on more than one occasion. As to the old farmer's warning, the only ghoulish thing I have witnessed is the state of Mr. Watts's living quarters.

Please relay to your husband my sincerest appreciation for his inquiries on my behalf. It is a relief to know that the master's reputation is generally honorable for "an eccentric new money type." His generous donations to "Counseling and Support for Veterans of War" seem in line with his hiring habits. While Mr. Reeves's full background is a mystery, I must assume him to possess some military pedigree. More than one night I have seen him patrol the halls as if waiting for the enemy to sneak upon us. Perhaps it is he who "left more on the battlefield than bullets and body?"

As to the master's behavior, if it were not for the trouble he causes me, I would think him a celibate! Lady Anton's numerous attempts to fling her six daughters at the man have been utterly fruitless. Then, thinking the master's tastes ran more masculine, she brought her nephew to dinner. The master gave his guest a phone number for a "gentlemen's only" club, wished him luck, and shooed him out the door. Last week, a Miss Ravensport of Drighton, Malsworth, and Illestrad spent more of her meeting thirsting for Mr. Estrova than the wine she wanted to import. Never before have I seen eyes that cold or a rejection that quick. The poor girl is probably still crying. Though with her looks and her father's fortune, I am sure a suitable match will be found.

Lastly, though I will always cherish your ever unique advice, please refrain from writing things like: "get the money before you give up the goods." Despite what may be said about me, I am a servant, not a succubus. Furthermore—

As the hall clock chimed three in the morning, bloodshot eyes looked up from the letter. Heavy lids drifted closed before popping open again. With a sigh, you flipped off the light.

"Oh, forget it. I will finish this in the morning."

Mealtimes at Gravelorne were an odd affair. While breakfast was served to the master at exactly whenever he felt like waking up that day, gods above save the servant who was late to lunch. Alex Slater, the undercook, did not hover over a hot stove all morning to have ungrateful diners show up tardy. If one survived his lecture, then one faced Ellsworth. At that point, the only option was to politely beg the Dark One to take you below before the butler got hold of you.

As the hall clock chimed half-past twelve, you hustled down the long corridor to the kitchen. Before you could knock, the door pushed open from within. Out from the room swung a bear of a man with a deep tan and a tall mohawk.

"Oh! Sorry there!" Barnard Miller, the manor's chef, exclaimed with a rowdy laugh. "Didn't realize you were standing so close!"

The undercook glanced up from the stove. As always, his double-breasted coat was a crisp bleached white. "Serves her right. She should have said something," he stated, stirring the pot. With a firm rap on the side of the copper cookware, he glared at the short distance between you and his mentor. Brown eyes narrowed. "Rude to just barge on in."

"Mr. Slater is right," you agreed with a nervous chuckle. "It is rude of me not to announce myself."

Cook removed a long white cane with three horizontal stripes from the wall hook. He patted your shoulder and wagged a meaty finger. "Don't be worried about that, missus. Every day that you come here early and set the table is a day that I don't have to."

"I am the maid after all," you replied. "It is a part of my duties."

"Still, it gives me more time for my midday constitutional." He loosed a throaty chuckle and playfully slapped your shoulder. With that, he strode out the door, sweeping the corridor with his stick as he made his way to the bathroom.

"I hate it when you call me that."

You turned to face your remaining companion. "I beg your pardon?"

"I'm fourteen," he grumbled, adjusting the flame. "It's stupid for a woman who's older than me to call me 'Mr. Slater.' Sounds like you're just kissing up."

You smiled. "You are correct again, Alex. I am sorry if I caused offense."

"Good." He waved his hand at the food. "Now, either be useful or get out."

You ducked around the butcher's block island in the center of the room and grabbed the handles of the rolling cart. When you first learned that the chef was blind, you wondered how he could arrange the food so beautifully. As it turned out, Mrs. Norton created a textured, symmetrical bone china set just for him. It contained eight wide ivory blocks that were interspersed with platinum stripes. Lotus petals were etched in dotted filigree. Cook used these marks to plate his meals like a clock. The hearty potato wedges sat at five, the flawless sunny side eggs were at six, and the golden brown toast points lay at seven. Alex was left to place the porridge, fruit, and sausages.

Like his mentor, Alex pressed the meat with the spatula, checking to see if it was cooked through. The undercook insisted that the sound of the sizzle and sponginess of texture were more accurate than just looking at the juices. You watched him with a fond smile, secretly suspecting he wanted to mimic Cook in every way possible.

"Why are you gawking at me like some stupid owl?" Alex demanded.

Best not to say anything. He would probably run you through with the kitchen knife if you told him he was precious.

"I am waiting on the meats." You nodded to the stack of bowls in the wash sorter. "Would you like me to ladle out the porridge?"

"If it'll please you," he grumbled, rotating the links. "Just don't misplace anything. Cook needs things in proper order."

"Of course," you replied, dishing out the lumpy oats.

When the cart clattered into the servant's hall, Lyle was already seated on the end of the bench. He leaned into the smooth oak and waved at you as you walked in.

"Thanks for the tip about the mold," the mechanic said. "The grout in the shop bathroom doesn't look so terrible now."

You passed him his plate. "Just make sure to open the windows next time. The bleach will burn your nostrils."

"Right," he groaned, flopping his cheek into the varnish.

You shook your head before nodding to his left side. "How is your leg?"

Lyle rolled up his pants, revealing an angry red sore on the outside of his short knee. He flexed the limb and winced. "The vacuum suction helps keep the prosthetic better attached, but the edge of the brace is rubbing something foul."

"Did the nylon stocking inside the sleeve help at all?"

He shook his head. "A little but not enough, I'm afraid." Calloused hands cupped the worn flesh. "I think I need to make a double layer. Something with more give on the edges and a hard brace to hold the shape."

"What about calfskin?"

"Worth a shot." He wrinkled his freckled nose. "Full grain chafes, though. Dunno how Reeves stands having that shoulder holster strapped on him all day."

You mentally added that to the list of questions about the causally bizarre Mr. Reeves. It could come right after: "why would a footman need a jackknife in *both* boots when he carried a switchblade in his pocket?"

"Speak of the Dark One, and he shall cometh!" a cheerful voice quipped from the door.

"Mr. Reeves!" You glanced at the clock. Only two minutes left. "What brings you here on time?"

Reeves plopped onto the bench beside Lyle and wrapped his arm around the younger man's shoulders. Grinding his knuckles into ruddy curls, Reeves flashed you a sparkling grin. "Can't be late all the time, can I? I'd ruin my reputation for spontaneity."

"Get off!" Lyle protested, digging the heel of his palm into the brunette's cheek.

Reeves loosened his grip and folded his hands behind his head. "Try a moleskin liner. Helps cut down on the chafing."

The redhead shoved Reeves's shoulder. "Oh, and you're such an expert."

Reeves tutted, wagging his finger back and forth. "Nope, just know a lot of soldiers. Moleskin or nothing, so says my friend Jim."

The young man sneered and thrust his pointer into Reeves's chest. "You told me last week that Jim's arm keeps popping off!"

Reeves smacked his fist into his palm. "Whoops! You're right!" With the wave of a hand, he added: "Forget I said anything."

"Wish I could forget everything you said," Lyle shivered, rubbing his arms. "Promise me you'll let Ellsworth or Cook give Alex 'the talk.' I still have nightmares about you and Mr. Sicarius going back and forth like a pair of ruddy cucklocks."

"Mr. Watts."

The air turned to ice. Three petrified faces rotated slowly to face the voice. Cook leaned on the door frame, gasping for air as he pounded the hardwood. In front of him, back straight and gloved hands neatly folded, Ellsworth was a towering force of poise and grace. Despite the serenity in his words, his dark eyes were fixed upon the freckled servant. Watts froze on the spot. Playing dead was his only defense.

With a flourish of his wrist, Ellsworth bent the young man's ear. "Five drommands for using that language at the dining table."

"It ain't fair to short my pay for that when it ain't even a word, Mr. Ellsworth!" the mechanic protested.

"No, it is not a word." Ellsworth took a dignified sniff. "However, I can guess what it was *supposed* to be."

Poor Lyle. Another few "five drommand" dockings and he would not even make a drossler for the whole week.

You bit your lip and turned back to the serving cart. Cook tapped the bench and the edge of Lyle's wheelchair with his cane before wandering around the far side of the table. Reeves edged away from the scene, taking his plate from you with a fox's grin.

As the clock chime whirled in the hall, Alex appeared in the door. Without a word, he rounded the cart and held out the plate of fresh sausages. There was a red, blistering rash crusted over his palms. When his eyes followed your gaze, he stiffened.

You took the dish without hesitation and looked up at his face. "Thank you, Alex."

He turned his cheek and muttered: "You're welcome." Then, he bustled over to his place at Cook's right hand. As he took his seat, he scratched the inside of the elbow through the sleeve of his shirt.

"Another flare-up?" Reeves asked. "I thought you just got the last one healed?"

Alex wrinkled his nose. "Allergic to the new soap too, I guess."

"Ah…"

Ellsworth released Lyle's ear and took his customary position at the head of the table. At the moment of the last bell, he sat in his chair and scooted in with one clean sweep. The other staff took their seats at the bench. You dished out the sausages before following suit.

Ellsworth closed his eyes and folded his hands together. "Let us bow our heads in a moment of clarity."

You stood before your nemesis, clenching your weapon. The dull face gazed back, lifeless and tarnished by the oily evils of the flesh. Polish in hand, you attacked with the hatred of ten aching fingers. Steadily, the filmy beige gave way to gleaming silver. With a sneer, you shuffled back onto your haunches and crowed, "Not today, my worthy foe."

The faucet said nothing in reply.

Your eyes fell to the filthy red ring in the bottom of the bath. Slathering another heap of paste on your rag, you wagged a finger at it. "Do not think I have forgotten you. I do not know from where you came, but your services are no longer required."

The bone china basin you could forgive. Unlike the tap, it was only gaudy but not completely impractical. It scratched less than the carved stoneware most aristocrats preferred for their tubs. However, your master loved to lounge about in his long, scented baths like a cat before a fireplace. Between the salt and the humidity, the facet's silver tarnished within a few short days. Clearly, he only purchased the fixtures for the bragging rights that came with maintaining something so impractically ostentatious.

As the grit at the bottom of the tub yielded to your rage, you glared at the jars scattered around the altar of vanity. Hues from coral to amethyst crafted a devious membrane which would stain even the most excellent vitrified finish. Beside them, oils of peony, lilac, and rose taunted you with flowery proclamations of capricious spending. A thumb-sized bottle was worth a year's salary. These were as long as your forearm. Whenever you moved them, your hands shook.

Burning knees and shooting aches in your spine protested your hunched posture. You stretched your elbows behind your shoulder and rolled your neck. A satisfying crack made you sigh with relief. Pain postponed, you searched the gleaming white surface for any sign of your quarry. There, at the corner nearest the wall, you spotted the fiend. Its rosy crust screamed a challenge as surely as an ape beating its chest. Your eyes flashed as you raised your rag. All at once, you lunged over the cusp of the bath, a violent sneer pulling tight over your teeth. Your hips collided with the porcelain. One hand gripped tight to the edge of the basin while the other stretched to reach the corner.

"Your enthusiasm is charming."

Your fingers slipped, sending you headfirst into the hard ceramic. The resounding "thunk" was accompanied by grey spots at the edges of your vision. Hissing pain rushed through clamped teeth. You scrambled to right yourself but could not. There was no grip to be had on the smooth edges. Curse your polishing skills! This was a disaster of your own making!

Large hands reached under your arms and lifted you aloft. Your skin flushed hot as long fingers gripped at the side of your breasts. Sicarius set you upon the floor and gracefully draped himself along the lip of the bath.

"Are you all right? That was quite a clunk."

Unable to speak, you blinked at him like an addled-brained pile of mush.

His hand reached out to touch the crown of your head. You winced as he found the bruise. He smiled. Soft fingers stroked a stray strand of hair back into place. The tickle of his nails at the edge of your scalp sent goose pimples rippling down your skin.

"I will have Reeves bring you some ice. Wait here a moment."

Bristling with discomfort, you stammered out, "I-I am fine!"

Sicarius gave you a raised brow and a cynical stare. "You will obtain no praise for martyrdom in this house."

Your hands balled into your thighs. Through gritted teeth and watery eyes, you replied, "Yes, Master."

His thumb traced the shell of your ear. "Did you know you hiss when you are startled?"

"I do what?"

He retracted his hand and leaned back on his perch. "Like a kitten. It is rather endearing."

Skin sizzling with shame, you leapt to your feet. "I think I will go get that ice. Please excuse me."

A deep chuckle chased you from the bathroom.

Later that evening, you hovered behind your master's desk. The note he left crumpled in your cold grip. Deep inhales and slow exhales were the only things keeping you from screaming. There, written in a tidy scrawl, was a single taunting instruction:

Read me something about cats.

That man was testing you.

With an exasperated sigh, you stalked down the hall. As you passed by the east stairs, you heard the clicking of metal teeth. Lyle's chair descended down the gear lift. With a proud grin, he pointed to his seat. Unlike the rattling disaster it was last week, the magnetic clamps were well sealed on the bolt pegs. He must have adjusted it again.

Pushing the lever arm to hasten his journey, he waved a friendly greeting. "Ma'am! Ma'am!" the young man called. "Are you going to the library t—?"

One look at your thunderous expression sent his words writhing into silence. Slowly, so as not to attract your ire, he pulled the lever back. The chair arced around one click at a time. As soon as he was facing the other way, the gear lift whisked him back up the stairs.

You pushed the doors to the library open and closed them with a snap. There, stretched over the long sofa, was Sicarius. A book in one hand and his cheek in the other, he never even looked up. You were grateful. Your mask was slipping.

Turning to the natural sciences section, your hand trailed over the spines on the lower shelves. Walrus. Weather. Windmills. Wine. More wine. An empty gap. *More* wine. Wombats. Clearly, what you sought was not here.

You stretched to your tiptoes. Feathers. Fungi. Still not there. It must be further up.

You took a few steps back and craned your neck, pointer finger skipping from subject to subject. Aardvarks. Ants. Bears. Berries. General Biology. Birth. Botany. Calamondins. Wait, calamondins!? That was an oddly specific subject. How much would anyone want to know about *one* citrus fruit?

Rich people certainly were odd.

You inhaled sharply as your eyes fell upon the next subject. Aha! Cats! Right there at the— Oh… That was rather high.

You scanned the room. The ladder was all the way over by languages and customs. With a frown, you walked to the far end of the library. As you passed the couch, blue eyes stayed trained on their reading.

Grasping the ladder, you began the arduous task of relocation. Despite being well oiled, there were multiple places where the vile tracks got caught.

"Come on, *friend*," you whispered into the metal. "Move along."

Resentment and resolve heaved your unwilling ally to the field of battle. By the time you clanged back to the reference texts, your armpits were damp with perspiration.

With a yawn and a stretch, Sicarius rose from his seat. As you shoved the ladder into place, he appeared at your side. In his hand was a book on Kestania's wine region. He rapped on the brass bars. "I asked Lyle to have a look at that this afternoon. Have you seen him?"

You stiffened. "Yes, but he was heading in the opposite direction."

"Ah. Well. One cannot rush genius, I suppose." Sicarius nodded to the top of your head. "How is your wound?"

"It is a little tender, but Cook assures me I will make a full recovery."

"Splendid." Your master squatted down at your left and pushed his book back into its slot. As he hummed to himself, you glanced from the ladder to him and then down at your skirt. His lips mouthed a children's rhyme as his index finger bounced back and forth between the other two wine-based texts. Your brow furrowed, but you elected to say nothing.

Grasping your hem, you pulled it to your leg and started your ascent one rung at a time. Up past M, L, K, and J, you climbed. When your heel reached even with F, you stretched out your empty hand. Fingertips barely brushed the binding. You took one step higher.

Clink!

All at once, your world spiraled backward in a gut-wrenching rush of adrenaline. A hiss of pain flew from your mouth as your ankle slammed into a metal rung. Nausea coursed up your throat, and you prepared to hit the ground. Instead, you collided with something warm and firm.

"I am about to call my insurance company to take out a policy on you."

When you realized who was holding you, the feel of his hands on your thighs made you throb with humiliation.

You turned your cheek, pretending to examine the ladder. A bolt was missing. The step swung loose in the air.

Sicarius hitched you higher in his grip. A stab of pain shot up your leg. You tried to move your limb but rocking the ankle only brought more agony.

He frowned. "Are you all right?"

You grimaced. "I think I twisted my ankle."

The master walked off towards the center of the room. You gripped his jacket, hiding your face as best you could. When he reached the sofa, he laid you down and took a seat beside you. You shuffled away from him, but he consumed every bit of space you gave up. The edge of his hip pressed against yours as he untied the laces of your heels. He tugged the shoe off, setting it gently on the floor. The tight nylon of your stocking only accentuated the swelling. Sicarius pulled at the sheer fabric.

"We need to take this off before it gets worse."

You sat up, trying to grip the silky hosiery through your long uniform. It slipped from your fingers. You wrinkled your nose and tried again. The fiendish fabric tented for only a moment before it snapped out of your grip. This would be easier if you could lift your skirt but not in front of—

All at once, your master's hands crawled under the hem of your dress.

"What are you doing!?" you demanded.

"As I said: taking this off before it is too tight to remove."

You scrunched your face and shoved at his arms. "I can do it myself!"

"Clearly not."

His hands rounded the side of your knee. Long fingers slithered up your thigh. Your breathing became a panicked series of tight inhales.

Sicarius gripped the edge of your stocking and slipped his hands below the fabric. Smooth skin glided down your bare flesh. He peeled the clothing away with a suspicious lack of haste. The palms of his hands caressed your calf before dancing down to the injured joint.

Blood pounded through your veins like the beat of a drum. It was as if his hand was coiled around your heart, not your hosiery. When warm fingers tapped your injured ankle, your breath caught in your throat.

"This may hurt some."

He palpated the edges of your bones, carefully squeezing from your shin to your toes. As tender touches rolled down your leg, your stomach flopped.

"There does not seem to be any lasting damage," he stated, lifting his hands. "I am glad."

Deep in the cockles of a long-numbed heart, there was a feeling too blatant to ignore. Eyes the color of aquamarine locked onto yours. Entrancing facets cast their spell, leaving your brain in a fog. Your tongue clenched tight to the roof of your mouth before any words could escape.

His voice was soft. "Are you going to keep falling like this?

Your chest spasmed. The trance broke. Balling your hands into the sofa, you whipped your head away. "I am not doing this intentionally," you muttered.

Sicarius examined your embarrassed expression before humming with satisfaction. He rose to his feet and strolled to the intercom near the door.

"Lyle, when you come down, bring some ice." Sicarius's smirk was sinful. "Our maid has had another accident and it has left her rather bothered."

CHAPTER NINE

Melt Season – Day 32 of 90, 48th Year of Creipus the Pious

Stumbling through a snowstorm to fetch flowers would never be your favorite activity.

In the mountains, the first third of the melt season was just more snow season thanks to the bitter northern winds which whipped up harsh ice storms. While Illestrad would soon blossom, Gravelorne's outdoor bulbs stayed tucked deep in their beds. Despite this, fresh flowers were expected throughout the manor. At first, you assumed they were brought from warmer climates. Sicarius Estrova was a shipping magnate, after all; connections and imported goods were his specialties. However, Gravelorne manor, much like its owner, prided itself on a certain degree of self-sufficiency to complement its affluence. Therefore, a private glasshouse garden was the perfect extravagant luxury to combine with your master's conspicuous consumption.

As you trudged down the large south lawn, biting gusts tore at your wool cloak. You crunched your way across the open yard. Thick snow tumbled over the edge of your ankle boots. Cold, wet toes were accompanied by a distinct and unpleasant slosh. Teeth chattering and fingers frozen, only one thought filled your mind:

Sicarius and his stupid flowers could go below.

Despite the trail that Mr. Norton blazed earlier that day, plenty of heavy snow still blocked your entry. Rage-fueled determination stomped the fresh powder into a flat carpet. The frosty door to the glasshouse fought you with every tug. Grasping the handle with both hands, you braced yourself on the slick ground. Whether it was friction or the firestorm of unkind words that melted the icy hinges, you did not care. Beaming with victory, you collected your basket and strode into the building.

Nearly ten massive archways in length, the glasshouse was heated by the same steam as the main property. Underground wires supported sun-bright lights hanging above the plants. Small aqua tanks fed the soaker hose system that snaked through the massive beds. Over the twelfth row, you caught sight of salt and pepper hair and a leathery neck.

"Mr. Norton! How are you today?"

The weathered man never looked up from his pruning. His deep wrinkles barely moved as he replied with a grunt.

"Do you think the strawberries in the conservatory will be ready soon? The master has had me reading about shortcakes for two nights."

Another grunt. Gnarled hands clipped away a side bud. It fell to the floor amongst all the others.

"Which row may I take from?"

A dirt-encrusted finger pointed one bed over. You walked to the closest pathway and shuffled through the small gap between piles of greenery. In a small basket at the end of each row was a pile of well-oiled, razor-sharp shears. Careful to leave a long length of the stem, you snipped enough flowers to refresh the vases.

As you wiped the sweat from your brow, your finger bounced over the rows. Carnations. "Grave Beauty" tea hybrid roses (Norton's prized cultivar). More roses. Back to the carnations. Huh…

"Mr. Norton?"

Grunt.

"Do lilies also grow well in a glasshouse?"

An affirmative grunt.

"Why do you not grow those too?"

Norton set down his shears. With a tired, ambivalent stare, he gave a stiff nod to the manor. "He don't like them. Poisonous to cats."

"Ah…" You picked up the wicker bassinet. "Well, you have a good day."

Grunt.

After being in such a warm building, heading back into the storm was painful. Clutching the basket to your breast, you lifted your hand to shield your eyes against the powder clouds. Every breath felt like lead in your lungs. By the time you reached the servant's entrance, your skin was raw and sore. Wet socks disappeared down the chute with a splat. You set your winter boots upside down in the bath to drain.

After changing into a short pair of heels, you shuffled off to refresh the vases. Only a few of the lower hall bouquets needed replacement. The front parlor looked fine. The dining room you would renew Friday morning, before the master's dinner party. As you finished plumping the blossoms in the library, there was a rattling squeak from the patio doors. A stout white cat dragged her tiny pink paws down the glass. Yellow-green eyes looked from you to the handle and back again.

"Oh!" You bustled over to the door and unlocked the latch. "Hello there, kitty! Would you like to come in?"

The cat swept past you, shaking off the snow. As you closed the door, she plopped her ample backside down on the marble floor. You swore her eyes rolled before she groomed her plush fur with short, fervent licks.

You squatted down beside her. "I saw you when I first came here. Are you supposed to be in the house or outside?"

The cat stared at you from under her whiskers.

"I suppose, being a cat, you think all places you please to visit are where you are supposed to be?"

Her tail twitched.

You stood up and straightened your apron. "It was a silly question. I beg your pardon."

The cat lifted her chin, studying you for a moment. Her ear flicked. After a brief pause, she rose to her feet, and sauntered off to the sofa. It took one graceful leap for her to settle onto the cushions. She draped her front legs one over the other and yawned.

"Yes, you do suit it better than I could. It must be nice."

All at once, the cat's ears pricked. With a chirp, she jumped from the sofa and padded over to the entryway with a crooked tail.

The door to the library swung open. Sicarius paused in the frame. Tangling herself between his legs, the white cat purred and bunted all over his black suit. The expensive fabric was slathered with patches of fur.

Your eyes widened. "Oh! Master, I am so sorry! Your pants—"

Sicarius held up a hand. Your mouth snapped shut. The cat plopped herself down beside his wingtip leather shoes.

The master stooped low, scratching her round cheeks. You were certain you saw a haughty grin on her lips.

"It is quite all right. Lemon wanders the whole estate without restriction." He smiled at the cat as she curled her neck into his head. "I believe she owns it more than I do."

"Lemon?" You glanced at the yellow-green irises. "For her eyes?"

The cat flopped onto her side, kneading the air. Her long tail thrashed along the tile. Sicarius stood and walked around her.

"If you ask Reeves, it is for her sour temperament. He was hospitalized for ten days for trying to pet her stomach. His recovery rather disappointed Lyle. He had the design for a prosthetic arm all worked out."

You coughed. "I understand."

Sicarius smirked. "Stay above her collar, and you will be fine."

Lemon bounced to her feet as your master neared the library doors. With another chirp, she trotted to the glass and sat herself down. Wordlessly, Sicarius depressed the lever and let her out again. With all the confidence of a goddess, she strutted out into the storm.

A soft smile spread across your cheeks. "You really do like cats."

"I spent a lot of time with them." Sicarius turned back to the shelves. His long fingers traced the spines of the business section book by book. "My mother and I were refugees. We were forced to flee into the night, barely stopping to claim our shoes. Hotels and hostels do not take payment in promises. We slept in barns when we could."

Your master bent low and rolled up the sleeve of his pants. On his right leg were numerous pockmarked punctures as wide as a human hand. On the left was a deep depression with puckered edges. Cold fear rippled through your veins. You swallowed and glanced away.

"Once they know the taste of the whip, guard hounds are loyal to their masters alone. No amount of food or begging will distract them from their duty." He nodded to the storm. "Barn cats have no such allegiances. They are slow to trust and judicious with their regard. Cruelty cannot purchase their obedience, and bribery alone does not sate them. Any capricious whims will drive them from you." He rolled the fabric back down. His eyes were as cold as the weather outside. "There is an honesty in their nature, which I find rewarding. By contrast, I have no patience for slobbering dogs."

At his harsh tone, your skin prickled.

Selecting a textbook on macroeconomics, Sicarius rose to his feet. "Have I alarmed you enough for one day?" he teased.

"No!" As the blazing heat engulfed your neck, you laughed awkwardly and scratched your cheek. "I am unsure of how to respond to something so"—the final word stuck on your tongue—"personal."

Sicarius chuckled. "When information is offered freely, it indicates a desire to talk about the incident. Therefore, you could ask a question, if you like."

Inside your brain, thousands of queries flitted to and fro. Finding something appropriate was like trying to grab hold of lamplight. However, one particular thought rang out clear as a bell. "How did you earn her trust then?"

"Lemon?"

You nodded.

"Lemon's colony was attacked when she was a kitten. I killed the mad dog and kept her in my bedroom while she recovered."

Your eyes drifted to the doors where the capricious creature came from. "Would not a cat dislike such confinement?"

Sicarius laughed. "Yes, she resented it at first. However, once we established a deep bond, I did let her go."

"Why?"

"Why what?"

"Why let her go?"

Sicarius's smile widened into uncanny valley. "I knew she would be back. After all, there was no better place for her. She just needed time to realize that."

The story sent a shiver down your spine.

For five days after seeing Sicarius's scars, a fanged creature stalked your sleep. Whenever the ethereal hound bit your dream body, muscle cramps tore you from your rest. Counting clock ticks could not slow your racing heart. Much to your dismay, what warded off the terror was the recent addition to your dreams—a faceless man who drove the creature away with a muzzle flash and the smell of gunpowder. At first, you thought it was a subconscious image of your late husband coming from the recesses of your memories to protect you. However, when your savior spoke, his true identity became awkwardly clear.

"I have no patience for slobbering dogs."

Chasing that particular specter from your waking thoughts proved more troublesome than the nightmares themselves. Still, sleep deprived or not, you had a job to do.

With a stifled yawn, you pushed the dinner cart to the dining room. Reeves stood in the middle of the passage, head pressed against the door to the wine cellar. In his hand was an expensive vintage of dry red imported only three days ago. His quiet muttering spoke volumes.

You raised an eyebrow. "How's the dinner party going?"

"He's on the third bottle." Reeves groaned. "Ellsworth told me to be slow about bringing the next one for the wine cellar's sake."

"Major Payne?"

The footman nodded. "And if I hear Lady Eiden's goose honk laugh one more time, I'm going to drown myself."

"Have you decided on a location yet?"

"I was thinking about the fountain in the north hedge maze."

You nodded to the small window which overlooked the south lawns. "I think the reflecting pool is more romantic. The old white oak there looks ripe for a haunting."

Reeves's bitter laugh echoed in the hall. His smile was worn at the ends from overuse. "Starting to show your true face?"

You cocked your head and plastered on a brain-dead grin. "Whatever are you talking about?"

Reeves scoffed. "Women are terrifying."

You hummed. "Speaking of terrifying, will any of them be staying the night?"

"Sadly, yes. It's not safe to throw them out into the mountains after nightfall, even if he doesn't like them." Reeves sighed. "Why invite people you do not like to dinner, though?"

His words made memories of Professor Campbell spring to life in vivid color. You could picture the way he yawned when his daughter-in-law prattled on about the latest noble marriages. Snippy retorts at dinner parties painted with venom fit for a viper echoed in your ears. Clear as if he were still above ground, you saw Professor

Campbell sitting at his dining room table, checking his watch as guests fled before dessert.

"Thirty-seven minutes! My best time yet!"

"Perhaps, he just finds it entertaining," you offered. "If one has no real problems, inventing them might prove amusing."

Reeves whistled. "Cook has knives less sharp than your tongue."

You patted his shoulder. "Fare well in battle, soldier."

Reeves closed his eyes and chuckled.

As you approached the dining room doors, a ghastly sound wheezed between the cracks. Somewhere between squashed accordion, sinus infection, and tortured animal, it was not difficult to recognize Lady Eiden's voice. Steeling yourself for the show, you clamped your mouth shut and opened the door.

In the nearest dining chair, slapping her knee with glee, was the dowager herself. Her scarlet brocade gown matched the red and gold oriental rug. The yellow reflection from the mustard-colored drapes made her mahogany skin glow… or maybe that was just the second glass of wine.

"Oh, Mr. Estrova, you say the funniest things!" Lady Eiden gasped.

Beside her lurked her sullen teenage son. Hiding behind a pile of coiled hair, his eyes were averted as he tried not to stare at the painting of Lycenia on the far wall. The Goddess of the Feast was rendered in stunning nude surrounded by bounties of roasted meat, glossy fruit, and rich wine. Between his cackling mother and the buxom view, he drifted lower and lower into his seat.

Opposite to the Eidens, tugging at Ellsworth's elbow, was the greying war hero, Major Payne. Red as a tomato and swaying like a half-spun top, he smacked the table. "Don't *hic* stop pouring until I say so!"

Ellsworth's teeth looked ready to crack. In silence, he tilted the bottle until only the tiniest trickle filled the wine glass.

Next to the formerly heroic sot, basking in the glow of herself, sat the ever-perky Miss Hunt. Her tittering laugh was as shrill as the ringing of steel bells. Her mother, Lady Hunt, dabbed at her thin mouth with the linen napkin. As you watched her red lipstick ruining the white cloth, you understood why Lord Hunt had not smiled since his wedding day.

Pins and needles tingled in your fingers as you clenched the cart handle tightly. You parked the meals between the black and brass sideboards, trying not to gag at the sensuous purr in Miss Hunt's voice.

"So then what happened, Mr. Estrova?" the young heiress asked, leaning into the conversation. The folds of her cowl-necked dress unfurled to reveal fascination and flesh. She tucked a silken coil of auburn hair behind her ear. Coy eyes were half-lidded and unblinking as she stared at your master. "You mustn't keep us in suspense!"

You bit your tongue and served the hungry woman her plate.

Tonight's dinner was rosemary braised lamb shanks. They were draped in a mushroom reduction and served with creamy polenta and salt-kissed stacks of steamed root vegetables. Young Lord Eiden, the only vegetarian at the table, received a hearty portobello steak with balsamic vinegar glaze. When he saw his meal, he nodded at the host. Your master smiled and returned the gesture. Then, turning back to the Hunts, he swept his hand towards the plate.

"By that point, General Armitage realized he had made a tactical error letting his cook go instead of accommodating the blindness. After all, a good chef is as precious as any fine heirloom." Your master dragged his silver fork along the bone of the lamb. The piece peeled away as if it was made of butter. "A special courier arrived the next day offering Mr. Miller his old job back with *twice* the pay. Of course, what the general did not realize is that I had outflanked him."

"Do tell!" Lady Eiden insisted, flapping her wrist.

Wide-eyed, you dodged the flailing limb before she could send the brown sauce plummeting into her own lap. With a sigh of relief, you set the woman's meal before her. She never looked up.

Sicarius caught your eye and then glanced at Lady Eiden's expensive gown. His grin grew one tooth wider. "Mrs. Miller always dreamed of opening a bookstore, but the heavy inventory can be very costly to import." His shrug was as cocky as the owner of the winning horse. "Unless, of course, you own the shipping company."

The laugh that bellowed from Major Payne was like a tuba blast in a tin can. "Outflanked indeed!" the drunkard crowed, curling his fingers around some invisible ball. "Brilliant move, Estrova! Get 'em right in the—"

Lady Hunt coughed before the Major could finish the sentence.

Miss Hunt dragged her calf across her knee while fluttering her eyes. "You do understand women, Mr. Estrova."

Trying to keep the bile in your stomach, you took your place along the grey and gold mural wallpaper next to Ellsworth. The clock chimed half-past seven. At least another hour of this nonsense to go.

Reeves was a fool. Drowning oneself at the manor ran the risk that one's ghost might be forced to spectate at every dinner party for all eternity. The Dark One could not craft a crueler punishment than that.

Lady Eiden carved a piece of her lamb loose, scraping the china with a loud screech. Ignoring any damage to the beautiful dinnerware, she stuffed it into her mouth. "Miller? Oh! You must mean in that elegant shop on Flounce Street!" She tapped her dimpled chin. "Now, where does a cook's wife get that kind of capital!"

Your master placed a hand over his sternum and bowed his head. "There might have been a signing bonus."

The sallow Lord Hunt's lips smacked like a cow. Watery eyes vacant of logical thought, he stared at Sicarius and snorted. "Seems like a nuisance, employing married servants. Having their attention divided between your home and their families must produce substandard work."

"Perhaps if I hired substandard staff, but I do not," Sicarius remarked, sipping his wine. "Besides, I find talented people tend to draw in others with incredible skill. For example, my gardener is a superb horticulturist. Along with him, I obtained his wife, the former Royal Master Ceramist. All the bone china in this house is her custom craft."

"My word! No wonder it is so detailed." Lord Hunt adjusted his monocle and inspected the pearlescent plate. "I thought it looked similar to Duke Florence's set, gods rest his soul."

"Now, that is not to say I hire only married couples." Sicarius nodded to you. "Ellsworth there is a confirmed old bachelor, and my maid is a widow."

Miss Hunt wrenched her head around. She looked you up and down before settling upon the mother-of-pearl brooch pinned to your tie. Her nostrils flared. Green eyes narrowed. She lifted her chin and pressed a lone finger into her cheek.

"So you hire mature staff then. How droll!" Her giggle sounded like shattered glass. "I have such a time keeping a lady's maid since most of the young ones disappear after marriage. Tell me, Mr. Estrova, are the *older* ones any better?"

How such a charming creature drove off her servants, you would never know.

Sicarius folded his hands in front of his chin. "You misunderstand me, Miss Hunt. I have no such policy. My undercook is not yet fifteen."

Lady Eiden clasped a hand to her mouth. "So young!"

"I find age does not always correlate with talent." Sicarius nodded to you. "My maid, for example, used to work for Professor Campbell. By the time she was Miss Hunt's age, she must have read over three hundred texts. Many of the neoscience, historical records, and cultural works he translated were transcribed by her hand."

Miss Hunt froze. Her eyes rolled in your direction. You kept your gaze on the floor and your expression more neutral than a beige wall. The taste of copper was heavy as you bit your tongue, *hard.*

Sicarius beamed at the heiress. "It pleases me to keep only things of value in this house."

The Hunts did not stay the night.

CHAPTER TEN

Melt Season – Day 81 of 90

"*Ow!* Reeves, so help me, if you hit one more pothole I'm vomiting in your bag!"

Cook roared with laughter from the front seat of the Benson. He turned and smacked his pupil on the shoulder. "Hang in there, Alex, it's only half an hour more."

As the car bumped again, the teenager clapped his hand over his mouth and squeezed his eyes shut. Even with the wind whipping through the windows, everyone heard the nauseated gulp.

With a sympathetic frown, you rubbed his back. "Reeves, really, it is a bit rough back here."

The engine noise dropped as the footman depressed the clutch. He clasped the mahogany knob in his hand and thrust the shifter into the next gear. "Sorry, ma'am, but if we slow down, we'll reach Marinar after dark. You don't want to be on these roads at night, trust me."

You gazed out at the dense pine forest on either side of the car. Even though there was still an hour until twilight, the thick trees cast deep shadows on the carpet of needles below them. The air was rich with turpentine sap and drifting pollens. It made your nose itch.

"What about the master?" you asked.

Reeves rolled his eyes. "With the way Sicarius drives the Lacrima, I'm sure he's already at the townhouse. The only one to ever beat his time was Lyle." The engine dipped again. With smooth precision, Reeves dialed back the shifter for the sloping curve ahead. "I'm still convinced he has secretly worked out a teleporter. There's no way he made it from Gravelorne to Marinar in less than two hours."

From the top of the hill, you could see the long, winding coastline and low-hanging sun. Golden hour painted the world in hues of fire orange. Near the edge of the city, steam rose from the Grand Station of Marinar. It was only half a year since you rode the steam train to this place, but it felt like only yesterday.

Another lurch of the car sent your stomach flipping. Alex groaned and muttered something under his breath that would have cost him a week's pay if Ellsworth had overheard.

"Toughen up Alex," Reeves teased. "You're losing to a girl."

"Mr. Reeves." Your voice nearly frosted the windshield. "Would you like me to repeat that to your wife?"

Sinners pleaded for their souls with less sincerity than when Reeves begged for your silence.

Compared to the massive mountain manor, Sicarius's lean, tall townhouse was almost claustrophobic. Even halls twice as wide as the professor's domicile could not improve the cramped feeling. To navigate steep stairs, the gear cart was forced to cling to tight corners. Plowing into the cupboards and tables while dodging the other servants was painful, even if graceful waterfall lines meant the edges of the furniture were smooth.

It is a universal truth that closer quarters make for higher tensions. The Gravelorne staff was no exception.

Weary from the hills, everyone but Sicarius was on edge. Most of the infighting was resolved by each party tending to their area of expertise. Reeves handled the cars and visitors. Cook and Alex set about collecting food for the stay. You threw yourself into all the cleaning the town dust-mice could not accomplish. Despite everyone's best efforts to keep the peace, more than the kettle was boiling over when you went to collect the master's nighttime tisane.

"Don't touch that! You'll mess up Cook's labels!" Alex snapped.

The labels Alex mentioned were of little help to you. Like the manor, all the cabinets at the townhouse had a series of dotted markers to indicate their contents. However, the code was not any defined language. It was just a pattern that Cook created to help him sort his wares. Alex had years to learn all their meanings. You were barely permitted in the kitchen to pick up meals.

Alex shoved the cupboard shut and stabbed a finger towards the hall. "The tea set is in the parlor!"

"Come now, Alex. She was only at the townhouse once before." Cook waved his hand and filled the kettle. "She can't know everything."

"I'm just trying to keep things in proper order!" Alex protested. "I can't stand people messing up the kitchen and making your life harder than it already—"

"Now listen here, *boy.*" Cook's voice made everyone in the room feel two years old. There was a deep frown and a father's disappointment on his lips. "I appreciate all you do for me, but I am more than capable of handling my own kitchen even if a few things are out of place. I'm blind, not broken."

Embarrassed brown eyes refused to look at his mentor. "Yes, sir," Alex mumbled.

Standing next to the door, you watched the exchange in silence.

Cook sighed and reached for the cupboard by the stove. Inside were eight canisters, each encircled with differing numbers of rubber bands. Meaty hands stroked down the sides until he selected the container with four markers.

"Missus, would you go get the teapot from the hutch?" He patted the top of the can. "I'll get the water boiling."

"Yes," you replied. "Absolutely, Mr. Miller."

Cook crossed his arms and turned to the boy. "Alex?"

"Y-yes, sir?"

The older man cocked his head towards the groceries on the counter. His broad grin was back. "Stop sulking and help me get these biscuit tins marked before bed."

"Yes, sir!" Alex agreed, rushing to his mentor's side.

As the kitchen door clicked shut, you could not help but smile.

In the powder blue parlor, you located a smooth white cabinet with crystal knobs and diamond-shaped accents. Inside was a china set with gold rims and matte black collars. The round, ladle-like cups were etched with cream-white bearded irises. For a moment, you stopped to admire their delicate blooms. Mrs. Norton was a true artist. Every tea cup you drank from was as lovely as the last, and seeing such pretty plates always made meal times a pleasure. Breaking from your thoughts, you collected the tall, tapered pot and bustled off to the kitchen.

By the time you returned, Alex was pasting rubber dots onto each of the new boxes. When you entered the room, he would not look at you.

"Mr. Miller, I have the teapot," you announced.

Cook waved you over to the stove. You skirted the preparation table, removed the lid, and handed him the china. Feeling the pot's edge with one hand, he poured the water with the other. "The silver serving tray is in the lower part of the hutch. I'm sure it wants a polish while the scones finish browning."

Alex squatted down to a cabinet below the sink. There was a clattering of glass and some scraping sounds. He tossed you a rag and the silver restoring preparation. You scrambled but managed to catch them.

"Hey."

"Yes, Alex?"

He turned to his glue-work, giving you his back. "Sorry… About before, I mean."

"We are all tired." You shook your head. "All is forgiven."

In the reflection from the window, a small smile slipped onto the boy's weary face.

After a quick polishing job and the ring of the oven timer, you set out on your next task: feeding the master his evening snack. China in hand, you rapped twice on the study door.

"Enter."

You carried the heavy tray to the maple desk and set it down. The smell of grassy chamomile and sweet cream swirled through the air. As you poured, you could feel Sicarius's eyes dragging over the exposed skin from your brow to your throat latch. Gaze fixed on the painted china plates beside the window, you tried to ignore the way your skin prickled under his scrutiny.

"How is everyone after the drive?" Sicarius inquired.

"Tired," you answered. "Alex was nearly sick from the hills. I am worried the stress is going to make his rash come back."

"And you?"

Were you overwrought from the car ride, or did the genuine concern in that question make your chest squeeze? You hoped it was the former. Your reputation was shattered enough without nonsense clouding your judgment.

"Well enough to work." You handed him his cup and clasped your hands in front of your apron. "Do you have a particular book selection this evening, Master?"

"Hm…" Blue eyes flitted to the sparsely populated shelves that curved along the walls. Most of the available options were business texts. Sicarius frowned and tapped his chin. "The townhouse selection is rather monotonous, isn't it?"

As he contemplated the inadequacy of his collection, your eyes drifted to the hollowed angles of his face. Curse the one who gave him those cheekbones. When he stroked his face like that, it made him look so—

You swallowed the feeling and pretended to examine the white wainscot for dust. "It seems adequate for the purpose. This residence is for trade relations, is it not?"

"Adequate?" he teased with a boyish grin. "My dear woman, you will break a man's heart saying things like that." Tugging on the drawer pull, he opened the top compartment of his desk, selected a business card and handed it to you. "Still, I am confident we can do better."

On the small linen rectangle was a handsome, silver embossed address and a simple store name: "Miller's Fine Books and Imports".

"Go see Cook's wife tomorrow. I am sure she will have a few selections that will improve our literary crisis."

"Yes, Master."

He leaned back in his leather chair and sipped his tea. "Oh, and one more thing." His cheeky grin made you sweat. "I need you to take a special order to Georgette."

Mrs. Miller's bookstore was located in the arts district of Marinar, not far from the prestigious University of Tramton. The old crabapples that lined its streets burst with fiery magenta blooms. Interspersed amongst handsome horses and monogrammed carriages, the latest steam-core saloons burbled up the road. Fashionable women clothed themselves in calf-length dresses with wide collars, kidskin corsets, and petite floral patterns. Men, no doubt mimicking the figure of their favorite athletes, preferred light linens with padded shoulders and tapered waistcoats. Patterns from tweed to plaid were all represented. Tall leather walking boots and round-toed kitten heels were almost as ubiquitous as brass embellishments.

Not unlike the well-dressed pedestrians, Miller's Fine Books and Imports was smartly trimmed. Though the front still possessed the dark colors of the coal age, its new windows were smooth and curvaceous as a stage dancer. Chevron-shaped glass inlays in the entryway allowed guests to peek at rows and rows of leather-bound wonder. The smell of ink and dust wrapped you in the feeling of home. You strode across a lattice-style blonde wood parquet. Ebony-diamond accents dotted the intricate patterns below your feet.

The shop assistant was a willowy creature with large wire glasses that engulfed her tiny face. "Good afternoon," she greeted in a breathy, high pitch. "How may I help you, madam?"

"I was sent by Mr. Estrova to pick up some packages," you explained.

The girl pushed her spectacles up a tall, pointy nose. "Yes, madam. Please follow me."

Up the cantilevered stairs you climbed, trying not to mind the hanging air between each stone tread. Alone on the second floor was a statuesque woman with dark hair. The champagne crepe of her A-line dress looked golden against her umber complexion. Unlike the plain corsets outside, the rich navy brocade of her underbustier was embroidered with vibrant peacock feathers. With an aquiline nose and deep brown eyes, her face would have been equally at home on a marble rendering of a goddess.

"Mrs. Miller?" the assistant called.

"What is it, Colleen?" the woman asked, straightening her flounce sleeves.

"There's a customer who says she's here on behalf of Mr. Estrova."

Mrs. Miller looked you up and down. "I take it you are the new maid my husband mentioned?"

"It is a pleasure to meet you at last, Mrs. Miller." You bowed your head. "Forgive any forwardness, but Cook hardly takes a meal without speaking of you."

The woman's eyes widened as she brought her hand to her mouth. "Oh, stars. What has the fool been saying?"

You waved your hands. "Only your praises, I assure you."

She groaned and pinched the bridge of her nose. "Somehow, that seems worse than the alternative."

Stifling the laugh, you continued, "My master feels his collection at the townhouse is bland. He said you would know what type of titles interest him?"

Mrs. Miller snorted and shook her head. "His pre-orders have arrived, if that's what you mean. Follow me."

On the far end of the second floor, taking up an entire wall, was a set of hand-sized novels in matte cloth binding. The shopkeeper crawled along the row, plucking one book after another from their homes. As she handed them to you, your face caught fire.

Ravished by the Rogue Regent
Succumbing to the Scoundrel
The Rake Takes His Bride
Bewitched by the Wicked Warlock
The Very Virile Viscount
Stolen by the Sea Captain
The Princely Consequence of Sleeping With the Duke
A Love Below the Shoreside Moon

Well, at least that last one did not sound so—

You flipped open the book and scanned the text.

As his tempting tentacles ravaged her buxom bottom—

You snapped the book shut. "Please tell me you are joking!" you protested.

Mrs. Miller scratched her cheek. "I wish I was. He's read most of the ones in print. These are the newest I have."

Next time you did Sicarius's shopping, you resolved to wear a deep cloche hat so you could hide in it.

As you staggered under the weight of your unwitting foray into fictional seduction, Mrs. Miller guided you down the stairs to the register. The shop assistant packed the books into a brown paper bag. Bending below the counter, her employer extracted a heavy pictorial bound in black leather. The gold lettering read:

Madam Millie's Illustrated Guide to Illustrious Sexual Prowess

You slapped your hand over the title. "There is a limit to what I will do for money, and this exceeds the bounds of it." You stabbed the cover with your index finger. "Under *no* circumstances will I be taking *this* book to *that* man."

"It's not for him," Mrs. Miller insisted. "It's the delivery for Georgette."

You clutched your chest and heaved a sigh of relief. "Thank the stars above."

Colleen opened her mouth to say something, but Mrs. Miller elbowed the girl in the rib. Handing over the thick paper bag, the shopkeeper waved goodbye with a tight grin. As the shop door slipped shut, the spindly girl approached her boss.

"Doesn't Mr. Estrova own the deluxe edition of Madam Millie's?"

Mrs. Miller's teeth gritted. "If you want to live, you will learn to be silent, Colleen."

By the time you reached Georgette's shop, the sky had turned a windswept grey. Clenching the paper bag shut, you hurried up the stairs. The buzzer cried out. Heels clicked across the hardwood floor. Blue eyes peeked through the chain lock. The sound of cheerful glee poured out from the crack. The door swung wide to reveal a leggy blonde with blue eyebrows.

"Come in! Come in!" she cried, snatching your wrist. "The tea is ready!"

Georgette's studio smelled like berries, oil, and alcohol. She dragged you to the plush velvet stool and pushed you down with a flick of her wrists. You dropped the bag on the floor as if it were filled with vipers. Your host hummed a bright show tune, swinging her hips to the rhythm. The ruffled bustle of her swallowtail skirt swayed all the way to the kitchen. When she returned, she was holding two copper striped ceramic cups and their matching teapot. She poured the deep purple drink with an extravagant flourish.

"Passionflower, blueberry, and rosehip. My own blend," she explained, draping herself over a cozy linen pouf. "It is the only thing to soothe the nerves."

"Oh! *Now* you are concerned about my nerves!" You kicked the bag of sin, spilling its carnal contents to the ground. "Tell me, how many of you are enjoying this farce of yours?"

Georgette raised four fingers before snatching up *The Very Virile Viscount.* "Ooh! I do adore a breeding kink!" With a coquettish grin, she waved the book at you. "You will tell Mr. Estrova that I *must* borrow it when he is done."

Seething, you sipped your tea.

Chapter Eleven

When you returned to the townhouse that afternoon, you brought with you three things: the bag of smutty books, a painfully fake smile, and the caustic aura of impending death.

"Mr. Reeves." Your voice was dainty as any virginal ingénue. "Where might I find our employer?"

The footman smashed himself flat against the wall. His finger pointed to the study faster than fire consumes dry tinder.

"Thank you," you replied with a bow before storming down the hall.

As you passed the kitchen, Alex screeched to a halt in the doorway. He began to protest his near trampling but snapped his mouth shut at the ghoulish expression on your face. When you reached the study, you knocked twice.

"Enter."

Just before you slammed the door shut, you heard everyone in the hall shuffle off to anyplace else.

Inside the office, Sicarius was standing at his bookshelf, finger gliding over the titles. Despite being fully dressed this morning, his black blazer was conspicuously absent. A pinstriped silver tie was loose around his neck, and his shirt collar was open to the bottom of his pectorals.

"Any promising titles?" he asked, nodding to the bag.

You set the bawdy books on his desk with a firm bang. The drawers rattled. "Enough," you insisted.

"Enough?" He raised a brow as a cocky smile dashed across his lips.

"Button up your shirt." An accusing finger pointed at his bare, well-sculpted chest. Your voice was flat as a squirrel under a tire. "We need to have a chat."

Sicarius whistled, pushing the book in his fingers back between its brethren. He put his hands in his pockets and strolled across the room. Perching himself on the front of the desk, he draped one leg over the other. Blue eyes sparkled with mischievous delight.

Your nostrils flared. With a snarl, you grasped the front of his lapel and stuffed the buttons back into their holes. Furious fingers twisted his tie into a hard knot and cinched it tight to his throat. Shaking hands clutched the fabric as you pulled his cocky face to yours.

"As was discussed during my initial interview, I am a proper maid, not some street cat purring for your attention."

His eyes drifted into a dreamy stare as he brought a hand to your cheek. "And yet I have always been tempted to call you kitten," your master declared. "Would that upset you?"

You slapped his fingers away. "You are an unrepentant scoundrel!"

He pointed to the bag of books. "Would you prefer a sea captain? I do own a fleet."

Your nose curled in disgust. "Do not confuse me for some starry-eyed waif who you can impress with your pretty figure, your preposterous finery, or your petty flattery."

"You think I'm pretty?"

You jerked his neck hard. "I am here to clean your house, read your books, and serve your tea. Pandering to your bizarre proclivity for sexual harassment is outside the scope of my services."

"How would you like a change of position then?"

The tie slipped from your hand. **"How do you sleep with yourself at night!?"** you shrieked.

"Sleep? You think I sleep?" Sicarius threw his head back and cackled like a storybook villain. "Why do you think I asked my maid to read to me?" he sputtered through cheerful tears.

"Whatever sordid fantasies you had for me can go straight to—"

"Now, now." Sicarius patted your shoulder. "There is no reason to call marriage 'sordid' just because you were widowed so young."

You froze. "Excuse me?"

"I am hardly the man to ask for forgiveness regarding such things. You will need to take that up with the clerics." He grinned. "Or was that not what you meant?"

With your lips pressed in a firm line, you watched him as a cat watches a squawking crow: simultaneously puzzled and alarmed.

Large hands groped for the brass ring of the right desk drawer. From it, he extracted a small oval box with gold trim. The crystal clasp flipped open with the flick of his thumb. Inside was a platinum sapphire ring with a round yellow gem embedded in a halo of marquise cut blue stones. The shape was reminiscent of a lotus blossom.

You staggered backward, staring at the jewelry as if it were a viper.

Sicarius looked from you to the box and back again. "Well, I told you I wanted to avoid diamonds." He huffed. "Mrs. Gause's dinner conversation is as relentless as it is vapid."

That ring… that *thing* had to be five years' salary!

Sicarius pushed off the desk and took your quivering hand in his. Your eyes bulged. He kneeled to the ground. The insufferable smirk on his face softened to a pleased grin. As he slipped the ring onto your left hand, bitter words flew from your lips.

"Stop with your games!"

"Games?" Soft lips pressed against your fingers. "Let me assure you, this is not a game."

"Everything is a game to you," you muttered.

Sicarius sighed. "After all we have been through, you still do not love me, do you?"

Love? Was he joking or delusional? You had only known the man a few months! First that "love at first sight" business, and now this. Sure, he was attractive. Yes, the attention was not *entirely* unwelcome after all these years of celibacy. However, a fleeting crush on a pretty face was far removed from "marriage material," let alone heart stopping, world ending, die-for-you love. Even with Piotr, that took time.

You tried to pull your arm out of Sicarius's grip, but his hold was tighter than a vice.

"Do you remember what I told you when we first spoke?" His warm thumb stroked over your cold knuckles. "I told you that, ever since I read the professor's letter, I wanted you."

The ring sparkled on your finger in the same way his eyes glittered in the lamplight. Its weight reminded you of the one Piotr had given you. A painful ache forced the air from your lungs.

"You are everything the professor was, you know? Astute. Efficient. Hardworking." He waved his tie at you. "A bit spiteful at times, but I find that rather exciting."

You shot him a suspicious frown. "You *want* a spiteful companion?"

"Say what you will, but I miss his barbs."

"You are completely illogical," you muttered.

"Really? I thought that marrying a woman whose company I enjoy was very logical."

The pounding of your blood made your ears ring. Stars. He might be a debauched eccentric, but he sure knew how to make a woman feel wanted. Maybe you should just—

No. Impulse decisions were for children. Even if he was being truthful—

Sicarius raised his index finger. "If you insist on logic, then let me point out you would not need to worry about money or housing ever again. That is worth *something*, isn't it?"

Well, a broke, unemployable widow could hardly argue the merits of financial security, but…

As you stared at the sapphire's rich blue facets, your body felt heavy with the weight of reality. Marrying a man meant wedding yourself to his entire life. For a gamekeeper like Piotr, that meant loving his dogs, keeping a modest home, and providing a willing ear for a rainy day. For a wealthy man like Sicarius Estrova, the task would be monumentally different. Keeping a social calendar, managing a full estate, winning favor through charm and poise; those were things expected of a society wife. Those were the costs of wearing his ring.

Specters of doubt haunted you, spewing their cruel gossip into your burning ears. The tactless harpies from the funeral would be only the first in a long parade. Again and again, each one would repeat what you already knew: a ring like *that* did not belong on the hand of a *maid.*

Fingers balled into tight fists, you looked him dead in the eye. "I can not."

Sicarius raised his brows. "Can not?" He hummed. "Now, that's an interesting choice of phrase. *Can not* over *will not.* I wonder…"

"Let go of my hand."

He wrinkled his nose at you. "I *will not.*"

Shock quickly morphed into a deep scowl. "Let. Go. Sicarius." You yanked back against him with each punctuation.

"Sicarius?" His groan was low and erotic. "Oh, I do like the sound of that…"

More than your heart throbbed at the sensual tone in his words. However, adrenaline and good sense pushed that to the side in a few quick beats.

"Release me at once!"

The unflappable man climbed to his feet, pulling your wrist to his chest. His steady pulse thumped low and slow against your hand. As you tore at his fingers, a cocksure grin split his cheeks.

"First, we need to talk about *can not.* I find it a rather amusing little phrase."

You raised your free hand, palm wide for the slap. In an instant, your other wrist was wrapped in his clutches. Above the taunting sneer, his eyes swirled with fiendish calculations.

"You see, *will not* implies a refusal to do so but *can not* means the inability to complete a task even if one desires it."

"Release me at once, or I *will not* hesitate to bite you!" you fired back.

Sicarius leaned over you, and his hot breath fanned across your face. As he drew near to your cheek, your skin caught fire. The master studied the goose pimples on your neck. His pulse quickened against your fist.

"You *can not* threaten me with a good time, kitten."

Your jaw dropped. "What is wrong with you!?" you demanded.

Never releasing your hands, he tapped your nose with his pointer. "Why should I elaborate? You *will not.*"

Your head spun. Eyes raw with angry tears, you finally snapped. "I can not marry you because rich men marry fine ladies, not maids!"

"Holding my money against me are you?" He snorted. "In all my years, only you and Professor Campbell have done so."

A quick yank pulled you chest to chest with fine silk. Wide eyes stared into his wild grin. Just before your lips met, he whispered, "I do not want a fine lady. I want a good woman."

Sicarius's caramel sweet kiss was tantalizing and slow. Your body melted like sugar over a flame. He nipped at your mouth, letting soft skin coax you under his spell. Deep inside your core, a spark of something long forgotten flickered to life. When he pulled away, you fell into his chest. The silver-tongued fiend loosed your hands and wrapped his arms around your waist. With delight, he added: "—and the woman I want is you."

The sincerity of his words was like an ice pick to the cold cockles of a frozen heart. It had been years since someone said those words to you. When Piotr mumbled them, your whole body tingled. Now, when Sicarius declared them, your knees buckled.

He poked the tip of your nose, pushing you out of your thoughts. When you looked up, he waved his hand in a prompting circle. "This would be the part where you say yes?"

Slowly, your head shook back and forth.

He curled his finger under your chin. "Well, even if you do not love me, it clearly is not a lack of attraction creating your hesitation."

"I—" You gulped, forcing your wobbling knees to stand. "I am not a society wife. I do not know how to manage a household or how to dance or how to hold silly conversations or how to flutter my eyes like some"—you snarled in frustration—"bejeweled butterfly!"

He laughed. "I do not recall listing those talents amongst my requirements."

You stabbed a finger at the door. "Society does not approve of people like me marrying people like you. In their eyes, I will always be some money-obsessed social climber. What kind of life is that for either of us?"

"Is that all?"

You glared at him. "Oh, yes. Just utter social ruin. That is all."

Sicarius moved his hands from your waist to your shoulders. He turned you around and sat you in the large, plush chair opposite his desk. As the fabric sank beneath your bottom, your knees rose above your thighs. He rested his elbow on the arm and raised his fingers one by one.

"One: Ellsworth can teach you management, and I am confident you'll be a better student than Reeves. Two: I can teach you to dance. Three: I like your conversation the way it is. Four: Georgette can dress you and teach you all the eyelid fluttering you want. Finally," he winked at you, "I will simply tell everyone seeing my maid bent over my desk was too good to pass up. They will just chalk it up to my eccentricity and go along."

"Y-you... Oh, Stars..." You buried your steaming face in your hands. "I beg you not to repeat that in any sort of company, reputable or otherwise."

"Can I repeat it in your company?"

You groaned. "This day can not get any more bizarre."

A finger tapped you on the shoulder. You looked up. Sicarius pointed to the ring, then to his nose, and then fixed you with a toothy smile.

This man was clearly a bit touched in the head. He could make any excuse he liked but what sane person would rush into a lifetime commitment like this? It was almost like he—

Oh... Oh, no. Seriously? The man was in his forties. There was no way... right?

As you eyed his childish excitement, the hairs on the back of your neck rose.

"You have never been married before, have you?" you murmured with astonishment.

He shrugged. "I never found anyone else enticing enough to propose to. Why do you ask?"

Stars above. Sicarius Estrova, *the* eligible bachelor of Coriland, really only wanted you? Okay, that was as precious as Piotr sleeping with his puppies.

"Are you going to keep falling like this?"

Butterflies fluttered in your gut. Your voice was halting and cautious. "Do you even understand what it takes to be in a marriage? It is not some happily ever after from one of your books."

"What it takes?" A wicked look overtook his face. "Oh! Are you worried about my performance in the bedroom? If so, let me assure you that I—"

You slapped your hand over his lips. "Please, for the sake of my sanity, stop talking."

A warm hand engulfed yours. As a wet tongue slid up your palm, you rocketed backwards over the side of your chair.

"Stop it!" you yelled.

"Well, how else was I going to prove the point without talking?"

"Listen here you farcical pervert—"

"Farcical pervert?" He snorted. "The professor does nice work. You are better than a thesaurus."

Shaking hands ripped the ring from your finger and flung it at his face. Sicarius snatched it out of mid-air as you stormed to the door. You depressed the handle. The crack to freedom widened. All at once, a pale arm reached over your shoulder and snapped the door shut. Sicarius leaned against the exit, his mouth hovering above your ear.

"I am sorry."

You crossed your arms.

"I enjoy teasing you. Your reactions are entertaining." He turned your cheek to face him and gave you an apologetic grin. "I went too far with the sex jokes."

"Yes, you did," you replied flatly.

"I *can not* promise you that I *will not* upset you ever again. I am far from perfect." The master reached down, taking your hand in his. He slipped the ring back onto your finger. "I *can* promise you that if you marry me, you *will not* be bored."

"What if I prefer being bored?"

His eyes glinted. "You *do not.*"

A snort of laughter flew from your lips. You glanced across the room. On the smooth desk sat a brass and enamel phone. Rebecca's face flashed across your mind.

Sicarius's eyes followed yours. "If it would help you decide, you are welcome to borrow it and call a friend."

As he read your mind, your cheeks burned. "Servants do not use the master's phone for personal calls."

He lifted your hand, bringing the ring to eye level. "Do you really think I hold to those types of rules?" His other arm slinked around your waist, scooping you off the door. Sicarius guided you across the room and pulled his chair out. You grimaced and lifted your skirts. He pushed the chair forward and rolled you to the desk. The huge wooden frame made you feel like a child.

"You may call as many people as you like." He patted your shoulder. "I will be in the parlor if you need me."

When he turned his broad back towards you, your throat felt tight. You parted your lips to object, but it was too late. As the study door clicked shut, the sapphire ring sparkled in the afternoon light. You groaned and set your overheated forehead on the desk. Still reeling from the world's most ludicrous marriage proposal, you stared at the telephone.

"Do you think financial security and a handsome husband is worth all his nonsense?" you asked the machine.

Indifferent to your plight, the rotary phone sat on the desk in silence.

With an exhausted sigh, you snatched up the mouthpiece. Stuffing your finger in the zero, you spun the dial.

"Operator," greeted the woman on the other end.

Your uniform skirt wrinkled in your grip. "Please connect me to The Worn Elbow Pub in Illestrad."

"One moment, ma'am."

As the line hissed in your ear, you clenched your teeth. Nervous eyes searched the clock for the time. Three in the afternoon. Would she even be there? Was she at the factory today? Should you call back later or—

"Worn Elbow Pub," a male voice answered.

"Lee? Is Rebecca there?"

"Oh!" Mr. Baylord, the proprietor of the bar, yelped into the phone. "Stars! Of all the people who would call! Wait… I thought you liked sending letters better?"

"I do!" Nervous laughter filled the line. Your toe dug into the floor. "It is just… Well… I have a very odd situation and—"

Lee gasped. "He proposed, didn't he! Oh, I knew it!" His voice was muffled, but you could still hear him calling across the room. "Becca! **Re-be-cca!** Get over here! You owe me a foot massage!"

"Y-you were betting on this?" you stammered.

"Yup, and I won!" Lee crowed. "Becca thought it would be sooner, but I told her you were a bit gun shy. Besides, spring is more romantic. Tell me he got you flowers! Oh! Wait. Here she is. Hang on."

The other end of the line popped with an excited squeal. "About time!"

"You were betting on this!?" you demanded.

Rebecca huffed in mock annoyance; the undercurrent of her voice brimmed with glee. "Why did you think I told you to hold out for the coin?" She paused. "You did hold out, right?"

You snarled into the mouthpiece. "I did not 'hold out for the coin.' I was *blindsided!*"

"Yes, yes. Thank the stars your rich boy-toy doesn't mind someone oblivious," she replied dismissively. "Cough up the details, or I am breaking up with you."

You sunk into the chair, massaging your aching temples. "I fear for your children."

"Pish posh. They'll grow up stronger this way. Now, what did he do? A carriage ride? Romantic dinner? Bent you over the staircase and—"

"No!" You coughed as the dry air hit your throat. "It was not romantic at all! He sent me to buy some smarmy books."

"…which ones?"

"Rebecca Jane Baylord!"

"Sorry! Sorry! Go on!"

You sighed. "When I got back from being *utterly humiliated,* I went to his office and told him I would not tolerate this behavior anymore."

"Ooooh! The feisty approach!" Lee called from the background. "Good idea! Treat 'em mean and keep 'em keen."

"Lee. Darling. She's trying to speak."

You scowled at the receiver. "Rebecca, he wants me to marry him! I can not *be* a society wife!"

"Of course you can. Just complain about how good help is so hard to find these days. Then you can slather on that judgmental stare, and you'll blend right in."

Oh, you had a judgmental stare slathered on, all right.

"Please be serious for a moment," you whined. "What would you do if you were in my position?"

"You mean if I was a poor widow being blackballed by decent society and some handsome, rich, crazy man told me he wants to marry me despite all that?"

Thank you, dearest Rebecca, for that rambling piece of sarcasm.

"Does he hit you?" she asked.

"No."

"Has he ever touched you more than you were comfortable with?"

"Yes, several times. That is part of the—"

"Under your clothes?"

"Well..." you curled the cord around your finger.

"Well...?" She sounded too excited.

You cupped the phone speaker, face ablaze with shame. "He... he reached up my skirt and took my stocking off when I fell from the ladder."

Lee whistled. Rebecca hushed him. "But nothing more, right?" she asked.

"It was quite enough!" you argued.

"Exactly how far was he from your undergarments at the time?"

"Rebecca!"

She clicked her tongue. "Exactly my point. He could'a, and he didn't." There was a small pause and a hum. "Is he as romantic as Piotr?"

"I do not want a fine lady. I want a good woman, and the woman I want is you."

"Sometimes," you admitted.

"I heard he is handsome."

"Can I repeat it in your company?"

You winced. "The flesh may be in good condition but the mind is rancid."

Rebecca laughed. "Rancid as it may be, his mind seems pretty devoted to you. Turned away all them other suitors, didn't he?"

Your stomach twisted in knots as she touched upon the next problem. "Think for a second what that means, Rebecca. He has never been married before," you stated. *"At all."*

She paused. "How old is he?"

"Forty-four, I believe."

"That's either creepy or adorable and I'm not sure which."

"Exactly!" you agreed. "He says I am the first he ever proposed to but—"

Rebecca squealed into the phone. *"Definitely* as romantic as Piotr then!" she insisted. "Stars! Doesn't that just make you feel special?"

It was at that moment that you realized having a friend who understood you completely could be a really terrible thing.

"Bet'cha could fall for him if he played his cards right," she teased.

You coughed. "I admit that, *on occasion,* he can be *intermittently* charming—"

"Oh?" she sneered into the phone. "Go on."

"—and there is a certain appeal to the security of marriage—"

"—especially when it comes with that kind of money. No more worrying about being a gutter-girl."

You gritted your teeth. "However, this whole scenario seems suspect."

"We're talking about a man whose other servants adore him! Think for a second! How many servants *like* the people they work for? Don't you think they wouldn't if he really was shady?"

The silence from your end spoke more than words ever could.

"Hm…" Rebecca's smirk was audible. "What do you think, Lee dear? How should I advise her, as a friend?"

There was a long pause on the other end of the line. Hushed whispers hissed at the speaker. After a time, you heard both of the Baylords answer: "Get knocked up as quickly as possible."

For a moment, as they went silent, you swore you heard a low, stifled laugh. You raised a brow and pressed the receiver tight against your ear.

"You all right?" Rebecca asked. "You got really quiet all of a sudden."

"Did Lee laugh just now?"

"Huh? No…? Why?"

You pinched the bridge of your nose. Must have been the static. Clearly, the stress was making you hear things.

CHAPTER TWELVE

Though the conversation with Rebecca persisted for half an hour past what your hammering heart could handle, it did little to ease your concerns. Her arguments were logical, if a bit crass. Sicarius was ridiculous but generous. The long nights you spent waiting for him to finish his work told you he was capable of diligence. Repeated business from his clients showed that he followed through with promises. He was well respected amongst those below his station, a rarity for a wealthy man, and possessed an affable demeanor. As you already knew, there were far worse fates than marrying a charming clown.

So why were you so restless?

Staring at the attic ceiling for hours yielded few answers. As the sun crept over the edge of your curtains, you lifted the cord around your neck and looked at the ring. The lotus blossom was small enough to be unobtrusive for daily life but large enough to command attention. Its band was smooth and soft as if it begged to belong on bare skin. This piece was clearly crafted, not made. Still, the delicate details looked like something better fit for a fae princess than a maid.

"Do you expect the likes of the Hunts and the Eidens are going to look at your finger and forget you were bringing them their meals a few months ago?" As you pictured a dubious stare from Miss Hunt, you loosed a bitter snort. "Not likely."

Then again, had Sicarius not called their attention to you, they may not have even noted your existence at all. That was simply how far a maid was below a mistress.

Knees tight to your chest, you buried your head in the mattress. As you laid there, stomach in knots, a single string of words clipped across your mind.

"I want a good woman, and the woman I want is you."

Irritated tears burned your hot cheeks. A frustrated fist hit the lumpy linen stuffing. "Why did he have to say something like that!?" you demanded of the night air.

The dark before the dawn refused to answer your question.

"Exactly how many times are you going to polish the same thing?"

Red, tired eyes rolled to the footman in the doorway. It was about two in the afternoon, the day after the proposal. You sat at the long mahogany dining table, rubbing the rag up and down a hexagonal candlestick. The polish had long since spilled onto the green enamel rim. Its once glowing surface looked hazy and dull.

Reeves scratched his cheek. "Wow… You look terrible."

"Your compassion is overwhelming, Mr. Reeves," you rasped.

"Alex was worried when you missed lunch. We all were."

"Thank you for informing me. I am sorry to have troubled you, and I will apologize to Cook and Alex at a later time," you stated.

"Did you sleep?"

You stared at him through swollen lids.

"Right…" He tugged the lyre back chair out and took a seat beside you. "Why don't you go back to bed and try to nap? I'll go tell Sicarius that you are—"

Your chair screeched across the pale wooden floor. "I will be fine. Please, allow me to continue my work unimpeded."

Reeves's face contorted in a mixture of pity and pain. "What happened?"

You clenched your teeth tight.

"Do you need a doctor?"

"No!" you insisted, setting the candlestick on the tabletop. "No, I… I am physically well." A shaking hand curled into your chest. "I am having difficulty with a decision. That is all."

Reeves cocked his head. "Let me guess; logic isn't lining up with your gut feelings?"

Your eyes widened. "Yes, that is exactly right."

He crossed his arms and hummed. "That's a tough problem."

"What would you do?"

He tilted back in the chair. A long pause filled the quiet room. "Probably whatever I felt would make me happy," he answered.

"And what if I do not know what would make me happy?"

The footman hunched over, grabbing his stomach as he sputtered.

"I really appreciate it when you laugh at my expense," you grumbled.

Reeves grinned at you from under knitted brows. "Sorry, sorry. I've been rather envious of you this whole time for being so good at your job. Sometimes I swore you were another of Lyle's machines. Seeing you like this—" He laughed again. "You seem so *human.*"

"I do have feelings, you know!"

"So follow them," he taunted, wagging his finger. "Stop being a servant for five seconds and be a little self-serving."

Your heart thudded in your chest. The words felt like a battering ram, smashing through the dark doubts in your mind. How long had it been since you did something for yourself? Not because it was the safest option. Not because it was the least likely to make trouble. Not because of any societal expectations or gratitude towards someone else. When did you last choose to *really* do what you wanted?

The heavy ring felt like ice against your skin. Your hand grasped it through the front of your dress.

Reeves sighed. "Look, I'm not trying to tell you how to live your life or anything, but whatever it is, you look miserable over it. If it's going to be trouble no matter what, then you might as well pick whichever way is worth the challenge."

Your fist clenched. Lifting your head, you gave the footman a tired smile. "I think I will try to get some rest, after all. Thank you, Garrick."

Reeves's stunned expression morphed into a cheerless chuckle. He pressed his cheek into the tabletop and closed his eyes.

"Did something I say upset you?"

He shook his head. "Just not handling the shock of you

calling me by my first name well, I suppose. It's like we're becoming friends."

For the first time since the marriage proposal, you laughed. "Have you had too much of Cook's dandelion wine again?"

He winced. "Too much of something for sure."

With a frown, you placed the back of your hand against his forehead. "You feel clammy. Do you want me to bring you an antacid?"

When Reeves lifted his face, his grin looked painful. "Nah, I need to suffer for my own actions."

When you awoke around seven-thirty, the sky outside the attic window was a golden haze. Sleep had soothed the burning in your eyes, but your mind was still a fog. With a few pops, you stretched your neck and climbed out of bed. As your fingers finished tying the apron's bow, your empty stomach loosed a low growl.

"Yes, I know," you replied, patting the irritable organ. "We shall go see Alex about some food." You gripped the whitewashed railing of the back stairs and descended the passage with caution. Until something was in your stomach, you did not trust your brain to keep you steady.

When you reached the kitchen, the smell of tomato curry filtered through the air. You rapped on the door and the voices inside quieted. Alex peeked through the crack. He scratched his arm and tugged the entrance wide open. "Did you get any sleep?"

"Three hours, perhaps." Your stomach growled again. You rubbed the back of your neck. "Might I trouble you for a small snack?"

Alex cocked his head towards the stove and walked back into the kitchen. You trailed after the teenager, taking a seat on a tall wooden stool. Cook hummed along as he stirred the pot of simmering vegetables. You folded your hands in your lap, taking care not to touch their workspace. Alex retrieved a small earthen pot. He set it in front of you and handed you a wooden spoon. You lifted the lid. Fresh steam scented with carrots and parsley wafted to your nostrils.

"You made this just for me?" you asked.

"Wasn't a big deal," Alex muttered, crossing his arms. "Just didn't want you throwing up my hard work 'cause of your sour stomach."

You took a bite of the rice porridge. The taste of celery, salt, onions, and something buttery made your mouth water. Warmth filled your belly, and not just from the food. You set your spoon down and smiled at the teen. "Alex?"

"Yes?"

"Thank you."

The undercook turned away, but not fast enough to hide his blush.

It was a good thing Alex fed you such a light meal. By the time you reached Sicarius's office, the food in your stomach felt like lead. You slipped the ring from the cord around your neck and pushed it over your knuckle. Though your gut was still twisted in tight, the weight of the band was not unbearable like last night. Rethreading the knot, you tucked your key back into your collar. Then, with a deep breath, you knocked on the door.

"Enter."

Sicarius was hunched over his wide desk, head in his palm. On his right was a heaping mound of papers stacked tall as his shoulder. Furious scribbling filled the room. When the door clicked shut, he looked up. Blue eyes flashed from your face to your left hand. His pupils dilated. He placed his pen in yet another bone china cup and rolled back his chair.

"Did you sleep?"

You shook your head. "Did you?"

The master's long legs crossed the room in three slow strides. He stopped an arm's reach away, running his fingers through his short hair. The circles under his eyes were dusty purple against pale skin. Sicarius's seemingly endless smirk was weary in the orange light that filtered through the blinds.

You looked away, fingers fiddling with the smooth metal band. "I am sorry that I faltered in my assigned duties last night. I was overwhelmed."

The soft touch of a large hand radiated up your skin, soothing raw nerves like a lullaby made of heat. His voice was low and calm as if he were whispering to a frightened animal. "There is nothing to forgive. I am the one who overwhelmed you." An impish sparkle flashed in his eyes. "Let us be honest; anything you threw at me was the product of my own actions."

A wry smile tugged at your cheeks.

Without breaking the intoxicating stare, he lifted your hand to his lips. Electricity fired down your flesh. "Since you are wearing my ring now, I assume your opinions have changed from last night?"

Worried eyes fell to your shoes. "Please understand, I do find the offer of marrying you enticing. It is just..." Your voice trailed off.

"You are still concerned about the social implications?"

"To be blunt, yes."

His gaze flicked to the ring. "But you're willing to talk this through?"

You nodded.

He squeezed your hand. "Then let us talk."

Sicarius led you to the guest chair, placing you between its thick scroll arms. The smooth grey fabric felt rough under your sweaty palms. A close mimic of smoky wood and vanilla, Sicarius's cologne reminded you of marshmallows over a summer bonfire.

"What do you propose?" he asked.

As you sank into the cushion, a tense discomfort ached down your shoulders. Though the silence dragged on, his face was as peaceful as a child playing with his favorite toy. Your hands balled into your skirt.

"I will marry you on the condition that the wedding stays secret from the noble circles."

The hairs on your arm bristled. In an instant, the calm, genial expression on your companion was gone. His lips dropped into a hard frown. Phantom shadows below smooth cheekbones deepened until they looked like pools of night. The hand holding yours tightened its grip.

"I *will not.*"

Your stomach jumped at the ice in his voice.

A Gamoidian curse spilled from his lips. His brow knitted until deep wrinkles formed around his eyes. "I *do not* understand why you are so ashamed of yourself, but I want *you.* I want you to be *my* wife."

You started to explain, but like a loose cart horse, he plowed right over you.

"You expect me to stay silent and pretend that I do not care for you just to please the gossip-mongers? Let them gossip. It would make me all the happier to hear 'Mrs. Estrova' again and again from their lips."

A white-hot fire burned up your throat. The words waiting on your tongue tasted like bile. Your nails curled into your palm. In a bid to control your bite, a mental ten-count ticked away one number at a time. With each click of the clock hand, your temper swelled.

Sicarius's fingers gripped his scalp. He snarled his next words. "Honestly, of all the things you could have asked—"

Out of patience, you snapped like a frozen twig. "Are you done?" you demanded.

Sicarius whipped his head around.

In the chair, back straight and hands folded, you glared at him. "I was under the impression that talking through a problem involved two people, not one. Is that not correct?"

Pale digits slipped from his hair. Blue eyes raked over your body from head to toe. Your stately aura of seething annoyance choked his rage to the floor. All the complaints on his lips died out.

"Let me be clear. I am not ashamed of myself." Your face was as hard as marble and just as cold. "I am a respectable woman in a respectable profession, and I am excellent at what I do. That is *why* I have no interest in being a source of amusement for the nobility. You offered to train me to deal with them. I will accept on the condition that you do not subject me to their offensive behavior before I am prepared to counter it. Is that clear?"

A puff of air filled his cheeks. He brought his hand to his mouth as his eyes wrinkled in delight. All at once, a blast of laughter roared from his throat. He tossed his head back, gripping his aching stomach. "Stars above, you are a masterpiece."

"Thank you."

Sicarius laughed even harder. Body still shaking with glee, he took your hands in his, kneeling down before you. Pride and delight swirled in his expression. The low baritone that poured from his mouth may as well have been fae wine. "Come with me."

A spike of raw heat shot through your core. Intoxicated by his words, you could barely breathe.

When Sicarius rose to his feet, he tugged you over. In one great heave, you were in his arms. He kicked the chair out from the desk. Even as he settled you across his lap, he never broke his gaze.

"Since I find pleasure in indulging you, I will agree to your conditions for now. However, know that this arrangement of ours *will not* last indefinitely. After all, I *can not* pretend I *do not* care when—"

A villainous smirk coiled onto his features. The airy tickle of his breath on your skin made your body throb. Seductive blue eyes drifted into a half-lidded stare. His low voice reverberated from his chest, leaving a tingling ache under your skin.

"—when you are *mine.*"

Unlike the slow indulgence of yesterday, Sicarius's kiss was ravenous. His large hand cupped your cheek, guiding you to his mouth. Soft lips devoured yours as hungry moans spilled from his throat. Between your thighs, a restless itch sprung to life. You leaned into his chest as loose fists clutched his shirt.

Against your backside, something hard pressed into your skirt. The hand under your knees trailed down your leg. Short, sharp nails traced along the swell of your calf. A gentle lift of your hemline broke the trance. You jolted against him and pulled away.

"Wait! What if the others—"

"Hush now, it is not like we could keep it a secret from

the staff anyway," he whispered, nibbling at the shell of your ear. "Since you are preventing me from preempting my nuptials with my fiancée, I insist on taking this opportunity to ravish my maid."

An excited tingle rippled down your body. Sicarius groaned as your shiver hit his pants. His hand climbed up your thigh, skimming over the fabric of your stockings before unhooking the garter straps. The toothy grin looked positively cannibalistic as he rolled across the high-cut blush-colored panties.

"Georgette does know what to do," he murmured, toying with the lacey hem.

Before you could say a word, his fingers plunged below the edge. The pad of his pointer dragged the moist heat up and down your delicate flesh. When he clipped your clit, you gasped.

"My, you are sensitive," he purred. "And so wet."

Pressing his thumb to your swollen bud, he stroked his way lower and lower. Long fingers dipped between your folds until they found your core. Back and forth, he traced the edge of your entrance with languid, teasing strokes.

Your twitching hands clasped his shirt like a lifeline. Pants heaved from your chest as you buried yourself in his sweet scent.

"M-Master..." you murmured.

Sicarius's body stiffened. A hiss filled the air. All at once, you found yourself heaved over the edge of his desk. Your tailbone hit the wood with a sharp thud that ricocheted up your spine. The master swept the papers onto the floor and rolled his hips into yours.

"I love it when you call me that," he growled.

Pressing the hard bulge into your thigh, he ground his hand against you. Your nipples pebbled against your silken bra as each flick of the smooth fabric against your sensitive skin drove you mad. All at once, he curled his pointer into your body. Sicarius grabbed your chin and pulled it to his face. Another blistering kiss silenced the needy sounds spilling from your mouth. His tongue lapped at you with the same firm pace as a second digit slipped inside. You whined against his lips.

"Something on your mind?"

Your hand reached down grasping the edge of his dark twill trousers. "What about—" The words choked off as he stroked the front of your walls, sending a flutter through your heart.

"What about what?" he teased.

Heavy lids drifted low. You pressed your thigh to his hardened cock.

Sicarius took a rattling breath as you shifted against him. His free hand slid from your cheek to the soft curve of your neck. The palm of the other twisted into your clit, making your back arch.

"We'll get there," he hissed in your ear. "Don't rush a good time."

You moaned as his fingers resumed their steady pace. Waves of pleasure wracked your body. Each slide of your soaked cunt against his supple skin had you writhing in his grip. Your hips began to shake as pulses of electric heat coursed up your stomach. Weak kneed and wanton, it was all you could do to clasp the slippery wooden desktop with slick palms.

As your thighs tensed tight, a rough grind from his hand tilted you over the edge. Grey swirls engulfed your vision. Your body fell around his fingers. Sicarius pressed a kiss to your neck, pumping you through your orgasm until you were spent. Chest heaving, you collapsed cheek first into his shirt. He pulled out, wide hands cupping your backside.

"Worrying about her master's pleasure before her own?" he mused, kneading your soft skin. "What a truly excellent maid I have."

With one scoop, he lifted you off the desk. As if he was positioning a beloved doll, he guided you to your knees on the plush white rug. The seam of your panties was soaked and cold against blazing skin. Sicarius's fingers drifted to his waistband. The clink of metal on metal was followed by the whisper of leather pulling through linen. His belt dropped to the floor. He leaned over and took your hand in his.

"Help your master undress," he commanded, pressing your palm to his pants.

In a hazy fog, your fingers fiddled with the clasp at the top of his waistband. It clicked open. The zipper fell. He hooked his thumbs into his boxers, pulling them down his legs. Soft fabric pooled at his feet. The smell of musk and arousal was heady in the air. His thick cock twitched in front of your swollen lips.

"Go on, kitten," he instructed.

"Then, you do not want—?" You looked down between your legs and nodded to the desk.

Sicarius shook his head. "Oh no, I very much want to." He stroked your cheek. "Call me old-fashioned, but I would just rather wait until we're married."

"If you are concerned about my perceived virtue, I do not believe any rational person expects a widow to be a virgin on their wedding night," you pointed out.

"It is not because you are a virgin that I am holding back," he explained with a wink. "It is because you are not."

You blinked at him. "I do not understand."

The silver-haired man tsked and wagged his finger at you. "If I give you everything right away, then what incentive is there for you to marry me?" He crossed his arms and declared, "Say what you like, but I *will not* be taken advantage of. I want it all. That's just the type of man I am."

At his words, you burst into laughter. "How did I go from being ravished to being the rake?" you demanded.

Sicarius grinned. "For tonight, you'll have to be content with the appetizer." His thumb paused on your lips. The heat in his eyes seared you to the core. "After the ceremony is complete, I will feed you the main course."

You sighed and looked up at him from under your lashes. "Master, I think you enjoy your teasing all too much."

"Not as much as I'm going to enjoy taking you on our wedding night." His thumb tugged at your lower jaw. "Now, why don't we put that delicious-looking mouth of yours to better use?"

As Sicarius guided you forward, you complied with his enticing suggestion. Wrapping your hands around the base of him, you pushed your lips past the soft tip. The taste of salt slid over your tongue. You rounded your mouth, letting your cheeks sink around his cock. As you gazed up at him, he stroked your skin.

"Go on."

Your hand squeezed his balls, letting them slip through your grip. Index finger and thumb ringing his shaft, your swollen lips plunged down. Keeping firm pressure, your hand rolled along his length. A moist tongue flicked across the notch of tissue below his head.

"Fumē!" The exotic expletive flew from Sicarius's mouth. "Good," he praised. "A little deeper now."

Moist clicks filled the air as saliva spilled from your lips. He rolled across the roof of your mouth. You angled him down, centering him in the middle of your throat. Your tongue curled around him. He slid between the slick rolls of muscle that cupped his cock.

With each hushed gasp from your master, the ache between your legs returned. Sicarius sped up the pace. You splayed your fingers wide across the wing of his hip. Trimmed coils of salt-and-pepper hair scraped against your palms. The taste of him made your head spin. A tight grip on the base of your skull guided you back and forth, setting the pace at a short, bobbing pulse. Under your ministrations, the muscles of his hips pulled taut. He twitched in your mouth.

When you looked up, his eyes were dark with greedy hunger. He groaned, and his lids drifted shut. A shudder wracked his body. Sicarius's soft head jolted against your throat, forcing raw tears from your eyes. With three quick thrusts, hot, salty cum spilled into your mouth. He clutched the back of your neck.

"Swallow," he commanded.

With his swollen member filling your mouth, you choked down the load. As he watched your throat bob, a pleased smile split his cheeks.

"My good girl," he murmured.

Your chest ached at the words. Letting him go, you licked your burning lips and sat back on your haunches.

Sicarius staggered back two steps to his chair, falling into the seat. He patted your cheek. Your thighs shifted against each other. He chuckled. "Does my maid need a little bit more?"

Unable to look away from his flushed face, you nodded.

He leaned back into the leather and coiled his finger into his palm. His hypnotic gaze called you to him like a fae song in the night.

"Come here."

Chapter Thirteen

Melt Season – Day 84 of 90

As morning rain tip-tapped on the window sill, angry squawking chased away intoxicating dreams. At first, you thought the sound was the storm crows fighting over snails in the courtyard garden. A thick cloud of colorful curses wafting through the open pane alerted you to the truth: the laundry maid next door was warring with the linen pins on the clothesline.

Blurry eyes turned to the clock. It was already past eleven. You rolled into your pillow, trying to catch your sleep as it slipped into the grey light. A chorus of raucous laughter echoed up the stairs. Your only reply was a disgruntled moan.

No one deserved to be that happy in the morning.

After last night, it was all you could do to put on your uniform and limp your way down the stairs. Cheery jazz music drifted through the halls. Every brush of the silken underwear left your raw skin throbbing again. The back of your neck itched from small scratches hidden by carefully styled hair. With all the dignity a woman walking side-to-side could muster, you knocked on the kitchen entry.

Alex's scowling face greeted you through the crack in the door. "I am not bringing out any more champagne, so you idiots will just have to get drunk on your—" He stopped, blinking at you as if he had seen a unicorn. "Oh, sorry! I thought you were Reeves again."

You clutched your head and squinted into the bright electric lights over the stove. "At this point, I would pay to be anyone else." You pointed to the cabinet on the left of the oven. "Could I have two aspirin, please?"

Alex's gaze rolled to your left hand. Every muscle in your body stiffened. There, sparkling bright even in the dull light of a rainy day, was the ring. Snatching your collar, your hands dove for the cord around your neck. With unbridled haste, the ring disappeared down your shirt.

Alex nodded to the parlor door where a swinging clarinet solo was blaring from the phonograph. "Don't bother. Sicarius has been bragging all morning." The teen snorted. "He took the whole day off work to celebrate. I closed the stupid door so you could sleep."

Well, so much for "secret."

Another burst of laughter exploded behind the glossy wood. Turning back to the only sane person in the whole household, you managed a grateful smile.

"Thank you, Alex."

Alex looked from you to the parlor. Loud whooping and bawdy conversation better suited for an Antellisian speakeasy than a luncheon rolled down the hall. He raised a brow at you. "Congratulations?" he offered.

You groaned.

After the two aspirin and a honey biscuit, your will to fight returned. You raised a hand to knock on the parlor door only to pause. Knuckles hovering over the tortoiseshell inlay, you shook off the well-trained urge.

Mistresses did not knock on their own doors.

As the entryway crept open, the full scope of your fiancé's vainglory was on display. The warm oak floor was covered in a cream and gold rug made of wavy lattice-like shapes. A pure white baby grand piano sat in the corner, polished and tuned but never touched. Reeves stood at the glass and gold sideboard, pouring Georgette another flute of champagne. She giggled, snuggling into his chest with the same effervescence as her drink. In front of the large picture window, Cook had his arm wrapped around the back of his wife. His fingers drummed on the mahogany frame of the Chippendale sofa while his Mrs. Miller lectured your infernal fiancé.

"—the look on her face when I handed her the books, Sicarius! I thought she would sooner murder you than marry you!"

"You would have deserved it too!" Cook chimed in, waving his glass at a man across the way. "Rotten thing to do to the poor woman."

Draped over the ivory damask settee with a remorseless smile on his lips, was the master himself. When he saw you, his smirk crept one tooth wider.

"Shall we ask the lady of the hour? She just arrived."

As all attention turned to your way, you felt naked despite the three-layer uniform. Reeves scratched the back of his neck. Mrs. Miller waved. Cook took another gulp of his champagne. Georgette pinched the bridge of her nose and flew to her feet. Long fingers grabbed you by the shoulders.

"Oh no. No. I did not make you such a lovely dress for you to arrive at your engagement party wearing your uniform!" she insisted, marching you out the door.

"If I knew I was having an engagement party, I would have worn it!"

"Mr. Estrova," the blonde called over her shoulder. "Do not worry. I will fix this."

"Georgette! Unhand me at once!"

As the seamstress shoved you up the stairs, Sicarius's laughter chased behind you. When the door to your attic room snapped shut, Georgette's eyes glinted with something heinous. She waved her hand at your left side and grinned at you. "Why are you not wearing it?"

"It was supposed to be a secret."

Georgette strutted off to your closet. "Secret from those who do not need to know." She wiggled her blue brows at you. "But how do I design the wedding dress when I do not know?"

You frowned. "There is not going to be a full wedding. Sicarius is just having a cleric come to the manor in a few weeks."

She extracted your cream and red gown, thrusting it into your arms. "So?"

"This very lovely dress will be more than enough," you pointed out, tossing the aforementioned frock on the bed.

As you pulled your headband off, your companion rolled her eyes. She lifted the dress from the sheets, unzipped the side seam, and waited for you to remove your apron. Once your uniform was laid aside, Georgette guided your hands into the ruffled creation. The curve of the waistline followed your body like a glove.

Georgette patted your stomach. "Stand up and breathe in. I need to see how it hangs."

As you held your breath, she fluffed the waist bow. A glimpse of the elegant cotton frock in the dressing mirror made you freeze. Was that really *your* figure? Stars above, the woman did nice work.

"Bias cut is very in," the seamstress remarked as she straightened your hem, "but I like A-line best. It is flattering on most and leaves room for good food and better wine."

"Georgette..." you warned.

She lifted your arm and stared at your skin. "Now for the color... Not white. Too virginal. Champagne, perhaps? Ivory?" She cocked her head, letting the silky bow on your back slip through her fingers. "We could do red. Every woman has a shade of red that just devastates."

You gathered up the soft skirt, swaying it back and forth. The dreamy image in the mirror made you smile. "I could wear this dress, which I like very much."

"Bah!" She pinched your cheek. "Do not worry; Georgette will handle everything."

You winced and brushed her hand away. "How would I survive without you?" you muttered.

As her attention flicked to your neck, the blonde stiffened. You looked down at the ring dangling on the leather cord near your latchkey. Slender fingers snatched up the brass object and shook it before your nose.

"What is this!?" she demanded.

You looked into her horrified eyes as puzzled as a parrot with a slide rule. "The key to the rooms at the manor?"

She whirled you around, snatching at the string. Kestanian curses poured from her mouth. The words were smooth enough to sound like pillow-talk if it were not for the undercurrent of agitated panic. The makeshift necklace pulled free. She handed you your ring. Then, straining with her slender arms, she knotted the leather so tight it might never come undone. Panting from her efforts, she thrust the key into your chest.

"Put that on a waist chain where it belongs!" she commanded, waving at your uniform.

With raised brows, you tucked the key down your collar. "Are you all right? You look pale."

"Never do that again." Georgette cupped your hands, her wild gaze filled with beseeching horror. "Please. You must never let him see you do that!" she begged.

"Him?" You cocked your head. "Who? Sicarius?"

Stone faced, she nodded.

"Why ever not?"

A cherry red nail tapped your neck above the notch of your collarbone. "The throat is a very special place. It carries blood, air, and the voice; it is a vessel that contains our whole life." Her words were mournful, like she was talking about death rather than a simple key. "He will not like to see you use it as a storage container. Not when he has—"

As you stared at the terrified expression on her normally playful face, your stomach was filled with ice. You swallowed. Georgette's eyes snapped to yours. Realizing your concern, a nervous smile danced across her cupid's bow lips. She swooned and gripped her wig.

"Oh! I am so silly. I think it is the champagne. Forgive me, forgive me." She pouted her lips and blew you a kiss. "So," her hands rolled down your arms. "Gauze sleeves or something else? Which do you prefer? I think it should be flowy for summertime, yes?"

As the bubbly blonde plied you with endless questions about taffetas and lacework, the delicate ring on your finger felt like a ball and chain.

By the time Georgette finished drowning you in breathless waves of opinions and options, the two of you reached the bottom of the stairs. Her eyes gleamed with excitement as she cooed about your soon to be dress. Your eyes looked like you had been dragged halfway across Marinar behind a horse and trap. As you rounded the corner to the parlor, there was an eerie quiet. The music, once blaring raucous and rowdy down the hall, had stopped. Through the door, you could see Mr. Reeves beside the gramophone, holding the needle above the vinyl diskette. Georgette raised her brows. Her husband nodded to the side table.

Sicarius leaned on the arm of his perch. In his hand was a black enamel phone with a white jade handle. It matched the tassels of the heavy curtains by the front window. Your fiancé's expression was carefree, if not a bit whimsical. Somehow, despite the fact that he was smiling, his lips were tense as if he were forcibly holding back joy under carefully groomed actions.

"I am thrilled you were able to call back so soon. Please give Lady Horitage my kindest regards for allowing me to purloin both your attentions in the middle of duty."

Lady Horitage!? There were only two people you knew who worked for that household. Alarm bells shrieked in your mind. Your face seized tight as a death mask. Every muscle screamed for you to run.

"Oh no, absolutely not, my good man. I will not hear of it." Sicarius coiled the cord around his pointer and turned towards the door. Wicked delight sparkled in his eyes as he waved the tips of his fingers at you like a child taunting a friend. "I will have my private rail car laid in for you, and you may meet it at Crossway Station. Once you reach Marinar, my footman will retrieve you. Do either of you get car sick? One of my fleet captains told me only last week that the local pharmacy has a pill that would make a tidal wave seem like a burbling brook."

Gobsmacked, you rushed to your fiancé's side and grabbed his jacket sleeve. Tugging on the grey linen, you shook your head furiously back and forth.

Sicarius smiled down at you and tapped the tip of your nose. "Ah! It seems my seamstress has finally relinquished her hold on the bride. Would you mind if I put you on with Mr. Reeves for a moment? He can tell you where to meet him when you arrive."

The footman bustled forward, taking the phone from your master. Before you could say a word, a tight grip wrapped around your wrist. Sicarius tugged you towards the door.

"What are you doing!?" you hissed.

"Well, while you were resting, I took the liberty of calling your parents." He wrinkled his nose and grinned at you. "Your father is quite a funny man. When I told him I wanted to marry you, he asked when the baby was due."

Your face burned hotter than the below flame. "Y-you told them!?" you stuttered in abject panic.

Sicarius stopped with his hand on the door to the study. "Well, I couldn't very well ask for their blessing and not tell them why I wanted it, could I?"

With a jerk, your devious husband-to-be dragged you into his office and snapped the door shut behind you. He plopped into the wide leather chair, settling your body between his legs. One arm clamped around your waist as the other delicately plucked the phone from its base.

"Now," he instructed, placing a kiss on your temple. "You *can not* leave until you have stopped worrying that poor woman into an early grave. She says she has not received a letter from you in two weeks!" He faked a sniffle. "Hearing her heartbreak nearly brought me to tears."

You scooted back and forth, trying to free yourself from his hold. It was no use. His arm was like a vice. Worse yet, as you struggled, a familiar bulge was forming between his legs. Sicarius held the phone out to you.

Furious eyes glared at him. "I will get you for this," you swore softly.

His grin looked crooked in the grey light. "Oh, do promise you will try."

Snatching the phone from his hand, you took a deep breath to steel your nerves. "Hello, mother?"

A chorus of banshee shrieks erupted from the mouthpiece.

"Yes, mother. No, mother. No. No. I sent you a letter the other day. Did you not receive it? You did? Well, then I fail to see—"

More yelling exploded from the other end.

You pinched the bridge of your nose. "I had every intention of calling you straight away, but I was up late last night, and I—"

Sicarius wrapped his arms around your shoulders and nuzzled your cheek. As furious accusations hurtled across the telephone wire, you swatted him away.

"Because it *only* happened last night. You can hardly—"

The lecturing continued. At first, it was the standard fare: lonely despair with a splash of guilt-tripping. However, as your mother kept up her blistering admonishments, you sat bolt upright.

"No, I am not pregnant!" you insisted.

Your fiancé was anything but helpful. His warm breath tickled the shell of your ear. "If they are so concerned about it, please give her my assurances that we can fix that quickly after the wedding," Sicarius purred.

You shoved his face away with the palm of your hand. "Stars above, mother! You sound like Rebecca!"

Sicarius hummed, dragging his finger down the side of your neck.

"You can not tell anyone! No! *Especially* not auntie! Tell her, and her bridge club will have it in the evening press!"

Sicarius pressed his warm lips to the soft skin where your neck met your shoulder. Your free hand pinched the inside of his thigh, hard.

"It is supposed to be a secret until I— No! No, I would never dream of keeping secrets from you! I just meant—"

Loud sniffles crackled across the line.

Your eyes narrowed. "Mother, I know you are faking it."

A honking sound was followed by a ridiculous, forced sob. You could not help but think that the jaunty swing songs from earlier would have been the perfect soundtrack for such a ludicrous conversation.

"Put on a show all you like, but you will not fool me!" you insisted, gritting your teeth.

"Just let her have her fun," Sicarius teased. "It's not every day that one's daughter gets married again."

Ignoring the fiend at your ear, you pulled the speaker away from your mouth and yelled, "I know because father is laughing in the background!"

A man's voice filled the phone. Your eye twitched. He continued on. All at once, your body stiffened. The heat coming off your face could have cooked an egg.

"Father!" you shrieked.

Barely containing his laughter, Sicarius plucked the phone from your cheek. "Drunk or a fool?" Your fiancé's chuckle reverberated deep in his chest. "Honestly, sir, at the moment, I might be both."

As your father roared with glee, you wondered if it was still considered mariticide if the groom was murdered before the wedding.

CHAPTER FOURTEEN

Heat Season – Day 14 of 91, 48th Year of Creipus the Pious

Five days before the wedding, you were unsure you would survive Ellsworth's estate management lessons long enough to say your vows.

"When hiring a tradesman, as a woman, you must assume he will attempt to cheat you. For example, paying more than five drossler per room to a redecorator is absurd. Obtaining multiple price quotes will help, but I strongly recommend taking Mr. Watts to any negotiations as he—"

As Ellsworth prattled on, your eyes started to cross. You bit your tongue, trying to straighten out the list of monthly expenses before you. Piles of words jumped in and out of focus: liquor merchant, greengrocer, fishmonger, butcher, jeweler, laundress, medical supplies, fromager, sharpshooters, steam-ore, car—

Wait a moment. **Sharpshooters!?**

"Mr. Ellsworth?" You held up the ledger. "What is this line item?"

"Oh, that." Ellsworth nodded his head to the window. The cloudless sky was a bright sunny blue. By comparison, the deep forest at the edge of the lawn looked like a carpet of shadows. "When the original Gravelorne nobles' debts grew too great, they could not afford their hunting dogs. Selling them would be dishonorable, so they elected to release them into the foothills. Thanks to their foolishness, there is a pack of ferals that makes its home in the pines. Once a year, we hire some hunters to thin them out."

"Thin them out?" Your throat tightened. "You mean—"

"If we do not tend to them, they spread the madness disease," Ellsworth explained. "Some will be stricken dumb and die quietly, but others become furious and lash out. It is not a risk we can afford."

You shuddered. In an old medical book of Professor Campbell's, there had been two images of a man with madness disease. Clapped in irons, his bulging eyes stared out of the pages and into your soul. In the first image, frothing drool sputtered from his spasming throat as he tried to swallow a small cup of water. The next shot showed the cup lying spilled in his lap. His face was contorted in agony. A single line below the twin pictures read:

In the later stages of hydrophobia, patients will beg for water but cannot drink.

Ellsworth watched your protests fade into heart-wrenching silence. He crossed his arms behind his back and turned to face the window. "Fifteen years ago, before Mr. Sicarius owned Gravelorne, a stray puppy entered the town at the foot of the hills. It was an adorable creature with long soft ears and button black eyes. You can imagine how the village children felt about it."

Your stomach clenched like you had swallowed burning oil.

Ellsworth's silhouette cast a deep shadow across the desk. "Adults know that the madness is incurable, and that a swift bullet is a kindness to the afflicted. Children do not understand these things. When it grew sick and began to bite, they hid the animal, fearing their parents would kill it. It died of the madness and took fourteen of them with it."

An icy tremble rippled up your arm. "Can not all warm-blooded creatures also catch the madness disease?"

Ellsworth nodded.

"Then, what of Lemon and the other cats?"

"Unlike the skittish feral dogs, cats like Lemon allow us to vaccinate them. The village dogs and livestock are also protected by our master's order." He pointed to a line item at the bottom of the list, which read: "medical supplies."

Your hands curled into your lap. "So it is only the ferals then?"

"Yes."

As the implications of the story rattled in your head, something Sicarius had told you months ago crept into your mind:

"Lemon's colony was attacked when she was a kitten."

"Is that what happened to Lemon's family then?" you murmured.

"Yes." He turned back, examining the weary expression on your face. "Perhaps we should stop for today. We need to prepare for the dinner party."

"Of course." With a shaky inhale, you bowed your head. "Thank you for your help, Mr. Ellsworth. I know that this is not enjoyable for either of us."

The butler's lips twitched upwards. "At least you are more determined than Mr. Reeves."

When the two of you reached the dining hall, Reeves's arrangements for the evening guests were "underway." The glossy mahogany table smelled like lemon oil. Jade napkin rings with Sicarius's spider seal clenched the fan-folded serviettes. The footman himself was nearly crossed-eyed as he scrubbed the scalloped crevices of the large serving spoon. Vague mutterings of thinly veiled curses poured from his lips like water from a tap.

"Mr. Reeves."

The footman jolted, a panicked expression on his face. "Oh! You two are done early?"

Ellsworth's eyes swept across the half-assembled display. He pinched the broad bridge of his nose. "I had expected you to have completed this task by now."

The footman stabbed his finger at the massive box of silverware. "Come on, Ellsworth! You can't be serious!"

"There are only six guests this evening. It is hardly a large affair." Ellsworth's eyes narrowed. "You will need to become accustomed to your job again lest you bring embarrassment on our employers."

Reeves looked at you, and a frown flitted across his lips. "Sorry, Mrs. Estrova."

"It is all right," you replied. "I am continuing my maid duties for a while, so you will have help."

Ellsworth stiffened so swiftly you swore you heard his neck snap.

"Is something the matter?" you asked.

Lips drawn tight, Ellsworth stared at you. He closed his eyes and inhaled deeply. "May I speak freely, Mrs. Estrova?"

"So long as I am wearing this, you are still my superior." You lifted your apron. "I am not 'Mrs. Estrova' yet."

Ellsworth massaged his temples. "Which is why I object to this situation. The lady of the house should not be doing a maid's duties. The longer you persist in your old life, the harder it will be to conceal your habits."

You hated that he was right. Imagine what the nobility would say if the mistress of the manor polished her own flatware. It would be the social scandal of the week! Still, standing in what was soon to be your dining room, your fingers ached to finish the place settings. Your eyes rolled over the mess, searching for a way to satiate your cleaning compulsion. At the far end of the table was an olpe vase made of dusty bone china. The white, hand-painted lilies that encircled its body resembled funeral bouquets.

"Mr. Ellsworth?"

"Yes, madam?"

You strode to the middle of the table and lifted the vase. Slick grey dust clung to the pads of your fingers. "Would arranging flowers be sufficiently lady-like?" you asked with a beaming smile.

Ellsworth froze. Reeves grinned and flashed you a thumbs up. The butler scowled at the footman. Then with a heavy sigh, he replied, "Yes, that is a habit of fine ladies."

"Excellent!" You backed away from the pair, one step at a time. "Then I will handle this."

Before anyone could protest, you darted into the hall.

"We shall get you properly clean," you whispered to the vase.

Despite your reassurances, the vase seemed unimpressed.

As soon as the dining room door closed behind you, the oppressive tension in your neck began to relax. You sighed with relief and hitched your captive higher in your grip. Now... which sink to wash your victim in? Ah! Yes! The bathroom at the end of the hall had a deep bowl.

As you turned the corner, Alex stepped out of the toilet and caught sight of the object in your arms. The blood drained from his face. Bug-eyed, he pointed a shaking finger at the vase. "W-where did you find that!?" he demanded.

You looked from the teen to the china and back again. "The dining room. Is something the matter with it?"

Alex's breathing turned into chest heaving panic. You set the vase down on the carpet runner and hurried to his side. As you reached him, the boy slumped to his knees. Veins bulged in his neck. He gasped for air. When you grabbed his hands, they were clammy and cold.

"Mr. Reeves! Mr. Ellsworth! Come quickly!" you shouted down the hall.

As if carried by wings, the footman flew to your aide. His arms enveloped the boy in a warm, gentle embrace. Reeves began to rub Alex's back, murmuring soft and slow, "Alex, you will be fine. You are safe. She cannot harm you anymore. Sicarius saw to that."

The undercook's gaze remained fixed on the china. Dry, raspy croaks rattled from his mouth. Alex's pulse hammered in your hands. His complexion had turned grey-blue. Wide pupils eclipsed the brown of his irises until he looked like a button eyed rag doll.

Silent as the grave, Ellsworth appeared. He looked at the scene before collecting the china. Then he vanished down the hall, taking the vase with him.

"Alex, listen to me," Reeves continued. "You will not die. If you pass out, your body will take over your breathing unconsciously. You have no control over that. No matter what you do, you will live through this, okay?"

Alex's stilted nod looked more like a tremor than an affirmative.

Reeves's brows wrinkled, but his smile remained calm. He continued to rub soothing circles in the boy's back. "Good kid. You'll be fine. We're going to wait this out together, okay? We're right here."

Tears spilled down Alex's cheeks.

Down the corridor, you heard the hurried tapping of metal on wood. Cook burst around the corner as if he was pursued by a Shadowhound. "Alex? Alex, where are you, boy?"

"About ten strides up on the left side," Reeves called.

Behind the chef, you caught a glimpse of Ellsworth's tailcoat disappearing beyond the bend. Cook counted as his cane clacked on the floor. When he reached nine, he slowed and squinted at the group. Reeves loosed his hold on the teenager and tapped the cane with two fingers. Cook kneeled to the ground. Big, calloused hands climbed from Alex's elbow to his arm.

"Dinner is on a simmer, so don't get yourself all worked up." Cook patted his apprentice's shoulder. "Did you put the tarragon away for me?"

Alex's breathing began to even. With trembling lips, he looked into Cook's eyes. The thundering pulse slowed. Freezing fingers gripped your hand back. With one deep inhale, Alex replied, "Y-es."

Cook broke out into a wide smile. "There's a good lad. I knew you wouldn't let me down."

"The—" Alex gulped. "The vermouth—"

"Already reduced. Needs to cool before I can add the cream anyway."

"M-ushrooms?"

Cook winked. "They are perfect. Wanna come see?"

"Yes," Alex wheezed.

The chef's ringing belly laugh filled the hall. As he leaned on his cane, a loud crack snapped from his back. "Reeves, help an old man up, would you?"

Reeves grabbed Cook's hand and scooped under his shoulder. With a smooth heave, both men stood. Your toes tingled from kneeling so long. One leg at a time, you climbed to your feet. As you steadied yourself, Reeves helped Alex up.

Cook smirked and rapped his cane on the floor. "Well, with all you people hustling and bustling, I'm apt to smack someone in the shin before I can dodge 'em." He held out his arm. "Be my eyes for a moment, boy."

Alex took his mentor's arm and wrapped it over his own. Despite the fact that he was still shaking, the teen's expression was smooth and determined. One step at a time, the pair walked towards the kitchen. Reeves tapped your shoulder and cocked his head towards the dining room. You trailed after him, casting quick glances back at the others.

"What just happened?" you whispered.

"I screwed up. That's what happened." The footman gripped his temples. "Sicarius said to use a container with white flowers. I just grabbed the first one I found. Totally forgot that it was Lady Milton's vase." Reeves groaned and smacked his forehead. "Stupid! The lilies should have been a dead giveaway!"

"Who is Lady Milton?"

Reeves paused with his hand hovering over the dining room door handle. A bead of sweat rolled down his brow.

"Lady Milton is Alex's former employer." Both of you jumped at the sound of Sicarius's voice. He held the vase, his sharp eyes staring at the footman. "Garrick, Ellsworth requested your presence in the dining room."

Reeves's jaw clenched tight. His hand started to shake. "Yes, sir."

As the door snapped shut, your fiancé turned back to you. "Thank you for taking care of Alex until Cook could come."

A cold wave of guilt rolled through your veins. You shook your head. "Reeves did all the talking. I only held his hand."

Sicarius took a step closer, taking your fingers in his. He pressed a soft kiss to your skin. "You know as well as I do that just having someone by your side can be enough to ease the pain."

Worried eyes glanced back down the hall. "I still do not understand why that vase caused the boy that much panic."

"I assume you never met the late Lady Milton?"

You shook your head.

Sicarius snorted. "Lady Milton was a client of mine for a time. She had only two loves: cleanliness and fine china. Alex was a hall boy in her home. You have seen his rash."

"Yes?"

"It is not contagious. Merely an allergic reaction which must be managed," Sicarius explained, tilting his head back to stare at the ceiling. "I was there the day Lady Milton first saw it. She thought the boy brought a disease into her home. In a rage, she attacked Alex. Her butler and I managed to get her off of him, but she broke his arm long before we could stop her."

Your breath caught in your chest.

"I took my wares and Alex back to the townhouse and reported her to the police. Before they could arrest her, she disappeared. The authorities have not located her since."

A numb cold prickled across your palm. "It is a pity she will never face justice for her actions."

He cupped your cheek, stroking it with his thumb. "I would not worry. Her deeds no doubt caught up to her."

"What will you do with the vase?"

Sicarius tucked the china under one arm and held out his hand. In the depths of his gaze, ego swirled with glee. "Let me show you."

Sicarius guided you up the passage until you crossed the threshold onto black marble floors. Warm afternoon sun bounced off the aluminum leaf above, making the ceiling glow silver. As windswept clouds drifted away outside the great windows, stray beams caught the edges of the golden tree's branches. The rough surface scattered the light into the air, making any floating dust sparkle like fireflies under a full moon.

Speaking of dust, was anyone ever going to tell you how to clean that gaudy thing without breaking it?

"Did you go to temple as a child?" Sicarius asked, leading you under the winding tendrils of the sculpture.

You snapped out of your frustrated thoughts. "Oh. Yes. Lady Horitage is very religious. She required it of all the servants and their families."

He set the vase down on the edge of the artificial pond. "Then you must know what lives inside the Fae Tree?"

Without hesitation, you recited the famous lines from the Holy Text: "Before the modern era, the eternal fae treated mortal humans like play things. As punishment for their greed and cruelty, the gods locked the fae's souls away in a golden tree, deep in the underbelly of the world."

With a bright smile, Sicarius clapped. The sound echoed like gunshots in the open hall. "My Fae Tree is not guarded by Shadowhounds of course," he explained, climbing over the railing onto the hard crystal waters. "However, I did ask the builders to make it as authentic as possible."

Watching the man pick his way through the field of delicate jade and capiz was a nerve wracking affair. Every time his pant leg brushed the edges of the fragile flowers, your heart stopped. Somehow, he managed to make it to the base of the tree without breaking any. He caressed the bark, tracing a single seam between the ridges.

Click, whirr.

With barely a vibration, the glass shifted and split, leaving a smooth path to the center of the sculpture. On Sicarius's right, at the end of the new passage, the tree itself parted to reveal a hollow compartment.

"Since the gods could put things inside their tree, I wanted mine to be capable of the same," he explained patting the trunk. "Lyle helped with the mechanisms."

You stared at the vase, still sitting on the edge of the pond. Despite all the movement, it was undisturbed. Your jaw dropped, eyes lighting with excitement. "That is incredible!"

His lips curled into a proud grin and pointed to the china. "Would you be so kind?"

Picking up the container, you walked up the path between the parted waters. When you reached the open hole, you peeked inside. Large enough to fit three grown men, the compartment filled the base of the tree. Lining the wide roots were a few remnants of chipped bowls and broken plates. In the center of the floor was a steel door with a large handle.

"Where does that go?" you asked, handing him the vase.

Sicarius set the china inside the sculpture. "Out to the Nortons' cottage. I commissioned it during the reconstruction." He winked at you. "All proper manor houses should have some secret passages, yes?"

"I fear I have read you too many novels," you teased.

Sicarius shooed you back past the edge of the false water before pressing the hidden button again. With the same whisper quiet whirling, the statue shifted back to its proper place. Despite the movement, not a scratch marred the marble floor.

When Sicarius returned to your side, his eyes were brimming with anticipation. He clasped his hands. "So? Do you like it?"

A beaming grin broke out on your face. "Yes. Very much."

He pressed a kiss to your forehead. "I knew you would."

"There is one thing I do not understand." You pointed to the tree. "Why keep the broken ones? You have enough china, do you not?"

"I am a bit sentimental," he explained, slipping his arm around the back of your shoulders. Smooth as cream, he steered you towards the south lawn. "So… the bearded night irises are in bloom. Why don't we go find some for the table?"

"Suddenly, you are free when you have been working all morning?" you asked, smirking at him. "Are you trying to make me forget that affair with Alex?"

"You wound me," he declared with fake offense, resting one palm flat against his chest. "Can a man not spend time seducing his fiancée with flowers anymore?"

You stared at him from under a raised brow.

Sicarius laughed and tapped the tip of your nose. "Fine, you suspicious creature. I admit I am tired of paperwork." Letting go of you, he stepped in front and swept into a ridiculous formal bow. "Allow me to use you as a distraction, my good woman." He lifted his head and extended his hand out to you.

You weighed the choice for a moment. He was being so obvious in his efforts. A little sucking up here, a little razzle dazzle there, and then suddenly you would forget Alex's terrified expression. Still, between what had transpired in the hall and Ellsworth's horrifying story, the thought was not unwelcome…

"I know you are lying," you told him, taking his hand.

"Do you now?" He wrapped your arm around his and placed a kiss on your temple. "Then why are you coming with me?"

You hummed and leaned into his shoulder. "Twice today I have heard stories that will give me nightmares." A frown crossed your lips. "Honestly, after all that, I want to forget."

Sicarius nuzzling your head. "You'll enjoy the flowers," he promised.

You sighed. "I just hope this evening is less trying."

Within two hours, it was clear that this evening was not less trying.

Lady Wilford, the matriarch of the oldest titled family in Marinar, smacked her wrinkled lips as she polished off her fourth glass of expensive Beruché wine. "As I just told Lady Foster last week, good help can be *so* hard to find nowadays."

Clasping your hands in front of your ruffled apron, it took all you had to stop your eyes from rolling.

"Quite so!" Lord Dankworth agreed, ruddy faced and wagging his fork in the air. "All these fiddly little girls with cotton stuffed heads trying for men's work in the factories. It's as if the world's gone mad!" He turned to his wife. "Do you not agree, my dear?"

Beside the bombastic politician, the mousey Lady Dankworth nodded her head. She was a painfully young slip of a thing, all long bones and painted cheeks. There was a distinct lack of substance about her, both on her body and in her manner. Her perpetually doll-like expression was as empty as her thoughts. Fortunately, her husband preferred her that way.

On the opposite end of the table and political spectrum, Mrs. Westcott, leader of the Marinar suffragettes, dabbed the edges of her tight smile. With well-practiced poise, she flipped a few stray box braids behind her shoulder. "Really now. The way you two go on, one would assume that any woman who holds a job outside of housewife or housekeeper was destined for the brothels."

"That is wholly unfair." Lord Dankworth's scoffing laugh rippled across his belly. "I have never spoken a word against governesses."

As only one half the table erupted in laughter, your teeth clenched. In stiff silence, you made your way to your master's side and refilled his tisane. The steaming heat of the chamomile was nothing compared to the burn deep within your gut.

Lord Dankworth shook his finger. "Look at what happened to the Hunts! They let their precious little girl go sailing, and poof!" He clapped his hands. "Next thing they know, she's gone missing. I tell you, no daughter of mine will be doing something so dangerous!"

Sicarius sipped his drink. "It is fortunate then that you have only sons."

"Quite so!" Dankwoth agreed, slapping his own thigh.

Mrs. Westcott gripped her napkin tight with her scarred hands. "I do not see the harm in allowing women to stand beside their men. The war proved that both sexes were capable of performing under gunfire."

Dankworth stabbed the table with his pasty finger. "Yes, but that was war, and this is now. Things are back to normal. Women should return to their proper places in the home."

Mrs. Westcott looked up the table to her husband. With a slow nod, he set down his drink and folded his hands. "I say, Dankworth," Captain Westcott pointed out, "it is rather bad form to infantilize half the population."

The ever-opinionated Lady Wilford grinned into her glass. "I am sure the fact that you married your nurse has not affected your opinion in the least."

Sicarius's shoulders shook once before a well-timed cough hid the laugh. You took two steps back from the table and held your breath.

The captain lifted his dimpled chin and stared down at the stubby society dame from under thin blonde brows. "Unlike some, I am not too proud to change my opinion when I am proven wrong."

The lady scoffed and waved her hand. It was freshly tanned from her recent trip to the sunny southern isles. "A joke, my dear man. It was merely a joke."

"A joke rather requires others to find it funny, does it not?" Mrs. Westcott remarked coolly, her thick lips pursing.

Sicarius's grin was as wide as the nude painting on his wall. "My goodness, what a spirited debate."

"And what is your opinion, Mr. Estrova?" Darkworth insisted.

Sicarius folded his hands in front of his face. "That a good companion is as precious as a fine gem."

The ring on your keycord scraped against your breast.

"Agreed!" Darkworth declared, pushing a lock of his wife's silky hair behind her ear. "Women should be properly molded, polished, and then kept safe like any other valuable."

"But Lord Dankworth, you have left out one thing."

"Have I?"

Sicarius closed his eyes and chuckled. "The finest gemstones are prized precisely because they can cut as well as be cut. To forget that would be a grave error indeed."

Lord Dankworth paused, staring at his host over thick, round frame glasses. As a bead of sweat rolled down his red face, he turned slowly to his young wife. She looked up at him with the button-eyed bemusement of a toy poodle confronted with calculus. He breathed a sigh of relief.

On the other end of the table, Mrs. Westcott's eyes rolled away. The creeping smile on her face spread like ivy up a wall, threatening to tear off the last of her crumbling façade. The captain took a bite of his ganache cake and said nothing. He could barely chew through the stifled laughter.

Lady Wilford lowered her glass and raised a greying eyebrow. "Upon my word Mr. Estrova, you make it sound as if all women are lurking about waiting to tear their husbands to pieces."

"Not at all, my dear lady. I said 'companion,' not woman." He smirked into his cup. "I find good men capable of the same."

She huffed. "It rather defeats the purpose of polite society if we start behaving like vicious animals."

Sicarius's blue eyes flashed. "Lady Wilford, you know as well as anyone that the *right* society can be both polite and vicious."

Mrs. Westcott and Lady Wilford sized each other up across the table. Both wore narrow eyes and a knowing smile.

"So what do you recommend, then?" The often silent Lord Wilford asked, leaning into the table. "That we all go out and acquire partners that bite? Hardly seems domestic at all."

"I find a pleasing relationship more like taming than domestication," Sicarius stated.

For the first time all evening, Lady Dankworth's tiny voice escaped her mouth. Her head cocked this way and that, trying to process words far too large for its capacity. "Taming? Domestication?"

"Fear not, Lady Dankworth." Your fiancé extended his hand to you. "My maid was assistant to Professor Campbell. I am certain she can give you the definition."

As all attention in the room turned to you, a burning heat engulfed your cheeks. Sicarius grinned. You curled your fingers into a fist to keep them away from his throat. With a cough, you explained:

"Domestication is a generations-long process in which a species is bred to a specific desired trait or personality. It is a purposeful genetic modification that leaves the target species unique from their wild counterparts. Taming refers to making existing creatures tractable to the presence of humanity. A tame animal is still wild and while friendly, may exhibit wild behaviors."

"Much like the professor himself," Sicarius joked.

This time, you could not conceal your grin. "Yes, Master."

Lady Wilford huffed. "Having been to a dinner party with the late professor, I can not disagree."

"Does that make more sense, my dear?" Lord Dankworth asked his wife. "Domestication takes longer but produces more consistent results. It's a matter of breeding."

The young woman's eyes flickered to life for the briefest moment at the word "breeding." Her voice was barely a whisper: "Ah. I see."

As you watched Lady Dankworth return to her sea cucumber like state, you were suddenly grateful not to be a purpose-bred lady.

"Well," Sicarius rose from his seat. "Shall we retire to the parlor for some drinks and cards?"

"Oh yes!" Lady Wilford replied, rubbing her hands. "Gin and gin rummy would do nicely."

Sicarius waved his manservant over. "I'm sure Ellsworth can accommodate you."

Ellsworth looked like he would rather accommodate a sharp pike up his anus. Lips pressed into a thin line, he opened the door of the dining room and ushered the guests towards the front parlor. As you began to trail after them, a large hand caught your elbow.

"Go take your nap, kitten," your fiancé purred in your ear. "This dinner has been rather stimulating. Once the guests are in bed, I will need you tonight."

You shivered. "Of course, Master."

CHAPTER FIFTEEN

It was half-past midnight when the door to the master's bedroom opened. You looked up from the book in your hands. Sicarius hummed a swinging tune and latched the bolt behind him. When he turned to you, two things caught your attention: his self-satisfied smile and a ruddy flush on his cheeks.

"How did the rest of the party go?" you asked.

"By the fourth round of cards, Mrs. Westcott was one drink away from strangling Lord Dankworth. Sadly, her husband cut her off." Sicarius strolled toward you with a drunken swagger. "We used the gear cart to get Lady Wilford up the stairs. I have every hope she will take her heels off before losing consciousness."

You shook your head. "Now I can see why you and the professor were friends."

The bed sunk beneath his weight. "Because we both possess a charming sense of humor?" he asked, tossing his shoes towards the wardrobe. They hit the door with a bang and rolled to a stop on the sumptuous wool rug.

With a sigh, you rose to your feet. Plucking the black leather oxfords from the floor, you set them in the row on the bottom of his closet. "You both enjoy baiting people."

Sicarius leaned onto his elbow, resting his head in the palm of his hand. He smirked at you. "And you clearly enjoy watching, my little voyeur."

You turned your cheek. "When one sees a train about to crash, it is hard to look away even if watching is not enjoyable."

"Tell yourself whatever lies you like," he declared, waving you off. "At least I am honest about my nature."

You hummed and began thumbing through the expensive clothing. "What color do you want tonight, Master?"

"You are not going to call me Sicarius?"

"You like 'master' better when I am in uniform."

Greedy blue eyes glowed in the din. "You are not wrong." A long finger pointed to the left side of the closet. "To answer your question, brown sounds perfect."

"You do not own a brown set."

Sicarius chuckled before flopping back on the bed. "I was looking forward to seeing you bent over, searching for it anyways."

You pinched the bridge of your nose. "You are consistent in your behavior, if nothing else."

"I am told my steadfast nature is one of my finest qualities."

"I suppose that is more believable than claiming humility amongst your virtues," you muttered, looking through the monogrammed night clothes.

With your employ—er… *financé* of little help, you selected a cream cotton pajama set with golden embroidery. There was a rustling behind you. From under the bed, Sicarius extracted a striped silver box with pale pink ribbon.

"I bought you something new," he explained, holding out the package. "For the warmer months."

You bristled and stared at the elegant wrapping. "If I was not clear—"

"Yes, yes. I know. You are 'not a fortune hunter.'" He rattled the present. "Humor an old man. If I'm to marry, I want my wife kept in pretty things like the rest of the house."

"Forty-four is not old."

He patted the bed beside him. "Flattery *will not* get you out of this, kitten. Open the box."

You took a seat on the marshmallow soft mattress. The slippery ribbon tugged loose with little effort. Delicate coral paper crinkled in the quiet room. At the bottom of the extravagant packaging was a blush-colored creation of silk georgette crepe and leavers lace. The bias cut nightgown had a gathered empire waist and wide, soft straps. Touching it was like holding air in your hands.

"The woman at the boutique said that shade looked good on everyone." He thumbed his chin, looking from you to the negligee. "I am pleased to see she was right."

A gnawing discomfort engulfed your gut.

With two fingers, Sicarius lifted your chin. "Now, what is that look for?"

"It is lovely. It is just..." your voice tapered off into reticent silence as nervous fingers played with the sumptuous fabric.

He turned your head, forcing you to look into his pale gaze. For a moment, there was a hard irritation that made you freeze. As your neck drew tight, his face faded into a soft, jovial expression. He laced his free hand with yours, rubbing the lotus ring with his thumb.

"This dress is suited for my wife. Do you understand?"

You laughed, scratching your cheek. "I suppose I must become accustomed to this."

Sicarius smiled and pressed a gentle kiss to your forehead. "It will be my pleasure to help you with that."

Soft lips peppered your skin with slow, indulgent worship. His large hands found their way to your neckline. First, he unfastened the lock on the brooch. Then, the ruffled tie slipped from your collar. One by one, bronze buttons started to fall. As he reached the third notch, words of warning seared across your mind.

"Please. You must never let him see you do that!"

"Wait!" you protested, pressing your palms flat against his chest.

"You are torturing me, kitten," he grumbled, nipping his affections down your cheek. With a raspy growl, he jerked you into his lap, rolling his hips against your thigh. Through his pants, a firm bulge pressed into your leg. "I have already waited a very long time to see you on my bed wrapped in silk and if I wait anymore I might explode."

You shoved again. "Sicarius, hold on a moment!"

"There is no need to be so skittish, kitten," he purred. "It is just a little—"

The master's voice choked to a dead halt as the key around your neck drifted into sight. In an instant, the warmth of the room vanished, leaving behind a frosty vacuum of confusion and silence. As the bedside clock ticked off the seconds, the shadows of the room seemed to lengthen and dance like fiends in the night. Sicarius's blue eyes were hard as block ice. With a powerful jerk, he tore the leather cord from you, leaving a stinging rope burn on your skin.

His voice was a terrifying whisper. "What is this?"

Like a housecat confronted by a wolf, you started to back away.

Sicarius hands snatched up your jaw, squeezing tight enough to make the bones creak. "Explain yourself."

You tried to jerk out of his hold, but a sudden grip on your left wrist held you like a vice. Your skin prickled as you realized how much stronger he was than you. As his fingers ground into your flesh, bubbling irritation crept through your veins.

"What possible explanation could you want for a key?" you demanded.

"Why is it around your neck?"

"I needed a place to store it."

A burning ache shot down your jaw as his hold tightened. "Why there?"

"Why not?"

He dangled the key in your face. "If you wanted something to put around your neck, why did you not just ask me? Why wear—" He glared at the key. "—this *trash.*"

"Where else am I supposed to put it?"

The smoldering, dark gaze did not match his deadpan tone. "In your pocket."

With a frown, you stabbed at your lap. "This uniform does not *have* pockets!" Your free hand grabbed his wrist and squeezed sharp nails into his arm. "—and you are hurting me."

Sicarius finally blinked. With a deep inhale, he loosed his hold and cupped the side of your jaw. Gentle strokes traced across the tender skin. When he touched one spot, you hissed in pain. His eyes widened. The fearsome gravel in his words was gone, replaced with reticent shock. "I hurt you..."

"Yes, you did," you agreed with a snarl.

As your fiancé stared at the sore area, his teeth clenched. "I am sorry, kitten," he murmured, eyes flicking from you to the aching flesh. "I did not mean to do that."

"What you meant is irrelevant," you snapped. "Tell me! Is this the sort of treatment I am expected to tolerate as your wife?"

"Certainly not." His hand dropped from your cheek. "I plan to take good care of you."

You eyed him with a raised brow. "Then give me your word that you will not do it again."

Blue eyes stared into your soul. "I *will not,*" he vowed.

In the ringing silence that followed, your heart beat pounded in your ears. Sicarius never broke his gaze. A bead of sweat slipped down your neck. You coughed and turned your head. From the corner of your eye, you watched him warily. His face was dead serious.

"I…" You licked your lips. "Then I suppose I will take you at your word."

Sicarius smiled. Long digits laced themselves between yours. "I will make it worth your while."

Well, this was new. Sicarius being serious instead of a wanton degenerate for—

"As far as I am concerned, I only want to hurt you if you ask me to."

Ah… Never mind.

You blinked at him. "If I ask you to? What are you—" As the meaning dawned on you, a throb between your legs sent tingles up your body. "Sicarius, you pervert!"

Sicarius lifted your hand to his mouth with a slow, seductive stare. As he pressed his lips to your fingers, bewitching blue eyes wove their spell. He worked his way up your palm, kiss by kiss. When he reached your inner wrist, an impish lick wet more than your skin. "If my promise proves unsatisfactory, I'm sure you'll find an unreasonable demand to which I will, inevitably, acquiesce."

Laughter spurted from your throat. "I would suggest divorce but they only allow it if both parties agree," you pointed out, jabbing him in the chest.

"Hmmm…" He tapped his chin. "Well, that might be a sticking point since I have no intention of letting you go."

"No matter. I bet I could make you beg for it if I put my mind to it," you teased back.

Sicarius pulled your arm aside and leaned forward until lips hovered above yours. His free hand snaked around your waist, bending you against his body. Like a hypnotic drug, the smell of his sweet, woody cologne intoxicated your senses.

"Please do not make me beg, kitten."

The feel of him nibbling on your ear blanketed your mind in hazy pleasure. Logical thought faded into the fog, leaving only raw craving in its stead. A hungry hum vibrated from Sicarius's chest and tickled down your skin. Blazing want pooled in your belly. You pressed into his firm body, aching for his touch.

"This needs to go," he growled, grazing your skirt.

Warm hands slid up the curve of your bottom and tossed your petticoat away. Your vision turned dark as the uniform tugged over your head. The dress crumpled to the floor in a heap.

Sicarius laid you against the mattress, insistent teeth nipping at your neck. You gasped as he slipped below the cup of your bra. Your fiancé toyed with your nipple, rolling it between his fingers before pinching it tightly. Soft thighs rubbed each other for relief as you squirmed in his grip. A muscular palm rolled up your spine. The back snap on your bra sprung free. He dragged the silky material from your body and tossed it to the floor. You lay on the blankets, chest heaving and body craving his touch like a drug.

Sicarius trailed his finger down the center of your breasts. "I rather like you just like this." He chuckled. "Oh well, the silk will have to wait."

One of his hands dipped between your legs. Electric pleasure fired across overstimulated nerves. A needy whine slipped from your throat. His thumb found your clit, rubbing in tight circles. You arched into his touch as grasping hands clawed at his pants.

Sicarius took your wrist in his free hand and laid it back against the sheets. "Have a little patience, kitten."

Before you could protest, he wrapped his lips around your breast. You gasped, seizing the blankets. As sharp teeth teased the sensitive skin, he rolled over your clit again. You shuddered, drowning in the heady scent of arousal and the sweet smoke of his cologne.

A long finger dipped between wet folds, pumping into your body little by little. Your thighs clenched around him, desperate for the friction. It was not enough. More. You needed more. More of his touch. More of his kiss. More of his bare skin against your chest.

"Please..." you begged, grasping at the front of his shirt. Your free hand fumbled for the buttons. "Please, I want to feel you."

With a pop, Sicarius released the raw flesh between his teeth. His pupils were blown wide, leaving his eyes dark as night under a pine forest's canopy. Loosing your wrist, he stroked your cheek. His other thumb ground against the swollen bud between your legs. "Not yet, you needy thing," he taunted.

You grumbled and wrapped your arms around his neck. As you tried to tug him into you, he laughed in your face. Your bitter frown shattered as his fingers stroked a spot on the front of your walls. Each touch left your vision riddled with speckled grey.

Sicarius leaned down, sucking hard on the delicate skin near your throat latch. Choked sobs fluttered from your lips as he worked your body into a writhing heat. Tight coiling in your core begged for release.

"Come for me," he whispered.

Your walls clenched tight on his hand as mind-numbing bliss engulfed your senses. The tension snapped free, leaving you pulsing around his thick digits. You whimpered, clinging to him as you tumbled down from the high. By the time your ears stopped ringing, you were a puddle of addle-brained goo in his hands.

Sicarius turned your head to face him. His tongue dragged along his wet finger. He grasped your wrist, tugging it to his aching cock. As he stroked your palm down his length, he shuddered.

"I cannot wait to be inside you," he groaned. "But this will have to do for now."

The slimy tip smeared across your belly, and the silver-haired man wrapped his hand over yours. Squeezing you tight around his shaft, he began to pump his weeping member. With each thrust, the head slid along the soft skin near your navel. His eyes clenched shut as his body began to vibrate. Pale cheeks flushed pink. Sweat beaded on his brow. The sight of him thrusting against your body like a wanton teenager made your brain feel like it was dipped in a boiling pot. There was no rational thought, only the burning desire to see him fall apart.

Each panting breath sounded raspier by the second. A string of foreign curses slipped from his lips. His hips jerked. His muscles stiffened. Wet pulses of slick cum painted your skin with his ecstasy. Sicarius collapsed to his forearms, nuzzling his cheek into yours. Writhing snuggles smeared his climax across both your bodies. He moaned your name, followed by some string of half-groaned gibberish, which was not fit for polite company. Amongst the mutterings, only one was clear: "Mēnue" — the Gamoidian word for "mine."

As his chest hairs tickled your breasts, you giggled and shoved at his shoulder. "Sicarius, stop it."

He clutched you tight to his overheated body, burying his nose in your hair.

"You *will not* be rid of me that easily, kitten."

CHAPTER SIXTEEN

Heat Season – Day 19 of 91

"Can I open them now?"

Georgette's reply was muffled by the pins in her mouth. "No."

As the rain outside drummed on the windows, you clenched your eyes shut and listened to the tapping noise. The Kestanian's nimble fingers tugged at the buttons of your dress, pinching and pulling her creation into submission. She had been alternating between humming and grumbling for fifteen minutes. As a rumble of low thunder shook the glass panes, a cold thimble grazed the edge of your spine. You jolted.

"Do not move, or you will bleed," the seamstress warned.

Goose pimples erupted across your skin. You tried not to squirm.

A gust of hard wind rattled the window again. Georgette sighed. "This weather is beastly."

"That is what we mere mortals get for planning an outdoor ceremony," you replied. "Still, they say rain on a wedding day nourishes future happiness."

"Do you really believe that?"

"My last marriage was sunny, and my husband was dead in less than two years."

Georgette patted your shoulder. "Perhaps a storm is best then."

The gentle tug of thread on fabric tickled across your back. You bit your lip to contain the giggle. Her cool, slender hand laid itself on your shoulder. A quiet snip was followed by a coo of excitement. Georgette brushed the hem of the dress straight before turning you around to face the looking glass.

"Now, you may look."

When your mirror image swam into focus, your breath hitched in your chest. Before you sat an ethereal parody of yourself, polished and primped to perfection. Her luxurious ivory gown was a long, tailored piece with a fitted bodice made of scalloped bobbin lace. The seashell-like trim extended over your collar bone and melted into tapered translucent sleeves as thin as butterfly wings. Shaking hands lifted the draped crepe skirt. Gossamer waves of delicate chiffon looked like they were woven by fae hands. As it slipped from your fingers, you wondered if clouds felt as soft to the touch.

"Oh Georgette," you murmured, turning to face her. "How did you finish this in so little time?"

She fixed you with a coy grin. "Because I am the best," she declared with a huff. "Even with his silly pockets."

You raised an eyebrow. "Pockets?" As you trailed down the side seam to the top curve of your hip, a silky cavity trapped your fingertips. "Pockets in a wedding dress?"

"He called four days ago and demanded I add them." Georgette shrugged and threw up her hands. "I do not question; I just fulfill the request."

Your heart squeezed as a small smile crept onto your lips. "That may have been my fault."

"Your fault?"

Before you could answer, the door to the parlor opened. Wearing his ink black swallowtail tuxedo, Sicarius strolled into the room. A sweet gardenia, fresh from the garden, bloomed on his lapel. It matched his white vest, bow tie, and pocket corner with perfect accuracy. The impish grin on his face reached all the way up to his brows. You stiffened. Georgette flew to her feet.

"Mr. Estrova!" She rushed to the entrance, setting herself between you and your fiancé. "It is bad luck for the groom to see the bride before the wedding."

Sicarius wagged a finger at the frazzled tailor. "Ellsworth tells me I don't need luck." He took her by the shoulders and escorted her to the doorway. "Georgette, you look a bit drained from all your hard work. Go get something to drink."

She bit her tongue, looking back and forth between the two of you. With a tentative hum, she forced a smile. "Yes, of course. I will have some coffee."

As the door shut, Sicarius turned to you with a beaming smile and reached into his short coat. He made his way to your stool. "I have a present for you."

From his pocket, Sicarius extracted a dainty, double-chained platinum choker necklace. A fire blue marquise cut sapphire hung from the central loop. Before you could say a word, he latched it behind your head. Despite its feather-light construction, the cold metal ring lay heavy against your throat latch. As you touched it, he pressed a kiss to your temple. In the mirror, pale eyes met yours.

A shudder rippled down your body. "You did not need to buy me anything," you insisted.

He flicked the glowing stone, knocking it against your collar bone. "I enjoy the way it looks on you."

You frowned and raised your hands to the clasp. "Understand that I only require a comfortable life, not a kept life. While I would not marry a man with no prospects, I do not require excessive enticements to secure my affections."

Sicarius took your wrists in his hands. Resting his chin on your head, he smirked at your reflection. "What if I find pleasure in bribing you?"

"Then know that bribery alone will not keep me."

He lowered his lips to your neck, tenderly pressing against the slender chain. As sharp teeth nipped at your flesh, you squirmed in his grip. His hot breath flared against your skin. Your thighs clenched as quivering pleasure pooled in your gut.

"Y-you need not put that much effort in at this late hour," you continued, adjusting a stray strand of hair in the mirror. "The ceremony will be done by midafternoon."

As the edges of his smooth jawline brushed against yours, your cheeks burned hot. "I feel you are misunderstanding my intentions," he murmured.

Lightning flashed outside the window. You swallowed to steady your voice. "What intentions?"

Watching a grown man pout was simultaneously the most precious and most obnoxious thing you had ever seen. The way his nose wrinkled reminded you of an impetuous child. Still, there was a certain charm in the boyish sparkle of his blue eyes and the crinkle in his brow. His fingers drummed on your wrists, never releasing their hold.

"What if the entire point was keeping you happy?"

Stars above! Was steam pouring from your ears?

You coughed. "T-then I suppose I could forgive you."

"Could you indeed?" Sicarius chuckled and wrapped his arms under your chest. With a gentle squeeze, he murmured in your ear. "How magnanimous of you, Mrs. Estrova."

His words made your heart spasm. Giddiness fluttered through your body. How long had it been since you felt this way? It seemed like ages ago. Now, bathed in the tender affections you had long denied yourself of, you wondered how you lived without it.

You leaned your head back onto his shoulder. "I liked the pockets very much."

His fangs grinned against your flesh. "Only the best for my wife."

Two fingers touched the chains around your neck. "Is this the only reason you came?"

He patted your head. "I came to tell you that I reached my good friends Silus Hurst and Frank Pulzar of The City Press and The Coriland Times. They have agreed to 'miss' a certain entry in the Marriage Registrar for a few months."

Your stomach sank. "How much did the agreement cost?"

"A case of fifty-year-old single malt to the former and one of my places on the Lustras waiting list to the latter's wife." He tapped your nose with a wink. "Reeves was able to make a far more equitable deal with the local gossip rags. Two kegs to each office, and suddenly they all went blind. It was rather astonishing."

You shuddered. "I am sorry to have caused you so much trouble."

Sicarius shrugged. "It's only money."

Beastly guilt clawed its way through your gut. "Still, I—"

The warm pad of a long index finger pressed against your lips. You looked up only to find that roguish smirk right before your eyes. As Sicarius kissed your forehead, a tender ache squeezed your chest. Despite yourself, when he pulled away, you leaned forward. With a chuckle, he rose to his feet and flashed you a haughty grin.

"The ceremony will be done in half an hour," he teased. "Have a little patience."

Walking to the cleric for the second time in your life was simultaneously better and worse than the first. During the first wedding, your fumbling legs and weak will barely managed to carry you onto the platform. Had Piotr's hand not reached out, you would have tumbled from the temple's stage. This time, the temporary platform below the great golden tree was easier to climb. You were moving towards a secure future, not running from a cruel predator. Armed with the poise of a woman long grown, you approached your fate with rational certainty.

Sicarius was a ludicrous pervert, but he listened to your feelings *and* your words. The worries about your "poor widow" status were pointless. Any lack of connections or dowry was irrelevant in the face of his prodigious fortune. Concerns about him changing his mind were foolhardy. Your reputation could never be worse, and he demanded to marry you all the same. Sicarius truly liked you for who you were. No woman could ask for more than that. No woman could *want* more than that.

This was for the best.

As you placed your foot on the first step, another crash of thunder rolled across the roofline. You looked back at the large windows behind you. Murky grey clouds billowed across the sky, covering the manor in a thick carpet of shade. Above you, the curling boughs of the great golden tree were dull in the din. The delicate twigs of its terminal branches looked like hawthorn spines.

Sicarius Estrova's massive hand swallowed yours. "Are you afraid of storms?"

"Of course not," you insisted. "I am not some dainty sugar cube that will melt in the rain."

A saucy grin coiled across his face. His thumb stroked your hand. "Which is exactly why I want you," he murmured.

The sallow husk of a cleric before you looked like he had been resurrected from the crypt to execute the ceremony. Wrinkled, flat lips billowed with each stilted, cracking breath. The smell of cedar and dust lay heavy upon his ornate, yellowed wool robes. Every word was halting and painfully slow.

"Dearly beloved," he wheezed. "Under the sight of the gods above, we gather as one to unite as one a bond for all time. This bond, set forth in the highest of our traditions, is untarnished by the passage of time and unyielding in the face of disco—"

As the cleric coughed hard enough to turn blue, Sicarius slapped the man across the back. The gagging splatter from his mouth matched well with the dark deluge outside. You clenched your teeth to avoid laughing in the poor man's face.

"Thank you, mah boy," the priest stated, patting your fiancé's broad shoulder. In a monotonous drone, he continued, "Now, as I was saying, matrimony is a reverent and"—cough, cough, gasp, cough— "joyous occasion."

If the officiant lasted through his speech, it would be a joyous occasion indeed.

"It is not to be entered into lightly or used as an excuse for flummoxation."

"Your Holiness," Sicarius whispered. "I think you mean 'fornication.'"

The cleric waved his hand. "Calm yourself, child. You can get to that tonight."

You cringed into your dress. Stars, did he really say *that* in front of your parents? Now you would hear that on repeat for at least the next four family dinners.

As you looked across the room, the audience reactions were mixed. Georgette kept a polite smile on heart-shaped lips while her husband buried his head in her wig to hide the chuckles. Your mother hid her laughter in a handkerchief while your father simply bit his tongue. Rebecca's outburst was barely contained by her husband's hand clamped over her mouth.

"Do you have the rings?"

Sicarius removed two smooth sapphire and platinum bands from his pocket. On yours, five baguette-cut blue stones were accented by round, golden gem inlays. His was much the same, but the sapphires were double layered for a wider piece. It still seemed small in his grip. He held it out to you. As another flash of lightning engulfed the hall, blue eyes seemed to blaze in the dark. Your hand froze, fingers hovering above the ring.

"Ma'am?"

You jolted upright. "Y-yes?"

The old man's eyes narrowed. With an irritated frown, he tapped the certificate before you. "Is this your name?"

You nodded.

He jerked his head towards the silver-haired hellion who was laughing at your expense. "Do you want to be married to this Scarious Estoma fellow?"

Sicarius sounded like he might choke on his own throat. With little else to do, you nodded again.

The officiant sighed. "Then pick up the ring and try to pay attention."

"Yes, sir…" you mumbled, face burning with embarrassment. Shaking fingers plucked the ring from the pale palm.

"Now then." The cleric coughed to clear his throat. "Do you take this man to be your lawful husband, to have and to hold in sickness and in health, forsaking all others until death do you part?"

"Sir?"

"What now?"

You pointed to the script: "You left out the 'for richer and for poorer' part?"

With a roll of his eyes, the cleric jabbed his thumb at the ostentatious tree behind him. An odd howling noise was slipping around Lee's fingers. As Rebecca heaved with laughter, her husband stifled the sound with his sleeve.

An uneasy smile creaked onto your cheeks. "Right… Um… Yes." You shuffled your shoulders back. "Yes, I do," you declared.

"Good." The cleric snorted before turning to the man beside you. "And you Mr.—"

"Sicarius Estrova."

"Sicorous Estroka," the cleric bellowed with a grand wave of his hands.

"Close enough," Sicarius muttered out of the corner of his mouth.

Your cheeks puffed, but you managed to hold in the snort.

"Do you take this woman to be your lawfully wedded wife? To have and to hold in sickness and in health, forsaking all others until death do you part?"

A magnetic grin danced across Sicarius's face. "I do."

"Good. I pronounce you man and wife." The Holy Text snapped shut. The cleric rubbed his hands together. "Put on your rings, sign the paper, and let's have a drink."

Late that evening, after your parents had long retired to bed, you finally got to ask the question that weighed on your mind since the ceremony.

"Major Payne?" you groaned. "What possessed you to take a recommendation for a cleric from Major Payne?"

Sicarius smirked, flipping off the parlor light. "The Major said that this cleric was the most entertaining officiant to ever grace a wedding." Your husband nodded to the gear cart that rolled slowly up the stairs. Reeves had one hand braced on the sleeping cleric's shoulder. Loud, boorish snoring zipped through the hall, echoing off the high ceilings. Georgette trailed behind, lifting the long robe off the treads. Sicarius snickered into his hand. "You must admit, the Major was correct. It was well worth pulling the man out of retirement for *that* show."

The midnight chime played. You noticed the usually dark halls of the estate were lit by electric sconces. Bathed in the warm amber of flickering bulbs, the Fae Tree's coiling branches seemed to glow as if they were lined with fireflies.

"Why did you never light the lamps before?" you asked.

"I hoped that you would cling to me in the dark."

You sneered at him. "As I have said before, I am not scared of the dark."

"I said it was a hope, not an accomplishment," he pointed out, extending his arm. "Would you indulge me now?"

You wrapped your hands around his biceps and leaned into his shoulder.

Sicarius's grin could have lit the entire manor.

Reeves and Georgette departed to the far west wing, towing the drunken clergyman to his quarters. After pausing to laugh at the elderly man's expense, Sicarius guided you down the long hall to the bedroom. The unyielding downpour pattered against the window sills. Quiet peace was only shattered by one terrifying statement:

"Your parents are quite entertaining."

Clutching at Sicarius's sleeve, you forced him to halt. "What did they say?" you demanded.

When he pressed a finger to his lips, your heart skipped. "I am sworn to secrecy," he replied, patting your arm.

"Scoundrel," you muttered.

Sicarius brought his lips to yours for a deep, wanton assault on your senses. His tongue dove into your mouth, feeding you a heady blend of passion and possession. As a large hand groped the edge of your hips, you moaned into the kiss. All at once, the world tilted and reeled. Strong arms hoisted you to his chest.

Eyes bulging, you clutched his lapel. "Sicarius! Put me down!"

"I *will not.*"

The door to the bedroom banged open. He shut it with his foot before setting you on the mattress. Behind you, a cold gust shuddered the glass panes. You jumped as fiery lips nibbled their way down your ear. He leaned his thigh between your legs, pressing the fluff of your skirt firm against your core. You groaned, tugging at his coat.

Sicarius slid behind you, plucking the buttons of your gown one by one. As soon as the bodice sprung free, you shuffled out of your sleeves. Hungry eyes watched the display with eager excitement. He hoisted your skirt to your waist, helping you slide out of your silken shell. The expensive dress became a pile of filmy fabric on the floor.

Sicarius's mouth blazed down the column of your throat as he pushed you backwards onto the bed. When you giggled and shoved at his chest, he growled and clamped your wrists beside your head. A hard bulge ground against your thigh.

"You have no idea how long I have waited for this," he grumbled against your skin.

"Then hurry up," you taunted with a coy grin.

He sneered at you. "A maid telling her master what to do? I think not."

Sicarius's lips cupped the peak of your breast. You writhed in his hold as he began to suckle on the sensitive skin. Tingling heat coursed from your gut to your brain. Your vision blurred at the edges.

"Stay there," he murmured against your chest.

The tailcoat was gone in seconds, followed shortly by the bowtie and patent leather shoes. As you lay panting against the sheets, he shucked his vest with ease. Sapphire cufflinks clattered against the nightstand. When his fingers reached the fasteners of his shirt, ice blue eyes stared into your soul. A warm hand cupped your cheek. Thunder rumbled outside.

"Look at me," he commanded.

One by one, he loosened each button, exposing his pale skin to the humid air. Rolling waves of graceful muscles slipped into view. Seeing the scar by his heart made yours burn. He followed your gaze. With a half-cocked smile, he guided your hand to his chest.

Your fingers traced the puckered skin. "What happened?"

He pressed his flesh into your palm. "A dispute with my half-brother," he explained.

"You have a brother?"

Sicarius moved your hand to his pants. "I will tell you the story some other time." The bulge behind the fabric twitched. "Right now, I am rather preoccupied with the thought of enjoying my wife."

With cheeks ablaze, you unhooked the latch of his trousers. Eager fingers dragged the zipper to its base before diving under the smooth fabric of his underwear. His hard cock sprung free with one sweeping tug. Your nails trailed down his firm backside. When he shivered, your grin grew.

"That was rather naughty," he purred, taking your wrists in his hands.

You shrugged and stared at him through half-lidded eyes. "You started it."

"That I did."

Sicarius captured your lips, climbing onto the bed. His full length pressed against your thigh, leaving a sticky trail of arousal on your skin. He scooped under your arms and hoisted you back onto the feather pillow. His hand groped down the edge of your body, dragging your lacey undergarments over your ankles. As he dropped to his elbows, the mattress creaked beneath you. Slow, tantalizing kisses peppered your neck.

"I want you," he moaned into your throat.

A large hand gripped his slick hard-on, pumping it a few times while the other slid between your thighs. As his thumb rubbed tight circles over your clit, you clawed at his broad back. Strangled whimpers sputtered from your lips. Sharp teeth pricked at the soft flesh below your collarbone.

When the first finger slipped inside, your body arched into his hands. Each thrust of the thick digit sent pleasure pumping through your veins. Sicarius's cock pressed against your stomach, hot and pulsing with need. He smirked at you with flushed cheeks and a feverish grin. Your heart lurched. As he stroked the front of your soft walls, toe-curling tingles fluttered across your skin. A second finger joined the first, driving what remaining sense you had clear out of your mind. Twisting into the blankets, your entire body burned with raw need. Any attempts at drawing breath quickly devolved into airy pants.

"Not yet, kitten."

When Sicarius pulled out of your body, you whined and smacked his back. "Villain," you snarled.

The fiend above you laughed in your face, lining himself up with your entrance. "Sweetheart, you have no idea."

The stretch of his cock filling you sent sparks across your eyes. Your arms clamped down on his broad shoulders. With each stroke, trembling muscles cried out for oxygen. It was impossible. Breathing seemed as foreign to your sex-addled brain as singing was to a turnip. Sicarius's steady rhythm lulled you into desperate surrender. Thrust by thrust, your hands loosed until they flopped on the pillow.

Inside your burning skin, coiling bliss snaked its way up prickling nerves. The rough scrape of coarse hairs on your sensitive clit made you mewl into his pectorals. Every driving pulse sent you higher and higher into ecstasy. When his length slid across one particular spot, you gasped.

Sicarius chuckled into your collar bone. "Oh?"

The head of his arousal prodded the front of walls. Your cunt clenched around him. Unbridled ecstasy swelled in your chest as he pounded you into the sheets. Sounds blurred into a soft ringing. As muddy delirium overtook rational thought, euphoric vibrations shook your body. All at once, the tension shattered, leaving you trembling in his arms.

"Such a good little kitten, taking my cock so well." His thumb swept the sweat from your brow. "Look at you. Just begging for your master to come inside."

As your hazy gaze rolled to his, greedy eyes drank in your blissed out expression. His arms wrapped tight around your shoulders, crushing you to his chest. Sicarius rutted into your limp body at a brutal pace. Before you could catch your breath, he shuddered and groaned into your neck. Three short pulses filled your sore sex with his seed.

The driving rain outside the window swelled with a strong gust of wind. After a few slow pants, your husband slipped out and rolled onto his back. Long arms groped across the bed, pulling you into his chest. Bristled hairs scratched at your cheek. A powerful, racing heart pounded in your ear. He cackled, squeezing you tight. As a bolt of lightning split the dark sky shadows, his blue eyes flashed black.

"Finally, you're mine."

CHAPTER SEVENTEEN

Heat Season – Day 31 of 91

"Mr. Ellsworth, have you seen the maste— I mean… my husband?"

Ellsworth paused, setting the dark red roses in the hall china vase. He faced you and folded his arms behind his back. "Mrs. Estrova, you have been the mistress of this manor for over two weeks. You may call me Ellsworth, as Master Sicarius does."

You scratched your cheek. "Old habits are proving hard to break."

"Indeed." Ellsworth looked you up and down, nodding with approval at your cream and burgundy dress. "How are your lessons with Mr. Reeves progressing?"

"Better than Mr. Wa— I mean Lyle's," you admitted. "Lyle moves the car as if it were an extension of his body. He tried hard to help me learn, but it was frustrating to watch him shift gears so effortlessly."

Ellsworth nodded. "Genius does not necessarily make one a good teacher. Often, it is the opposite."

You pressed your hands together like a prayer. "Please, do not tell him. I do not wish to hurt his pride." A dark grimace fell over your face. "Also, do not tell Reeves. His pride is too big already."

Ellsworth's lips twitched as he nodded to the west wing. A faint crooning filtered down the long hall. "To answer your first question, I believe Master Sicarius is practicing in the library."

"Practicing?"

"The trombone, madam." Ellsworth sniffed. "He used to play late into the night when he could not sleep. Fortunately, since you arrived, those occurrences have stopped."

Your ears perked, listening to snatches of song. "Would it upset him to have an audience?"

Ellsworth stared at you with a raised brow. "In the many months you have known him, what would you say is his most consistent personality trait?"

"He likes showing off." You massaged your temples. "Never mind. I do not know why I even asked."

When Ellsworth turned back to the roses, there was a wry smile on his lips.

As you strode down the hall, a brisk waltz wafted from the library doors. The minor melody was haunting, as if made for a carousel that only ran after nightfall. A tinny piano played the two-three beat while the trombone swung back and forth like a sailor singing shanties. By the time you reached for the handle, your head was rocking in time to the melody.

When you opened the library doors, the sound swelled to a sweeping chorus before tipping into quick stepping runs of cheerful notes. There, in the center of the room, your husband sat before the music stand. His arm flew along the brass slide. Each flick of his wrist was as graceful as a ballerina twirling across the stage. Eyes closed, he swayed to the gramophone's ghostly accompaniment. On the long notes, soft fluttering whirled from the wide bell. His rich tone filled the room from corner to corner. Every ringing note was as warm as a sunny day. As the piece came to an end, you shuddered.

"Beautiful," you murmured.

Sicarius looked up from his sheet music and shrugged. "A bit sharp in a few places. I fear I took too much time off."

You made your way to his side. "I had no idea you played."

"You never asked," he replied, taking the needle off the record. Cocking his head, he patted his lap.

You pointed to the long, hard instrument. "There is already something occupying that space."

A smarmy smirk split his lips. "I was under the impression you enjoyed sitting on my boner."

You slapped your hand over his mouth. "You are a monstrous pervert."

He kissed your palm and mumbled something that sounded suspiciously like "you enjoy it."

With a roll of your eyes, you grasped your skirt and took a seat across his thick legs. Sicarius locked the slide and set the trombone over a cone-shaped stand. As he wrapped his arm around your waist, you leaned your head into his chest. His heartbeat was as fast as the metronome.

You nodded at the instrument. "What made you decide to play the trombone?"

"My mother was a professional dancer before we immigrated to Coriland. When I was seven, she married a wealthy patron. He agreed to provide for my education in exchange for his beautiful young bride's continued adoration. She coaxed him into paying for orchestral lessons at the boarding school." Sicarius shifted you so that your cheek lay on his shoulder. His broad fingers stroked your bare arm. "I admit, I did choose this particular instrument for impure reasons."

"Such as?"

He raised his arms and stretched them long. The wrist of the right side flicked wide as three fingers gripped the invisible slide brace. "In the seventh position, the trombone is just long enough to hit the head of the person in front of you." He winked. "The esteemed Lord Caleb Walton played trumpet. The trumpets sat in front of the trombones and I always hated Caleb."

You slapped his arm. "You are evil!"

He grinned. "I never claimed to be good."

"If you were that terrible as a child, how did your mother put up with you?" you teased.

"At least in that particular instance, she approved. My mother did not like nobles either."

The image of the silver-haired beauty from the great hall drifted through your thoughts. "What was your mother like?" you asked.

Sicarius's smile was tainted with wicked delight. "Estella was like the nightmuse."

"She ate men's souls?"

He chuckled. "According to Mr. Hedgecoth, she was well worth the cost."

"What about your brother?"

"Ah... he's technically a half-brother on my birth father's side." Sicarius tapped his chin. "Come that you mention it, I do not believe I have ever met him in person."

You poked your husband in the chest. "Then how did he give you the scar?"

Sicarius's eyes flashed. "You're a curious little kitten, aren't you?" He patted your shoulder. "You know how boys are. We had a fundamental disagreement that became a bit heated. During the worst of it I said some rather rude things about him. One of his companions gave me this on his behalf. You can consider it mostly settled for now."

You raised an eyebrow. "Define 'mostly settled?'"

"I haven't heard from him since I hired Reeves," Sicarius replied with a shrug. "Speaking of which, how are your driving lessons going?"

You pursed your lips. "We practiced downhill driving today, and that was simple enough. I am a bit nervous about going up the switchbacks."

Sicarius wove his fingers between yours. "I can teach you how to shift through the hills if you like."

You eyed him suspiciously. "Why are you so insistent that I learn to drive when we have two capable chauffeurs?"

"If something should happen to your driver, I do not want my wife stranded." He kissed your forehead. "Besides, fine ladies should drive fine cars."

"Despite all your efforts, I still doubt I will become a 'fine lady' in the eyes of high society." The beautiful dress wrinkled under tight fingers. Your voice dropped to a disheartened murmur. "I was not born for it."

Sicarius lifted your chin. "You spent more than a decade handling Professor Campbell's whims and moods. Compared to that, you will find society rather polite."

As he stared at you with smooth self assurance, grasping envy clenched your heart. "You forget, I spent time in the presence of his esteemed daughter-in-law and her 'friends.' Noblewomen may be polite, but they are hardly cordial. I think they only keep each other's company to have enough backs for their knives."

Sicarius pressed a kiss to your temple. "Reeves tells me your words have a surgical precision that would suit that mood."

You glared down your nose at him.

His eyes sparkled with glee. "Yes, that expression will be perfect. You will fit right in."

You folded your arms. "How did you learn to handle the society crowd?"

"Excellent schooling helped," he admitted before wagging his finger. "However, as Mr. Hedgecoth put it: 'what gaps manners will not cover, money can smooth.'"

"Charming," you groused.

Sicarius squeezed your waist before nodding over his shoulder. With a sigh, you lifted yourself off his thighs.

One long digit tapped the tip of your nose. "You need only remember one thing about blood-born nobles." His eyes flashed dark as a cruel grin curled on his lips. "They are evil without exception."

The cheek that Hunter Highton punched ached at Sicarius's words. Though the wound was long gone, you could feel the blow as acutely as that night you hid amongst the hounds.

"You are not a dog."

With Piotr's words, you buried the ghostly memory deep under a sarcastic sneer. "You mean I have endured all the professor's lectures and Ellsworth's lessons so you can *purposely* take me into a den of corruption for your own amusement? I feel *so* much better now."

Sicarius escorted you to the gramophone and flipped the record over. The click of the metronome, set to the pace of a fast-beating heart, ticked across the room. A sharp two-three beat on violin strings led the way for a crooning alto-saxophone. As the eerie song swelled to life, he held out his hand to you. "I do believe you requested to learn the basics of dance, yes?"

When you took his hand, he guided your palm to his shoulder. As his arm wrapped around your waist, he drew you close to his firm chest. Half-lidded eyes stared into yours. Memories of his warm hands caressing your body flooded your thoughts. Face glowing hot, you looked to the hem of your dress. A single finger lifted your chin.

"Eyes on me," Sicarius commanded.

Your breath caught in your throat.

His grip drifted to your lower back. "Now, the steps follow the beat of the song: one-two-three. The first step is back—" He pressed forward with his left leg, forcing you to shift your right leg behind you. "Then, you take a step to the left." Applying a gentle pressure at your waist, he moved you to the side. "Finally, bring your feet together."

"This song is a bit fast for a beginner," you pointed out.

His warm whisper tickled across the shell of your ear. "Just follow my lead."

With a small grin, you nodded along.

"Good girl," he purred.

At first, your movements were contained to a small box. You stumbled, trying desperately not to smash his toes. All the sounds of the world dropped away until only the melody and the hammering of your heart remained. As the dark chorus swelled to the trombone, Sicarius swept you away. Though the step remained the same, he guided you into sloping turns as dizzying as walking in a dream. Your husband hummed along to the song in his low baritone. The spellbinding vibrations tingled across your skin, leaving your hairs standing on end.

When the song stopped, a raw hunger gnawed at your core. Sicarius's gaze dropped to your mouth. You bit your lip. With a smirk, he lifted the charm on your necklace, rolling it between his fingers. His pupils dilated, leaving only a thin rim of blue to surround the inky dark.

"When you look at me like that, it makes me want to put a collar around your neck and keep you all to myself."

"What?"

His hand trailed up to your jaw, cupping the side of your face. "You heard me, kitten."

The record player crackled and skipped behind him. The way his teeth flashed reminded you of fangs. Swallowing thick saliva, you stood transfixed by the sight of his eerie expression.

"I heard you, but are you serious or joking?"

Sicarius slowly pressed his lips to yours until raw need thundered in your chest. His intoxicating cologne smelled of caramel and powdery ash. As he clutched your waist, his free hand guided yours to his beltline. There, between his legs, you felt a hard bulge twitch against your skin. You jolted as he rubbed himself on your palm. He groaned and broke the kiss.

"I told you, I rather like it when you call me master."

Heat burned down the back of your neck. You took a rattling breath and licked your swollen lips.

"If you would like, you can accompany me on my next trip to Marinar," he said. "There is a little shop near the port that caters to those kinds of things."

"There are shops for that?"

He pressed his forehead to yours. "If one can dream it, money can buy it."

You toed the ground, eyes breaking away from his spellbinding gaze. "I am not sure…"

Sicarius nuzzled your cheek with his cold nose. "You know you are curious. Don't deny it."

"Stop!" you protested in a half-hearted whine.

Your husband gave you a teasing wink. "Come with me. If you decide to try it, I assure you that you will enjoy it." The hard-on in your hand throbbed as he cracked a boyish smile. "Though I reserve the right to make suggestions on what we purchase."

"And what will you be suggesting?"

He tickled his fingers up the back of your neck. "What do you think?"

You swatted his hand away. "I will be making the final decisions."

"That is fair," Sicarius wove his fingers into yours. "Though you already know I take good care of my kittens. Just ask Lemon."

"Oh, then I shall be treated very well indeed," you taunted back.

"Properly worshipped. I promise."

You smoothed his tie with a coy grin. "I suppose, on that condition, I will indulge your whim."

He kissed your forehead. "I do not deserve you."

You hummed.

"Cruel minx. You are supposed to deny that," he muttered with a fake frown.

You hummed again and tapped your chin. "What if I do not *feel* like denying it?"

Sicarius grabbed you by the shoulders and turned you around. As you stumbled forward, he playfully slapped your lower back. You jolted, flashing him an irritated sneer.

He patted his trombone. "Would you be a dear and go find the brown binder of sheet music? It is in the arts section under 'T.'"

Rubbing your back, you rolled your eyes and made your way to the winding staircase at the east end of the room. When you reached the arts section on the north wall, you sighed with relief. T was well within reach. No questionable ladders required. Plucking the binder from the books, you jumped as a scurrying shadow caught your eye. The folder fell, clattering to the floor.

"Are you all right?" Sicarius called from below.

On the top of the folder, sitting on a spiral web, was a brown, fat-bottomed spider. It stared at you with glossy black eyes. The creature seemed as startled as you were by the sudden encounter. You laughed at yourself and lifted the binder up by the other side. When you turned, Sicarius was already at the top of the stairs.

"Just a cobweb spider," you assured him with a hand wave. "Nothing to worry about. I will put it outside."

"Give it here," he commanded.

Puzzled, you handed the binder over. He flipped the music, his icy eyes settling on the small arachnid. The room turned frigid as a snowstorm. The hairs of your arm prickled. All at once, he slapped the folder to the ground, flinging the tiny creature from its home. His leather shoe came down like a hammer. With frigid brutality, Sicarius ground the spider into grey organ paste before your eyes.

"What are you doing!?" you demanded, grabbing his sleeve.

"I don't like spiders." When your husband looked at you, his face was as smooth as a glacier. "And it scared you."

"It *startled* me," you corrected, staring at the visceral splatter on the white floor. A cold regret coiled in your chest. "It was just a little thing. There was no need to slaughter it."

Sicarius fixed you with a frown. "They eat butterflies."

"They also eat other things like mosquitoes, flies, and fleas," you pointed out.

"They are predators." His voice was hard as steel. "Do you honestly believe they care what is caught in their webs?"

Your finger stabbed at the front of the house. "If you hate them so much, then why put one on your crest?"

A cruel smirk danced on his lips. "That is a special species."

"How is it special?"

Sicarius took your hand and pulled you towards the stairs. When you reached the first floor, he led you to the science section. Long fingers stroked the spines until he came to a thick, blue leather book titled: *Spiders of the Known World.* The pages turned in a whirl of ink and yellowed paper. Somewhere near the front of the book, he paused and handed the text to you. It read:

FAMILY: ARCHAEIDAE — THE ASSASSIN SPIDER

Assassin Spiders are a unique species of specialized hunters. Unlike the typically opportunistic members of the arachnid family, they exclusively prey upon other spiders. They are active hunters and do not build webs. Following draglines from orb-weaving species, they strum at the edge of the webs to lure in their prey. When the prey draws near, the hunters swing their long jaws out to impale the orb weavers on a venomous pike. Keeping the victim at arm's length, Assassin Spiders slowly wait for the prey to die. Then, they draw the body in and consume it.

"You put something that impales and cannibalizes its own kind on the front of your house!?"

Sicarius grinned. "The professor told me about them during our travels. I thought the idea was entertaining."

"Why am I not surprised?" you muttered, massaging your temples. "However, this still does not explain why you slaughtered that creature so viciously."

"I just want to keep my kitten safe."

"I doubt it was harmful," you mumbled.

He cupped your cheek, stroking his thumb over the soft skin. "After everything it took to lure you to my side, can you blame me? Even if it did not harm you, it must harm another life to survive. That is just the nature of a spider."

As you stared at the stain on the floor, a hard dread knotted in your stomach.

CHAPTER EIGHTEEN

Heat Season – Day 45 of 91

"Ah! My mistake," Sicarius laughed, thumbing over his shoulder. "That *was* the turn."

Your hand curled on the wheel of the Lacrima, fingernails digging into the expensive Peltian leather. Teeth grinding, you swiveled the shifter from second gear to first. Smooth and slow, your foot rose from the clutch.

"Why are you slowing down?" he asked.

You waved at the throng of people outside the windows. "It is a bit busy."

Military sailors in their striped sweaters and square collars swamped the sidewalks. Gaggles of working women traveled in packs, roaming through the whistling wolves without a second glance. Scruffy war orphans darted in and out of the lane, their hair knotted and faces painted muddy grey with dirt. In front of you, a horse and cart ambled down the street as if the beast was two pints into its afternoon. The driver slumped to the side again, and you prepared to brake.

Sicarius snorted, leaning into his elbow. "If you honk, they will move."

"What a kind husband I have," you muttered.

"Kindness is useful, but a display of force is sometimes more appropriate." He took your shoulder in one hand and pointed to a road on the left side. "Turn there," he instructed, bringing his fist down to bop the horn twice. When the staccato whine tooted from the Lacrima, the crowd parted like the tide had drawn them out to sea. His smug smile was contagious, but you still rolled your eyes.

The narrow side street was surrounded on all sides by wooden structures that seemed held together by mortar and prayer. Puffs of back coal smoke leaked from the patchy chimneys, both through the sides and the top. The air was thick with the smell of sulfur and the whisper of ashfall.

Sicarius nodded to the haphazard shacks. "The Ordango will be in the harbor for at least the next twelve months. Her Highness has decided that Marinar will be converted to steam, starting with the port district."

"So she sent her sailors to enforce the ruling?" you asked.

He sneered. "Who else do you think the people of this area will respect?" He pointed to a small turnoff. "You can park there. We shall walk the rest of the way."

Pulling past the drive, you lined the taillights up with the edge of the space. The clutch pressed against the floor as you shifted smoothly into reverse. Using only one toe, you eased the gas before lifting off the clutch until you felt it bite. You turned at the waist, licking your lips. The car rolled backward into the narrow spot with all the haste of an elderly pensioner digging for coins at the checkout counter. When the front tires rolled over the curb, you breathed a sigh of relief.

Slow clapping filled the compartment. "Very good," Sicarius praised with a broad grin. "Only a month in and on top of all your other lessons too. You are a quick study."

Heat flooded your cheeks as you rubbed the back of your neck. "I am just doing as I was taught."

The silver-haired man squeezed your shoulder before stepping out of the car. The driver's side opened, and he held out his large hand. With a pleased smile, you took it and climbed from the leather seat.

"Mr. Estrova!"

A wild whirl of dust and excitement slammed to a halt in front of the alley. Two young boys with faces covered in sooty smears beamed at the pair of you. The first was an olive-skinned child, maybe six years old. He had eyes of jade and a pile of oily ebony curls tied in a low ponytail. The second was a little older, with a deep complexion and neatly wrapped rows of black hair braided over his head. His brown eyes flared wide with glee.

"Michael. Thomas." Sicarius wrapped his arm around your waist and stuck out his other hand. "How are my favorite troublemakers?"

Thomas, the taller child, grabbed your husband's palm. "Real good, Mr. Estrova. McMurray's got me doin' odd jobs round ya boats whenever she's in port. Pays on time too!"

"I am glad to hear that," your husband replied, grasping the boy's hand and giving it a hard squeeze. "My! Your grip is getting stronger!"

Thomas leaned into the hold, his tiny arm shaking as he clutched Sicarius's palm tight. "Just ya wait, Mr. Estrova. I'm gonna be the head of your security someday."

Sicarius's proud smile stretched from ear to ear. "I look forward to it." He turned to face the other child. "And how are you faring, Michael? Getting out of the pickpocket business, I hope?"

Michael wiped his hand on his pants before taking your husband's. "I gots me a sponsor. That stuffy detective you sent along. I work for him now. Gathering info, being his ears, and the like."

"Ah, Detective Florris. He's a good man."

"Been teaching me to read and math all right, but he wants me to go to school next season." Michael pouted, crossing his arms. "Dunno that I want to be friends with all them nobles and rich folks, though."

Sicarius wagged a playful finger in the boy's face. "If you can learn to blend in with their fancy manners, it will make you all the more valuable later."

Michael threw a halfhearted punch into your husband's leg. "Ah come off it Mr. Estrova. Ain't no slum rat like me ever gonna be valuable."

Sicarius loosed your waist and squatted down to look the child in the eye. His hand gripped the boy's boney shoulder through the ratty old jacket. Blue eyes stared into green ones with such intensity that the child flushed and looked away. "You are valuable, Michael, just as you are." Sicarius ruffled the kid's messy hair. "Do not let anyone tell you otherwise."

"Screw off!" Michael whined with a laugh.

Heart throbbing in your chest, you stifled the coo which threatened to ruin the moment. All at once, the two boys' attention snapped to you. Both seemed befuddled by the pleated chiffon skirt and your high-neck guipure lace blouse. They frowned at the pearl buttons and flowing lantern sleeves before their roaming eyes finally settled on perfectly polished T-strap heels.

"Who's the honey?" Thomas asked.

Sicarius rose to his feet and grasped your shoulders. He shifted you in front of him, resting his chin on your neck. "Boys, this is my wife."

"You married a toff?" Michael muttered.

Sicarius grinned and poked your cheek. "No, I married my maid and gussied her up to look like a toff."

"Gussied her up?" you repeated with a raised brow.

He wrapped his arms around your waist and pouted. "Would now be a bad time to confess that I like a woman in uniform?"

Your stare was pointed enough to draw blood. "Do you lack a firm understanding of what the word 'secret' means, or are you just pretending to be an imbecile?"

Michael wiped his nose on his sleeve. "Sounds like a toff."

"She had a very excellent teacher," Sicarius replied, kissing your cheek.

Thomas snapped his fingers. "Oh! She's that one ya been pining over! The professor's maid!"

"Guilty as charged," Sicarius declared.

"Pining?" you asked, turning to the boy. "What do you mean pining?"

Thomas grinned. "Oh, he's been talking about ya, ma'am, for forever! Every time he came to see the ships, he'd be all like, 'my maid is so smart' and 'my maid is so cunning' and 'my maid looks so cute bent over my desk.'"

You rounded on your husband with the fury of a hurricane. As you grabbed his tie, he put his hands in the air. "In my defense, I said that before I made my promise."

"And that makes it acceptable?" you demanded with a glare capable of cutting steel.

"I may have been a bit drunk that trip?" Sicarius offered.

"Oh, he was stone-cold sober, ma'am," Thomas snickered. "Weren't he, Michael?"

Michael nodded. "Dry as Antellas on worship day."

The aura of rage pouring off your body threatened to suffocate the entire party. "Oh, *really?*"

"Now darling—"

You yanked the silk to stare him in the eyes. "Do not 'darling' me, you debauched reprobate."

"Geez, she's a pistol, Mr. Estrova," Thomas teased.

Sicarius winked at them. "Worth it, I assure you."

You glowered at him before releasing his tie and giving his chest a firm shove away from the car. With a huff, you reached for the keys in your purse. "I *will not* stand here and play babysitter to a child."

"That's hardly fair," Sicarius murmured, clapping the boys on their shoulders. "They are much more mature than many grown men."

"I was not talking about them," you pointed out, reaching for the door handle.

Sicarius's hand hit the door beside you, pressing it shut. Hot breath fluttered past your neck. His other arm wrapped around your waist, pulling you into his chest. When you turned your head away, he placed his cheek against yours. A low baritone, filled with sing-song remorse, rumbled in your ear. "I am sorry I embarrassed you."

"You ought to be."

"I was wrong."

"Yes, you were," you agreed.

He brought his hand to your jaw, turning your body to face him. Gentle eyes and an apologetic smile greeted your irritated scowl. "Forgive me, kitten?"

Your eye twitched. "Why should I?"

"...because he said you was smart before he said the stuff 'bout a desk?" Michael pointed out in a high pitched half-laugh.

"Very cute, Michael," you said with a shake of your head.

"Am I cute enough to forgive too?" Sicarius tried, pointing to his nose.

"No," you stated.

Kneeling to the ground, Sicarius swept your hand to his lips. Blue eyes twinkled in the smoky sunlight. "Please tell me, what sacrifice must I make to keep my goddess sated?"

Goddess, huh?

Your eyes rolled over broad shoulders, a boyish grin and bright blue eyes. Well… maybe he was not all bad… for an asinine pervert.

You stared down your nose at him. "Your promise not to talk about me so disrespectfully to others and a full, plated offering when we return home."

"Your wish is my command." He touched his heart. "No more lewd remarks about you except between us. As to the rest, I'll send Reeves for a goat."

"I was joking about the plated offering," you pointed out.

"Really?" He winked at you. "I *was not.*" Reaching into his pocket, he extracted two drossler coins and tossed them to the children. "Would you boys be so kind as to watch the car?"

Michael snatched the gold from the air and handed one to Thomas. "No problem Mr. Sicarius. Ain't anyone going to touch it while we're here."

Sicarius waved a hand over his shoulder before leading you out of the alley.

Walking three streets across the dock district with Sicarius Estrova was like being at a ball on the Queen's arm. Every sailor, whaler, and bailor of the raucous quarter crawled out of the woodwork to greet him on the way. When both a constable and the drunk he was arresting waved, your apprehension levels climbed through the roof.

"Why does everyone know who you are?"

Sicarius gestured towards a sea captain skipping off with a brothel girl. "I own two-thirds of the ships in the harbor. Many of these people work for me, either directly or indirectly."

You pulled your cloche hat down around your neck.

Sicarius peaked up the brim. "I assure you, none of them will tell a soul."

"Oh, not to worry then. If the whole of Marinar knows, that is hardly anyone!" you snapped at him.

He took your hand in his and squeezed it. "Allow me to assure you, the nobles of the town would never stoop to venture down here. Your reputation in society will be quite unaffected."

As another group of rowdy brawlers stopped to holler cheerfully at the scarred man, you buried your hot face in his shirt. If a simple trip down the street was like this, what would being on Sicarius Estrova's arm in "proper" society be like?

Oh stars, why did you ever agree to this?

"You regret agreeing to this, don't you?" The soft tone and hesitation in his words struck you. For the first time all day, he genuinely sounded upset.

"Yes," you confirmed. "Does that really surprise you?"

He shook his head. "Surprise me? No. Disappoint me? Yes."

"Then, perhaps, do not disappoint me so often," you muttered.

Sicarius stopped in the middle of the sidewalk, turning to face you. A soft smile played on his lips. "I *will* try."

All right. That was cute.

Dominique's Exotic Emporium was an unassuming grey building one street over from the Marinar port authority. Crowded amongst noisy bars and rent-by-the-hour lodgings, the peeling paint and dark tinted windows looked like any other rundown storefront of the dock district. Strong iron bars beyond the glass panes did nothing to ease your worries. However, the inside of the store was a pleasant shock. Beyond the mottled doorway was a welcoming, well-lit boutique. The floor was freshly whitewashed with painted walls of neutral cream. Chic floating shelves and reproduction nude oil portraits dotted the interior. Each section was separated with gold and red embroidered screens for private shopping. Crooning jazz crackled from the gramophone at the main desk.

"Mr. Estrova! How good to see you!" Across the floor, a statuesque, bronze-skinned woman hurried to your side. Her crinkled salt and pepper hair was tied in a tight bun and slicked back from her triangular face. She had a tall nose with a rounded slope and wide-set eyes, sharp as a blade. Bowing low to your husband, she looked at you from under painted lashes. "Is this the one?"

Your husband stepped aside, pushing you towards her. "Dame Dominique, may I present Mrs. Estrova."

She took your hand and rose gracefully to her full height. At least a head taller than the average Coriland man, she dazzled in a black leather dress that clung to her ample hips. The lines of her arms were smooth and sinewy like a wind hound.

"Dame?" you repeated. "As in—"

"As in Knight Supreme of The Rosen Guard," Sicarius confirmed with a wry smirk. "Or at least, up until seven years ago."

You shuddered. Seven years ago, just before the war, was the time of His Majesty King William Drossler the Third's assassination. It was said that the Queen's private army, The Rosen Guard, quelled more than fears in the weeks following the unexpected death. Several high-born nobles, who may have held claim to the throne, found themselves "escorted" out of the country in the middle of the night. By the time the dust settled, only the Queen, wholly of ignoble blood herself, seemed fit to take the reins of a Coriland in crisis.

Sicarius's voice was smooth, but his grin was pointed. "You were there that night, were you not, Dominique? How many assassins were there? The reported count has changed so many times one scarcely knows what to believe."

Dominique's smile was strained. "Why do you not ask your footman?"

Sicarius wagged his finger at her. "I will get you to share someday."

The dark-haired woman rolled her eyes and beckoned you across the room. Your husband wrapped your arm over his and followed in her footsteps.

"Why would Mr. Reeves know?" you asked, trailing along. "Was his battalion at the palace?"

Sicarius snorted. "She's just teasing. Those two had a difference of professional opinion many years ago, and their relationship has never recovered."

The shopkeeper paused beside a tall rack of leatherwork and fur. As your eyes widened, she turned to face you with a thoughtful hum.

"Now, which color do you find pretty?"

The collars came in a vibrant rainbow from sunset pinks to inky black. Some were studded with dull spikes, others embossed with delicate floral patterns. While most were leather, there were a few wide silk brocades. Towards the bottom were tall pieces with heavy boned construction, designed to hold the head in upright alignment. At the top, dainty pastel options with bows and ribbon ties hung from a gold rod.

"I..."You swallowed. "Should I just pick my favorite color?"

Dominique smiled. "If you would like that."

You rubbed the back of your neck. "This is rather new to me. I am not entirely sure what I *would* like."

"Avoid the posture collars then. Those take some getting used to," Sicarius remarked. He plucked a medium weight, pitch colored leather piece out of the center and held it up to your throat. "Black looks good on everyone, right?"

Dominique raised an eyebrow. "Traditionally one receives that color after they complete the advanced training."

Your husband hummed. "Perhaps something more casual then."

The woman beside you pointed her long finger at the next shelf. "You could choose the ears first and then decide on the collar."

Stacked in fuzzy piles were rows of animal style headbands of varying color patterns from solid white to tabby stripe. On the far left corner were some rubberized dog looking sets in matte black. Next to these, cream tipped red fox ears were followed by dainty rounded selections that reminded you of a teddy bear. With a terrifying grin, Sicarius made a beeline for the section labeled "kittens and cats." Scooping the entire lot of merchandise into his arms, he held them one by one against your hair.

"Too plain. Bad color. Too big. Too small." He paused, rubbing a bristly brown fur between his fingers. "This texture seems... itchy."

Dominique plucked a single headband from the available options. "Kittens' ears are smaller and more rounded than cats'," she explained, tracing the slightly domed triangles atop the thin black wire. "If you choose a multi-colored pattern, you do not need to get an exact match to the hair."

You eyed the patchy print. "Calico?"

She shrugged, handing you the set. "For accuracy's sake, it works best for women."

Curious, you slipped the band over your head and walked to the nearest mirror. As you tilted back and forth, the ears stayed nestled neatly in your hair. You shook your head to test them. Despite your efforts, they remained in place.

"Mr. Estrova imports that wire for me," Dominque declared with a proud smirk. "It is the best for serious roleplaying couples. After all, you do not want to lose them in the straw."

You flicked the tip of the ear, fighting down the heat in your cheeks. "I see. Well, that is a bit more adventurous than I was planning." Turning back around you started to say, "Sicarius, what do you—"

There, hands clutched over his bright pink face, your husband stood frozen. Blue eyes were watery with tears as a small trail of drool dribbled down his palm.

"Stars above, you have no shame!" you snapped.

"Shame?" he wiped his mouth with the back of his shirt sleeve. "What possible good would that do me?"

If your eyes rolled any further back into your skull you would be staring at your own brain.

"How odd," Dominique mused, stroking her chin. "I thought you were bringing your wife to see me?"

Sicarius snapped bolt upright, his face suddenly hard. "She is my wife," he declared, his voice tinted with a coarse bite.

Dominique's inspecting gaze drifted up and down your pretty clothing and confused expression. Pressing the tips of her fingers to her red painted lips, she let out a chuckling huff. "Forgive me. For a moment, I thought she was the mistress."

"The mistress?" you asked.

The raven haired beauty flashed you a coy smile. "His expression. Most men do not look at their wives like that."

"Hedgecoth did," Sicarius protested.

Dominique shook her head. "Estella was a trophy wife, not a first wife."

Your husband crossed his arms and declared: "I married my trophy wife first. Isn't it better that way?"

Oh stars… Did Sicarius really just say that about *you?*

You brought your hands to your cheeks, trying to hide the upward twitch at the end of your lips. There was no fighting it now. Your face was the temperature of the sun.

Dominique snorted before turning back to the rack of collars. She dragged her finger along the rows, searching for something. "I think we need a simpler design for her. Nothing too childish but with a little flare." She paused over a red piece. "This perhaps?"

Sicarius snapped up the collar. A small golden bell, sewn just below an ivory leather bow, dinged as he pressed it against your skin. "It's the right shade," he agreed, unbuckling the back. He reached for your neck but halted in his tracks at the wariness on your face. After a deep breath, he lifted the collar up to show you the inside. "It is padded," he remarked, tapping the spongy cotton liner. "May I put it on?"

As he looked at you like a puppy begging for a treat, you realized that this time, unlike the necklace incident, he was actually waiting for your permission.

"I will try."

You let your smile fly free. "Yes."

Sicarius's fingers caressed the smooth skin of your neck as he wrapped you up like a present. When his hands fell to the buckle, he turned to the shopkeeper. "Dominique, how tight do I…?"

The tall woman swept beside you, eyeing up the curve of your throat. "About here," she explained, tapping one of the holes. "Too loose and it will rub."

With your new accessory fastened in place, Sicarius turned you around to face him. His cheeks were taut, lips pulled wide over his teeth.

Was it painful to smile like that? It looked painful.

"You look…" He gulped, staring at you with a burning hunger. One finger reached out to ring the bell. As it tinkled, a shiver wracked his body. "…incredible," he moaned, licking his lips.

"Sicarius?"

"Hmmm…?" His unblinking stare was going to burn a hole right through your skin.

"Why are you so obsessed with my neck?"

A loud sputtering noise rushed from Dominique's mouth. As you turned to look at her, she was hunched over clutching her stomach. Wiping tears from her charcoal lashes, she waved at both of you. "Let me know when you are finished shopping," she laughed.

The touch of Sicarius's hand on your cheek drew your attention back to his excited grin. "Once you put a collar on a kitten, they are all yours." Long fingers traced the bow. "Seeing you wear anything but my collar…" His eyes flickered dark for a moment before he let out a soft, genial laugh. "Well, that's behind us now," he declared patting your shoulder. "Let's pick a matching tail and look at dildos."

…Maybe you gave him too much credit earlier.

By the time you made it back to the car, Sicarius's smile threatened to break his jaw. Any single pause in the drive earned an irritated hiss and a twitch of his brow. Against paper-pale skin, dusty blue veins throbbed with every heartbeat. Sicarius white-knuckled the steering wheel all the way home. When the car pulled into the garage of the townhouse, he bounded over to your seat, sweeping you up into his arms. His hold on your body was as tight as a constrictor around its prey. As he took the stairs to the bedroom two at a time, his voice rippled with excitement.

"The cream ones will match best," he insisted. "Wear the cream ones with the little flowers."

What were you really supposed to say to *that* face? It was a wonder the eerie grin did not tear his cheeks.

So it was that, fifteen minutes later, you sat on the marshmallow soft bed, hands splayed between your folded knees. As instructed, you were wrapped in a creamy silk bandette bra trimmed with bobbin lace. Its matching tap pants had lightly flounced edges accented by small, embroidered flowers. Sicarius finished fastening the buckle at the back of your neck and slipped two fingers underneath the padded red leatherwork. "Is it too tight?" he asked.

You touched the D ring and shook your head. The ears remained in place.

He rang the bell again. It tinkled in the warm air. "You look incredible."

You plucked at the hemline of your underwear. "The tail keeps tugging on the shorts."

Sicarius took a seat beside you on the mattress. "Well, there are some limitations with the aesthetic." His cocky grin darkened into something perverse. Curled fingers wiggled in the air as if they were itching to cast a terrible spell. "I did purchase the insertable kind if you would rather try that instead of the clip-on."

The smell of blood filled your nose. A long-suppressed memory of Hunter Highton's hands groping your backside lurked at the edge of your mind. With a hard swallow and a deep breath, you locked it away before holding up a flat hand. "I do not."

"Well now," he teased. "That *is* a firm denial. It would look so good on you too." He pouted and crossed his arms. "Poo."

The nervous tension melted as a giggle sputtered from your mouth. "Did you really just say 'poo?'"

Narrow blue eyes and a furrowed grey brow were a poor match for his taunting sneer. "It is *my* house, and I may say what I like," he declared in feigned offense. A long finger tapped you on the nose. "—and I will thank my darling wife not to make fun of me for it."

You flopped onto the bed, shaking with each peel of laughter. As you wheezed, Sicarius scowled.

"Keep that up, and I shall punish you, kitten."

Rolling onto your back, you pulled your knees into your chest and cocked your head at him. "What would that entail?"

Guiding you onto your side, Sicarius lifted your head to rest in his lap. A warm hand found its way to your back, stroking the bare skin. Goose pimples prickled down your spine. Your eyes drifted shut as a contented sigh slipped from your lips.

"Well, it certainly would not involve petting you like this," he murmured.

"You said you wanted me to be a kitten," you pointed out, nuzzling into his skin. "Are kittens not mischievous?" With a bratty grin, you added, "Why punish me for doing what you asked, Master?"

Sicarius dragged his short nails just under the band of your bra. "You have a point."

Breathy whimpers poured out as the itch you did not know you had was suddenly soothed. You leaned into his touch, fingers curling into loose fists against his taut thighs.

Sicarius stiffened. You looked up only to be greeted with dilated pupils and a hungry stare. Something firm twitched against your cheek. His hand pulled out of your bralette, and he cupped your face.

"Kitten..." he groaned, lifting your head to his.

The kiss was a ravenous blend of saliva and want. Bristling hairs from his five o'clock shadow scraped against your skin. When the pads of his fingers trailed up your thigh, you whined into the lips. Sicarius's tongue teased at your teeth until you complied with his demand for access.

As he stroked his velvety organ along yours, long digits dove below the edge of your lingerie. His pointer slipped between your folds, dragging the moist heat up to your clit. His free hand wrapped around the back of your neck, coaxing you deeper under his spell. When he circled the small bud between your legs, a squeak shot from your mouth. He took your shoulder in hand, breaking the kiss to lay you on the bed.

"Such a sensitive little kitten," he growled, keeping firm pressure on the bundle of nerves. He chuckled as your body throbbed against him. "So wet for her master."

Eyes shut tight, you writhed into the sheets, panting from the shockwaves of pleasure he forced upon you. His free hand worked at your bralette, peeling it over your head, piece by piece. He kneaded at the sensitive flesh and pressed a wet kiss to one of your pebbled nipples. As he began to suck at the supple skin, you moaned. His tongue rolled back and forth, toying with you. The light brush of teeth combined with a sharp pinch to the other breast made your back arch up to meet his mouth.

An eerie chuckle above you made you crack one lid. Sicarius's dark gaze was like a bottomless pool of shadows threatening to swallow you whole. A shudder wracked your body. Whether it was from excitement or apprehension, you could not tell.

All at once, your husband pulled away. You whimpered as Sicarius took your hands in his massive palms. "Paws up, kitten," he instructed, bringing your wrists to rest beside your head. Then he plucked a short, chain leash off the nightstand and held it taut before you. "I want to see how you look on my arm."

The clasp of the lead snapped into place. You lay on the bed, chest heaving. As the chain-link dipped between your breasts, his cheeks flushed a glowing pink. Arousal coiled through his features. He fixed you with that skeleton-wide grin. The cavities below his cheekbones looked like deep chasms.

"Mine," he moaned, stroking your cheek. "All mine."

Your heart hammered in your chest.

Sicarius leaned forward and lifted the leash up. His lips smashed against yours. With one yank, your shorts tore from your body, leaving you naked save for the fluffy ears mashed into your hair.

As he waited, Sicarius shucked his sports coat. "Get up here and undress your master," he commanded, winding the tether around his hand.

By the time you were sitting upright, a dizzy heat had engulfed your brain. Tumbling forward, you grabbed at his shirt for support. He stroked your back, toying with the chain between his fingers. With ragged breaths and ringing ears, you fumbled with the buttons of his shirt. When the expensive fabric finally unfurled, he pulled your nose to his nipple.

"Lick, kitten."

The tip of your tongue darted out, barely flicking across his blazing skin. As he shuddered, you pressed a soft kiss to his pale chest. Emboldened by the raspy gasp from above, you slowly licked again. The nails on your back dug deeper and deeper into your flesh.

"Fumē," he cursed in Gamodian, reaching for his pants. "Turn around."

You looked into his eyes with a wide-open panic. "W—what?"

He clenched the leash. "Turn around and stick your butt in the air."

A flash of phantom pain shot through your body. The long-forgotten feel of a drunken dick prodding at too tight a hole sucked the air from your lungs. You cringed away, but the chain caught, leaving you straddling his bulging pants. Trapped with cold fear coursing through your blood, you yelped, "It is not going to fit!"

"We already agreed to skip the anal plug for today. Why are you worried about—"

At the word "anal," all sound around you waned as painful ringing shrieked in your ears. Wide eyes stared at nothing. Hot tears poured from your lashes as warm snot leaked from your nose. Despite your heaving chest, there was no air in your lungs. Hunter was glaring at you. Your teeth chattered as a terrified sob ripped from your throat. His hands tore at your skirt. Your eyes slammed shut. Claws dragged across your leg, pulling your panties down to—

"Kitten."

Two warm hands clasped your shoulders. The leash hit your ribs with a dull thud. You glanced up through salty stinging. Black eyes burned with below flame. Sicarius's mouth was set in a firm frown. "Tell me what happened," he commanded.

Each breath felt stilted, like the weight of his hard gaze was crushing your chest. "S—Sicarius?"

The stare broke. His eyes softened as he wrapped his arms around you. "I am sorry. I did not mean to scare you."

You swallowed a choked whimper.

"Your first husband?" he murmured against your throat. "Is he the one who—?"

"No!" you cried, furiously shaking your head. "No, Piotr would never..." Your broken voice trailed off.

"Who then?" he coaxed in a deep, hushed voice.

Nervous fingers gripped the blankets. You buried your chin in his chest. "It does not matter."

Sicarius squeezed your shoulders. "It matters to me."

Trembling lips could barely form the words. The feeling of grasping hands tugging at your skirt seemed so real. You could smell Hunter's cloying cologne, something expensive and floral suited for a mature dandy, not a boy rushing to be a man.

"Hunter Highton," you murmured. "He was the second son at Fulston Manor. He—" Your throat clenched tight, as ropey saliva threatened to clog your airway. Burning cold shuddered down your limbs.

Sicarius rocked you back and forth in his arms. "Tell me what happened," he repeated, this time much softer.

You buried your head in his warm chest, inhaling your husband's ash and vanilla scent. Like the incense of the temple, it felt like the smell could drive away your personal demon. "There was a girl he fancied, Evangeline Calcraft. H-he said that he would not take my virginity but that he had t-to— *practice* on someone."

Sicarius stayed still as a rock. His firm arms held you tight against his body. The grip made your bones ache. As you continued to shake, he waited patiently for your next words.

"When he started grabbing at my..." you swallowed. "...at my butt I just panicked and started crying. He let me go but he never forgave me for hurting his pride, not even after they were engaged."

As the lingering silence lengthened into a pregnant pause, Sicarius stroked your back. The warmth of his hand spurred you on.

"P—Piotr beat Hunter badly that night. As long as I had Piotr, Hunter stayed away," you explained.

Sicarius's expression was cloaked in shadow save for a small smile on his lips. "Saviors, huh? So that *is* your type."

"What do you mean?" you asked.

"Just something I always suspected." He patted your shoulder. "Let me see if I understand this right: The boy tried to coerce you into anal intercourse, but stopped because you were crying?"

With chattering teeth, you nodded.

"And then Piotr beat the boy black and blue so Hunter wouldn't come back?"

Your lips trembled. Another nod.

Sicarius rested his chin to the top of your head, cradling you against him. He sighed, rubbing gentle circles in your back. "I am very grateful you told me."

As Sicarius's soft reassurances melted into your ears, a mellow warmth pooled in your gut. His cologne smelled sweet on his sweaty skin, like the strange honey trap plants the professor used to keep. The vague thought that you might be the fly flitted across your mind.

"Life brings so many troubles. Do not bring your own."

Against your better judgement, snuggled safe in his arms, you decided to take Georgette's advice.

"I am glad Piotr was the one who taught you about sex." Sicarius murmured. "Though clearly not everything was resolved by his care."

Embarrassed heat sizzled in your chest. "I am sorry for ruining the mood."

Sicarius shook his head and stroked your cheek. "Nothing ruined. I just want to know what triggered that reaction of yours."

You twiddled your fingers, staring down at his lap. "Your words were just so similar to what Hunter said that night..."

"It was not your fault," he cooed in a smooth, placating voice.

"When Piotr died... it wasn—" You choked on the contraction, letting out a wretched sob. "It was not safe to stay. I was so scared, I just— I ran."

Sicarius hummed. "It was not safe," he agreed. "I am very glad you left." He nuzzled his cheek against the crown of your head. "Had you not, you never would have found the professor." His voice became a low hiss. "—and I never would have found you."

The change in tone made your skin prickle. You shifted in his grip, trying to get a better look at his face. By the time your tear-blurry eyes could focus, there was nothing there but a smile.

Sicarius scratched his head. "Well, I suppose that answers my earlier question. Both jaded and deeply in love with *two* saviors— one romantic, the other fatherly. No wonder love at first sight seems hollow." His smile shifted, creeping wider and wider. "But I can work with that."

"Work with what?"

Sicarius's odd grin was right in your face. His expression looked like a jester's mask: all sharp lines and terrifying glee. "I can make you love me."

This again? Clearly, the man read too many romance novels.

"We are already married," you pointed out. "It is not necessary."

He cocked his head. "Love is unnecessary? For a couple? How old fashioned." Sicarius pointed to his chin and plastered on a school boy's sneer. "You and your pragmatism leave me at a serious disadvantage trying to win you over."

"Why do you need to 'win me over?'" You folded your arms across your chest. "I am tied to you for all time while you parade me around like a prized pet. Is that not what you wanted?"

"Ah…" he murmured. "You're still upset about the dock district, then?"

No, of course not, *darling*. Why would you be mad that two *children* knew you *"looked good bent over a desk?"* That *utter embarrassment* was such a *small* thing.

You sighed. "Reality is not a story book and I have not expected it to be so for many years. All I ask is that you keep your promises and provide me with a good life. There is no need to strain yourself trying to"—you made air quotes with your fingers—"make me fall for you."

Wild cackles filled the room, echoing off the tall ceilings until they made you wince. "Strain myself? You think I am straining myself?" He slapped your back. "Clearly, I did not express my intentions well enough when I proposed." Sicarius grabbed your chin between his fingers, forcing you to look into his dark gaze. "I am madly in love with you; every part of you from your snide little smiles to your sweet surrender. I want them all. That's the kind of greedy man I am."

Mouth agape, you stared into wide, sharp teeth. The gears in your brain clanked to a halt. Steam poured out your ears. As he brought your face to his, you could taste his sour breath.

"—and I will savor the look on your face when you realize you love me back."

When Sicarius kissed you, there was a possessive heat in his affections that made your flesh burn from ear tip to ankle. Lowering you to the bed, he tilted you onto your stomach. His arm wrapped under your pelvis, hoisting your hips against his as he crawled over top of your body. You jerked up, only to realize his hand was on the leash. The collar caught on the chain, holding you in place as he rubbed his cock on your inner thigh.

Sicarius's long digit sank into your hot core, trailing along your walls until you whimpered. A second followed, pulsing in your body alongside its brethren. He ground his palm against your sensitive nub. Your eyes squeezed shut as your heart slammed against your ribs. Every stroke numbed your mind, sending you deeper into a breathless fog. The smell of sweet, woody smoke captured your senses.

All at once, the fingers inside pulled away. You gasped as something wet prodded at your entrance. As he eased you back onto his dick, Sicarius's low voice rumbled in your ear. "The next time I tell you to put your tail up, the only thing you'll be thinking is how good it feels to be full of your master's cock."

On your forearms and knees, his every move was too intense. His hard-on stretched your body little by little until you could feel each thrust deep in your belly. Hand clasped around your hip, he settled into a steady rhythm.

"M—Master, that is—" The words choked off as he slid along the front of your walls. Shaking arms buckled. Your cheek hit the mattress, fingers clawing at the blankets as he pounded into you. Only his grip on your pelvis kept your legs from collapsing. The muscles of your thighs quivered as your vision swirled.

"Such a naughty kitten, shaking your hips like that. Are you going to come?"

Before you could reply, he wrenched you up to sink deeper inside. The soft 'pap' of flesh on flesh made your stomach clench. Locked tight under his solid body, it was all you could do to gasp for air. Wrapping the chain in his massive fist, he tugged on your collar. Your neck pulled up, back arching until he pressed against every piece of you.

"Come for your master like a good girl," he rasped in your ear.

One final swipe of his palm set you trembling into the sheets. As your walls clamped down, Sicarius groaned. His cock pulsed inside you, filling your core with his load. When you lay collapsed against the mattress, your husband gently coaxed the ears from your head, careful not to tug your hair. He trailed his hand down your spine, tickling across the tip of your tailbone before rolling up to your hip. With two soft pats, he pulled away and leaned over the edge of the bed. He returned holding his monogrammed handkerchief. You shivered as he reached between your legs, wiping the cum away. Once he finished with you, he did the same for himself, shuddering at the cold fabric against his hot skin. The silken square was quickly wadded up and tossed aside. Sicarius flopped back onto the mattress and pulled you into his chest. The warmth of his arm cocooning your dizzy, orgasm addled body was as potent as alcohol. Heavy lids drooped lower and lower. As your mind began to drift, he murmured into your hair:

"I will help you past this, kitten. I promise."

Chapter Nineteen

Heat Season – Day 60 of 91

With a gulp, you stared up the black drive snaking between the dark pines that cloaked the hill. Despite the hot sun, the shadows that pooled beneath the thick stone arch left a shiver on your skin. Your fingers tightened on the shifter. Sicarius strolled around the car and shut the door behind him. The heavy gate slipped open as wide as the maw of some great beast. The road before you looked like an oil slick. Throat tight, you turned to your husband. His grin was as taunting as it was bright. He tapped your hand with his index finger.

"Traditionally, one does not ascend a hill while in park," he teased.

Glancing from him to the winding switchbacks, you reached for your lap belt. "Perhaps you had better—"

His eyes were cold as ice as the smile stretched one tooth wider. "Now, now. How will you ever learn if I do everything for you, kitten?"

You pursed your lips.

Sicarius laid his hand over yours. "I can handle the shifting if you will work the pedals."

"That sounds needlessly complicated," you pointed out. "Also, on a hill this steep, why would I ever shift out of first gear?"

"Just drive faster, and second gear will do fine."

Eyes narrowed, you shooed his hand away. "I shall stay in first, thank you."

"As you wish," he replied with a shrug.

You depressed the clutch and pressed your right foot down until the engine began to purr. Once the sound reached the correct tone, you took a deep breath and shifted into first. Your foot eased off the clutch, linking the engine and transmission back together. While the Lacrima crawled forward, you pushed the throttle higher and started the ascent.

Slow, low claps echoed from the passenger side. "See? You did not need my help."

With a pleased smile, you rounded the first switchback. The driveway to the manor climbed at a steep grade which made your stomach ache. However, as the Lacrima continued to keep pace, some blood began to return to cold fingers.

Sicarius nudged your arm after the third curve. "Try second gear," he urged.

Feeling a little less panicked, you tapped the gas and over-revved the engine. As excitement got the better of you, your foot came off the clutch too fast. The car lurched into gear.

Sicarius laughed. "Easy, kitten. The car is no competition for you, so there is no need to kill her."

"Sorry," you mumbled, cheeks growing hot.

He patted your back. "Do not fret. There is nothing you can do that I *can not* fix."

By the time you reached the final switchback, a low buzz had begun to filter through the cabin. You raised a brow and turned to your husband. "What is that noise?"

He hummed and tapped his chin. "Probably nothing."

"Probably?"

Sicarius slapped the dashboard. There was a sharp *clunk*, and the droning noise became a violent rattle. "Ah…" he pointed out his window. "Perhaps I ought to investigate that before we continue?"

You revved the engine for the shift and moved back into first. The car began to slow just as you crested the turn. After you pulled to the side of the hill, your shaking hands yanked up the emergency brake before shutting off the engine. "What happened?"

Sicarius unbuckled his seat belt. "I do not know."

When the door clicked shut, he walked to the front of the vehicle. The black hood slid up, blocking your view. Small tings and sharp clanks echoed from the engine bay. Unbuckling your lap belt, you slipped out of the driver's side. Though it was summer, the thin mountain air was cool in the shade. You rubbed your arms and crept up towards your husband.

In a small voice, you asked: "Did I damage it?"

With one swift pull, Sicarius snapped the lid shut. Leaning on the glossy paint, he smirked at you. "Well, it will not burst into flames, but I think it would be best to have Lyle look at it before we proceed on."

You toed the ground. "So I did damage it."

Thick arms engulfed your body, and Sicarius spun you around to face the back of the car. "Now, now. It is called 'learning to drive,' not 'driving perfectly the very first time.'"

Nervous eyes glanced at the vehicle. It was more like a piece of art on wheels than a method of transportation. "But the Lacrima is your favorite…"

A pale pointer lifted your chin. Dazzling blue eyes stared into yours. "And you are my wife. Which do you think is more important to me?"

A soft smile tugged at tight lips. You buried your head in his tweed sport coat. "Thank you," you murmured. "I will not do it again, but thank you."

Sicarius chuckled in your ear. "I appreciate both sentiments." He glanced at your T-strap heels and looked up the arduous path. "Though, those might be an issue."

Kneeling down, you started to unfasten the buckle. He grasped your shoulder. Your eyes flicked to his. His grin was tense.

"Absolutely not."

You frowned. "It is only a ten-minute walk from this point."

He sneered. "Do you expect me to let my wife walk stocking-foot up the rest of the drive?"

You shrugged. "All right, then I shall stay in the ca—"

Before you could finish the thought, you were swept up against a firm chest. One arm wrapped itself around your shoulders while the other snaked under your knees. Your eyes bulged as you clung to his neck for support.

"Sicarius, put me down!"

"I *will not.*"

"You can not carry me up this hill!"

"Why not?" He bounced you in his strong grip. Your eyes clenched shut as zero gravity flopped your stomach. "It's romantic," he cooed.

"When you drop me, it will not be romantic!" you protested.

He pouted and pinched your thigh.

"Stop that!"

"Have some faith in me," he teased. "I am quite sure that I can at least mak—"

The word stuck in your husband's throat. Broad shoulders stiffened. The air felt heavy and silent, like a blanket of snow. Sicarius lowered you to the ground, keeping your face pointed to the Lacrima. One hand around your waist, he pulled you to the passenger door. When his thumb depressed the latch, it was chilled as a corpse. His tight grip on your hip ached like a bruise. Unblinking eyes stared at something up the road.

Sicarius's voice was low and firm as he nudged you. "Get in the car."

You turned to look where Sicarius was staring and wished you had not.

A scruffy red dog stood ten paces off the driver's side door. The long ears of the setter were matted with cockleburs. It stared into the air, snapping at some invisible fly. Thick ropes of drool oozed from its mouth as it slathered its way across the pavement. All at once, it made a retching, gagging noise and began to swipe at its face. Writhing and clawing itself to blood, it opened its eyes long enough for bottomless black to stare right through you. Like something from a nightmare, your heavy legs felt rooted to the ground.

"Kitten."

Your head snapped up, staring into Sicarius's patient expression.

"Get in the car," he repeated, his voice soft.

Without further hesitation, you crawled inside. As you tried to climb over the center console, the door clicked shut behind you.

"What are you doing!?" you demanded in horror. "Get in!"

With a smile, Sicarius shook his head and held a finger to his lips.

In confused terror, you watched him make his way around the back of the car. By the time Sicarius rounded the vehicle, the creature was seven paces away. Head tremoring, it swayed back and forth on unsteady feet, its empty gaze sweeping over the terrain before it. When its attention snapped to your husband, its black lips quivered into a drunken snarl.

Sicarius came to a standstill, his hand barely a finger's twitch from the handle to safety. Crusted furrows of fur and saliva curled around the setter's nose. Long ears swung back until they laid low upon its skull. It lowered its head, gaze fixed upon your husband. Jagged fangs flashed into view, gleaming from frothing mad rage.

Sicarius's eyes met the inky black with clinical regard. His nostrils flared and a dark shadow fell upon his face. Smirking lips pulled tight over his teeth, mimicking the creature's expression with eerie accuracy. He drew the door open, smooth and slow. Gaze locked with the mad creature before him, your husband slid into the driver's seat with only the whisper of his coat on leather to announce his arrival. As the door clicked shut, a great pause filled the empty gap between man and animal. The dog froze, its heavy lids drawing wide over its domed brow. Then, in a furious rush, the creature surged forward, lunging for the source of the noise. When its fangs found no purchase on the swooping fender, it staggered away, face rippling with fury.

It was only when Sicarius leaned over to your side of the car that you remembered to breathe.

"What were you thinking!?" you demanded. "I could have crawled across the center console. You should have just followed behind me instead of getting closer to it!"

"Yes, but the dog is on this side and there isn't enough room for us to switch places."

"Switch places?"

The glove compartment fell open in your lap, revealing a steel blue pistol with a dark rosewood handle. Inlaid with diamond shaped tortoiseshell grip embellishments, it reminded you of the geometric patterns on the study floor.

"I doubt you're as good a shot as I am," he explained.

Your eyes widened as he extracted the weapon and began to roll down his window crank by crank.

"Why is there a gun in the glovebox!?" you asked in horror.

He raised an eyebrow and let out a snort of amusement. "Because I put it there?"

You glanced back and forth between the cold metal and your husband. "Is it loaded?"

He smiled as he flipped off the safety. "Yes, but the manual guards are quite good." He patted your cheek. "Don't worry. I have seen a policeman drop it three stories off a roof during a tussle. The hammer broke off, and the round never fired."

His words brought you no comfort.

The gaunt dog stumbled, falling to the asphalt. There, it lay on the ground, curly tail tucked under its body. Through its thin red coat, you could see the heart hammering against its ribs. The animal staggered to its feet, staring at the car. A hoarse, croup-like howl ripped from the setter's throat. Your husband leaned into the window frame, pointing at the dog's left side, near the tip of the elbow.

"I can not shoot it in the brain, or it might spill the madness into the air," Sicarius explained, as if he were discussing how to scramble eggs. "Cover your ears. This may take more than one shot."

Curling into a ball, you buried your knees in your chest and clamped your hands over your head. It was not enough to conceal the sound. One dull pop was followed by a screech of pain and a long pause. Sicarius brushed against you. The car wobbled as the driver's door slammed shut. Two more cracks fell in rapid succession. Your blood felt like ice water. The door clicked closed. Your husband leaned past you, placing the gun back to the glovebox. When the car slipped into drive, the rattle was gone.

"It had to be done," Sicarius said. "It would have died in agony and taken others with it."

Your body began to shake.

A large hand squeezed your shoulder. "Calm down, kitten. You know I will always protect you from any wild dogs."

That was not it. That absolutely was not it.

It was impossible to decide which item was worse: your husband's unexpected weapon stockpile or the way in which he effortlessly used it. Your mind was a blur. Trying to absorb the information was like willingly drinking poison. As you stared blankly into your skirt, the now quiet car rolled up the hill.

When Ellsworth opened Gravelorne's front door, he was greeted by the master's weary smile. Sicarius carried your cold, quivering body across the threshold. Your eyes were glassy and listless. Breathing came in shallow rasps. Ellsworth tugged the door shut tight and threw the latch.

Sicarius hitched your weak body higher against his chest. "We had a run-in with one of the ferals. Would you be so good as to fetch the brandy?"

Ellsworth's fuzzy brows furrowed. "Shall I send for a doctor?"

Sicarius shook his head. "No. I think she will come out of it with some food. Poor thing is a bit shocked."

Ellsworth's eyes roamed over your dazed expression. Without a word, he bustled to the office and opened the great door. Sicarius strode past his manservant, kicking the entryway shut behind him. The tap of leather on marble faded down the hall. Your husband set you in the large wingback chair, kneeled beside you, and patted your hand.

"We are back at Gravelorne now. Do you understand?"

You nodded, drawing your knees under your chin. Your hands clamped around your shins, clutching your body into a tight ball. With your face tucked into your skirt again, the dull throbbing at the back of your skull became painfully apparent. A single hiccup erupted from your throat.

Sicarius's warm hand rubbed up and down your back. "You are safe. I promise."

The image of the unexplained *loaded* gun monopolized your thoughts. Your teeth began to chatter. Two quick raps on the study door sounded dull, like they were coated in mud.

"Enter," Sicarius called.

Reeves appeared, clutching a silver tray with warm brandy, steaming broth, and fresh bread. He hurried to the desk, setting the food down. Brown eyes searched yours for signs of life. Stilted breathing and a glazed stare were all he received in reply.

"She looks awful," he muttered, pouring a small glass of liquor. "What happened?"

"There was some trouble with the car. One of the mad ferals came out of the woods. I dispatched it."

"Right in front of her!?"

Blue eyes narrowed. "Should I have let it wander off?"

Reeves scratched the back of his neck. "Well, no… I mean—" He cast a sideways glance at your vacant, desolated expression.

Sicarius took the brandy and pressed it into your hand. "Have Norton collect the body for cremation. We can not risk a scavenger consuming it."

With a grimace and a nod, the footman made his way to the door. As the latch clicked shut, you sipped the brandy. The smooth drink tasted like apricots and oak.

Sicarius lifted the wide porcelain spoon to your lips. "Say 'ah.'"

Bloodshot eyes rolled to him. You clamped your lips shut and shook your head.

He smirked. "Well, at least you can manage that much." Setting the bowl aside, he waved one hand to prompt you. "Come along. You need to say it."

As you swallowed another gulp of the warm drink, your stomach began to burn.

"You are not going to ask why I shot the dog?"

The image of the poor creature violently gagging on its own saliva seared across your mind. You winced and mumbled, "I wish I never saw it, but I did not want to see it suffer either." With a rattling inhale, you set down the drink and pressed your brow into your knees. "I do not know what to feel about that," you admitted.

Sicarius stroked your cheek. "It is not the dog's fault that its previous masters were fools. However, as the steward of these lands, I can not ignore the threat it posed to my staff, my family, and the village below us."

"I know. I know." Your voice was cracking. "I know all that, and it still does not—"

As your words devolved into harsh sobs, Sicarius wrapped you in his hard embrace. "Pitying the dead will not bring the world to rights. Only action can do that." He pressed his cheek against your ear. "I promise you, the nobles who abandoned the dogs have already paid for their short-sighted actions."

His words did nothing to ease your mind.

A soft *clink* was followed by a hand lifting your head. "You need to eat for me," your husband pushed, pressing the bone china spoon to your lips. "A bite at least."

The taste of onions and carrots rolled across your tongue. Swallowing felt like choking. You threw your head back into the chair, clenching your eyes tight. The soup slipped down your gullet. Sniffing back the tears, you took slow, deep breaths.

His fingers wove themselves into your hand. "If you will eat a little more for me, I have something special to show you."

"W—what?" you stammered.

He scooped a fresh load of broth into the spoon. "Eat first."

By the time the master of Gravelorne finished coaxing you through the bread, warmth had returned to your skin. Climbing the stairs on buckling legs was a feat all its own. Sicarius stopped two stumbles before you managed to make it to the bedroom. He set you upon the bed as if you were made of glass. The faucet ran in the bath. Returning with a warm washcloth, he dabbed at your tear-streaked face. Each soft brush of the plush fabric sent tingles down your skin. When he smiled at you, your chest ached.

Satisfied with his work, Sicarius made his way to the smooth desk on the far side of the room. He depressed a concealed panel and a secret drawer popped out on the left. From the hidden chamber, he extracted a stack of old, yellowed letters on fine linen paper. The red binding cord slipped free. He shuffled through them one at a time until, at last, he plucked two from the pile. Tucking the others back into their hiding spot, he strolled to your side. When he held out the letter, you recognized the boar's head crest.

"That is—!"

Sicarius smirked. "I saved all his letters over the years. Most are bound in the library, but my favorites are up here." The paper waved back and forth. "Go on. Read it."

Rain Season – Day 10 of 92, 31st Year of Creipus the Pious

Sicarius:

I am sad to report my fool son has engaged himself to a pathetic farce of a woman. My new daughter-in-law is the only heir of a low-ranking noble house. She possesses great beauty and a title but little else. The woman finds joy in only two things: the society pages and the gossip of her hen-headed friends. She can speak for hours and say nothing at all. The endless blathering wears upon my nerves.

In other news, my eyesight continues to wane. The doctor informs me my retinas soon will be useless. The last employment agency in Illestrad tells me that there are no further applicants for the secretary position. Apparently, I am considered "difficult to work with." I replied that, had they in their possession a worker who was better than useless, I would be disinclined to correct their employee's failings. It seems that was an unsatisfactory response as I was asked to never return. I believe I hold the distinct honor of being the only man banned from all fifteen offices.

As fate would have it, I may have stumbled upon a potential solution to my problem. Yesterday, when leaving the city library, I found a bedraggled creature crying in the rain. Curious, I asked what she was sniffling about. It seems she was the chambermaid of some great house, but circumstances forced her from the occupation without reference. The whole thing had such a pathetic romance about it that I offered her a position.

As you would expect, my new maid is a disaster. Her speech is ghastly, and she is completely illiterate. She ducks around my house like an abused kitten whenever I walk by. I have never had a fouler cup of tea in my life than one brewed by her hand. Despite all that, she has two redeeming qualities: she possesses a ravenous efficiency when put to any task and a thirst for knowledge that rivals my own at her age. I set her upon a page of letters and was shocked to find it completed to my satisfaction in two nights. I am thinking of training the feral thing up and seeing what becomes of her. If she disappoints me, I suppose I can put her in a box and write "free to a good home" on the front.

Also, the next time your ship goes out, import me a better laundress. The one closest to my house starches my collars as if she wishes to slit my throat with them.

Yours sincerely,
Professor William Campbell

Blurry eyes looked up from the letter. The professor's snitty voice rang in your ears, clear as that day in the rain. You clenched your hand to your mouth as fresh tears rolled down your face.

Sicarius held out a second envelope. The paper was wrinkled with dog-eared corners. "Would you like to read the next one?"

With a strained smile, you nodded.

Snow Season – Day 89 of 90, 31st Year of Creipus the Pious

Sicarius:

I am glad to hear business continues to be prosperous despite the mutterings of war in Gamoid. I wish that I could travel with you, but alas, my bones are becoming thornier with each passing day. Getting old is not something I recommend. As to your two inquiries, I have news on both fronts.

First, I must commend you for finding the only thing my daughter-in-law truly excels at: gossip-mongering. She has confirmed that Lady Gravelorne's last ball gown was of "lower quality" and her new necklaces are "pathetically petite." My son reports the family's society appearances are becoming less and less frequent. While rumors suggest an illness is to blame for their inhospitality, Captain Payne reports seeing Lord Gravelorne in a drunken scuffle with a bookie at Pinesburrow Track. If you truly have designs upon Gravelorne Manor, open negotiations posthaste. My insurance agent tells me the eldest son increased the policy on the estate last week. An unfortunate "accident" may soon befall the property. However, if you wanted to negotiate a good price, that may be to your profit.

As to my "pet project," yes, the maid continues to siphon information like a vortex. If things progress well, I may yet have her reading elementary children's books within the month. After all those years of teaching fools, I find myself gratified to see one pupil who makes steady progress. When you are old, perhaps you will understand the fatherly pride that teaching a willing mind can give. I admit, I am coming to look upon her much like my own child, and I believe she senses it. Her manner becomes less skittish by the day. In fact, after witnessing a heated discussion with a pushy tradesman, I daresay the kitten has some claws. With a little prompting, she may turn out to be a very entertaining prospect. I wonder if I could teach her to hiss away "well-wishers" at the door?

Yours sincerely,
Professor William Campbell

You snickered into your hand. "I do recall him encouraging me to do that. I thought he was joking. It sounds like he was more serious than I realized."

Sicarius leaned back onto his elbow, resting his head upon your thigh. With a hum, his fingers rolled down the side of your leg. You inhaled and smacked his shoulder with a grin. He wrinkled his nose and stuck his tongue out at you. As your attention turned back to the letter at hand, you noticed a few smears at the edge of the page. You leaned over and held the paper against his hand. The marks matched the span of his fingers.

"What did you do to this letter?" you asked. "It looks worn ragged."

He closed his eyes and let out a contented sigh. "Do you recall when I proposed?"

You snorted and ran your fingers through his short locks. Your nails traced the edge of his long scar. "Quite viscerally."

Sicarius rolled onto his back. In the warm afternoon light, his eyes were a moonlike grey-blue. He lifted his hand to your cheek and trailed his fingers down the side of your jaw. "I told you that I wanted you ever since I read the professor's letter, did I not?"

You nodded.

He tapped the edge of the paper. "You thought I meant the recommendation letter. I meant this one."

As your eyes flicked to the date, your jaw dropped. "That was over a decade ago!"

He smirked, taking the letter from you. "I saw you once, about a month earlier. You were asleep in that club chair in his study, curled up like a cat. It made me want to pet you. I was interested, but rest assured, it was not love at first sight," he teased and waved the paper back and forth. "Hearing what he said in this letter is what made me fall for you."

Your heart throbbed in your chest.

Sicarius raised a brow, grinning at you. "Would you like to read some more?"

With a beaming, teary smile, you answered with one word: "Yes!"

CHAPTER TWENTY

Rain Season – Day 17 of 92, 48th Year of Creipus the Pious

Waking up in Sicarius Estrova's embrace on a chilly morning was a mixture of bliss and bother. While the warmth of his furnace-like body was comforting, being stabbed by a rock-hard cock was a bit much some days. Worse, if he realized you were awake, wet kisses and sour morning breath peppered your neck, dragging you from much needed sleep. His groping hand kneading at your breasts could either be ecstasy or torment, depending on how late he kept you up. Waking up this morning with a throbbing headache, four hours sleep, and something sliming up your spine was miserable. You groped for the heavy jaw above your head, pushing your palm against his throat.

"No," you grumbled.

He rolled his hips into the curve of your butt as one hand tickled down your thigh. "Are you *sure?*"

"I am not in the mood, Sicarius."

Long fingers toyed with the high edge of your silk undergarments. Despite cleaning up, the seam was crusted with his cum leaking from your body. Last night's adventures roosted like pigeons in your skull, pecking at your brain with every tick of the clock. Raw from your overindulgences, you curled away from your husband.

"I can fix that," he taunted, sharp teeth pricking at your ear.

Glaring at him sent another wave of pain through your head. You groaned, burying your face into the blankets. "Please leave me alone," you half begged. "I did not get enough sleep, and my head hurts."

Sicarius's hand pulled away from your core, drifting up to your temple. Firm circles followed the taut muscles from the base of your skull to the swell of your neck. As the tense tissues released, you moaned with relief. The bed creaked. Sicarius chuckled. The wonderful sensation of rolling relaxation slipped away. You cracked open one eye, only to see your husband tugging his trousers over a very excellent backside.

"You stay there. I will acquire some aspirin."

You tried to sit up, but another spike of torment sent you reeling into the mattress.

"Hush now," Sicarius murmured, patting your head. "You need to get some more sleep before this evening."

"Why?" you mumbled.

His nails dragged at the itch along your hairline. "I will tell you about it when you are feeling better, all right?"

A groan and tiny nod were his only reply.

"Sleep, kitten," he cooed.

As if a spell descended upon your body, every limb felt like it was sinking into a whipped meringue. Heavy lids closed. Slow, steady breathing formed a rhythmic lullaby. When the door clicked shut, you slipped into unconsciousness.

A few hours later, your headache-less brain lolled into the waking world. Squirting through dry, sandy grit, you managed to focus on the blurry bedside clock: one fifteen in the afternoon. With a groan, you sat up, ears popping as you smacked gummy lips. The aching stretch in your bladder drove you from the soft bed into the bright bathroom. Red eyes took in the woman in the mirror. Puffy lids, swollen lips and messy hair all said the same thing: last night was more than your body could take.

On the sink were a glass of water and two aspirins. You downed them in seconds.

After tidying your appearance, you returned to the bedroom and drew back the velvet curtains. Squinting your way to the wardrobe, you spotted a silver box with a red bow propped against the closet door. Bare feet padded across the carpet. The ribbon slipped free. Curious fingers lifted the lid and parted the cream tissue paper. Inside was a black, bias cut floor-length gown with a ribbon belt and draped neckline. Tucked under the dress, you found a lotus-shaped platinum wire brooch with an opal center. Your fingers traced the halo of pale accent aquamarines. They glittered in the afternoon sun. Beside a butter-soft silver pashmina, there was a note.

Had to work. Meet me in the study. Wear the dress.

With an amused grin, you made your way back to the closet to pick a pair of matching shoes.

Thirty minutes later, with your hair tamed and makeup painted to your taste, you descended the stairs to the main hall. Despite the short slits in the tapered skirt, your steps were elegantly stilted by the body-conforming shape. When you reached the marble floor, you let the long hemline drop. The rounded train drifted behind you, sweeping back and forth along the polished surface. It made you feel like the world's most expensive dust mop. Two quick raps on the study door were followed by one word:

"Enter."

When Sicarius looked up from the mountain of paperwork, his furrowed frown shifted into a proud grin. He flew from the desk to your side and draped himself around your body. His fingers teased the silk ribbon around your waist.

"Do you like it?"

You rolled your eyes but could not hide your small smile. "At some point in our marriage, will you allow me to choose my own clothing?"

"And lose the pleasure of decorating my wife to my tastes?" His nose wrinkled. "Never."

"Does your control fetish extend to all aspects of your life, Master?"

Sicarius hummed and pressed a kiss to your forehead. "You tell me."

Your fingers plucked at the neckline. "So, what is the occasion?"

Blue eyes flashed with scheming excitement. "Ellsworth reported that your dinner etiquette has been satisfactory for two weeks. I think it is high time we tested you on a few guests."

It felt like the Benson was parked on your chest. "No!" you protested, wrapping your arms around your ribs. "Sicarius, it is too soon! I do not feel confident enough for that!"

The grip on your waist hardened into a tight pinch. "You said the same thing two weeks ago," he snarled.

Your eyes narrowed. "That is because what was true then is true now!"

He took your chin in his fingers. "You promised me this was a temporary affair."

"You promised me that you would keep it secret until I was ready!" you fired back, stabbing a finger at the door. "You think all the staff, a plethora of shopkeepers, my family and friends, and the entire dock district is secret!?"

Sicarius drew a slow, irritated breath deep into his barrel chest. "We are discussing your behavior right now, not mine."

"They are not very much linked?" you demanded.

"We have been married three months," he pointed out, moving his hands to your shoulders. His words were sickly sweet, squeezed between gritted teeth. "I am trying to be patient, but is it so much to ask to have my wife come to dinner with me?"

"Is it so much to ask for you to uphold our agreement?"

With a string of Gamoidian curses, Sicarius's fist banged down on his desk.

"Beating the furniture fixes nothing," you stated, voice dripping with venom.

More rapid fire foreign mutterings paraded from his mouth. He ran his fingers through his silver hair. An irritated smile stretched tightly over his hard jaw. Wild, dark eyes stared at you as he leaned into your face. "Why are you like this?"

You sneered at him. "I thought you liked me spiteful?"

All at once, Sicarius threw his head back. Hollow, cruel laughter filled the room. It made your ears ring. When he finally stopped cackling, he pinched your jaw between his fingers. His other hand slipped up the slit in your skirt, bunching the fabric around your waist.

"Only so I can break you of it," he growled.

Sicarius lips crashed against yours, hard and violent like a punch to the side. You squirmed in his hold, muffled whines squeaking from your throat. Your nails curled into his chest, digging into the flesh below his shirt. It did not slow him down. He forced his tongue into your mouth, dominating the kiss with a ferocious heat. You shoved at him, but he was like a brick wall. His fingers dived past the edge of your short slip. Your skin bristled with rage as he began to stroke the sore folds, smearing his leftover cum across burning flesh.

All at once, you bit him on the lip.

Sicarius pulled back, licking the blood from the wound. His grin was bright as neon lights, but both eyes looked like black, bottomless pools. "Naughty thing. What was that for?"

"I am sore."

"So?"

"You *can not* solve every argument with sex, jokes, and bribery!"

He pouted. "Why not?"

"Sicarius!" you screeched.

With a sigh, he let you go. You stumbled backward, rubbing the sore spot on the crest of your hip. Straightening the silky dress, you felt wet heat between your thighs. While your brain screamed "traitor," your body craved more of those big, groping hands.

Stars, what was this man doing to you?

Your husband wagged his finger in your face. "A compromise then?"

Cheeks filled with wanton heat, you panted to catch your breath. "W-what kind of compromise?"

He pointed to his nose and then your chest. "*I* allow you to break your end of the bargain tonight, but *you* will accompany me to the Marinar orchestra on a night of *my* choosing."

...effectively letting Sicarius set the date of your societal debut.

You tilted your head with a quizzical frown. "Is there some reason why this is suddenly such a concern to you?"

"As you will recall, it has always been a concern of mine." He shrugged and leaned on the desk. "However, given the guests tonight, I thought this an excellent opportunity to practice."

A cold sweat peeled down the back of your neck. "Who is coming to dinner?"

Sicarius's smile sharpened in excitement. "The Highton family."

Twisting your handkerchief in knots, you walked up and down the front hall underneath the great golden tree. The long skirt of your maid's dress flowed back and forth, swirling around your calves. Your nails were chewed to ribbons. Each tick of the second hand was a stab wound to your nervous heart. Alex and Lyle, both dressed in their formal livery, watched you from their seats on the stairs. Ellsworth stood beside the door, monitoring the black drive below the glowing full moon.

Alex sighed, burying his head in his palm. "Making a scene isn't going to change the problem."

You glared at the teenager, eyes zipping up and down his uniform, looking for any flaw that might upset the picky Lord Highton. The collar was starched, each button was tight to the blinding white coat, and the apron was wrinkle-free. Even the boy's chef's cap was ironed and pressed. Your eye twitched. With no real critique to silence him, you crossed your arms and snapped, "Should you not be helping Cook?"

Alex's grin was snotty as he ticked off his fingers. "The quiche is done, Cook wants to know when the guests arrive so he can start the mushrooms, and this is *far* more entertaining."

Lyle elbowed the boy. "Oh, come on, Alex. Don't be a brat."

Alex harrumphed and turned his cheek. "It's her own fault, getting worked up over such a silly thing."

"Mr. Slater." Ellsworth's voice was a low, firm grunt. "Mrs. Estrova is your employer and could see you dismissed without reference should she so choose."

Alex's eyes popped wide. His throat bobbed with a tight swallow.

You sighed and waved a hand. "It is fine, Mr. Ellsworth. Just because I do not wish to hear it does not make the boy wrong."

Lyle grinned, his freckled cheeks wrinkling. "Yeah, Mr. Ellsworth, we all know that nasty criticism is Alex's way of trying to comfort someone."

Alex's face bloomed bright red. He stabbed the mechanic in the side with a sharp elbow. "Shut up!"

Lyle grinned at him. "Be nice to her. She worked for this family for *years.* How would you feel if you ran out on Sicarius and then suddenly bumped into him after all that time?"

The undercook frowned. "You know that would never happen."

Lyle wrapped his arm around the younger boy's shoulder and poked the side of his cheek. "Ah, come on, under all that attitude you've got an imagination, right?"

Alex looked from your tightly drawn expression to the darkness outside the front doors. His sneer softened as he watched your fingers clench the fabric of your sleeves. You paced the veins on the marble floor like a caged animal, only half-listening to his response. A sympathetic grimace curled on his lips.

"Fine. About like that," he admitted.

Lyle laughed and slapped his companion on the shoulder. His hand dug into Alex's scalp, roughly ruffling the brunette's hair. "Such an honest boy. The mistress may still like you yet."

"Get off me, you idiotic goon!"

You stopped your death march long enough to notice Alex's now crooked cap. "Lyle! Button your collar and stop disarranging your fellow staff. Lord and Lady Highton could be here any minute!"

With a pout, Lyle snapped the fasteners of his black collar and tugged down on his short, double-breasted chauffeur's jacket. Your eyes locked on to the leather belt of his high waisted trousers. It was one notch too loose. With a loud cough and a stabbing point, you gestured to the infraction. He groaned, tightening the band. You straightened his gold-trimmed pillbox hat. Lyle winced but said nothing.

Mr. Ellsworth smiled, peeking through the window pane. "They are here."

Like cockroaches scattering before a searchlight, the entire understaff ran for their places. Alex shot off down the hall to warn Cook. Lyle leapt to his feet and hurried to stand in the greeting line. You lifted your skirt and dashed around the corner to the master's study. The door clicked shut behind you as you pressed your stress-weary body tight to the wooden frame.

Sicarius looked up from his desk, taking in your shaking hands and fear-riddled expression. "Ah. Our guests are here, I presume?"

Your head snapped up as you clutched your pounding heart. "I cannot do this."

He slid to his feet, slipping his hands into his pockets. "You will be fine."

"What if they recognize me?" you hissed.

"What if they do not? Will you be disappointed?"

You shook your head. "I would be incredibly relieved."

Sicarius patted your shoulder. "Tell me, do most nobles recognize their lower ranked maids?"

"No," you admitted.

He smirked. "And after more than a decade and a half?"

"No, you are correct." Clutching your elbow to stop yourself from shaking to pieces, you sniffed back cold snot and tilted your head to the ceiling. "I am sorry. I know I am being irrational, but I..." Your voice trailed off.

Sicarius wrapped his arms around you, pulling you into the tuxedo coat. "See, this is exactly why I wanted you to be my wife tonight. I could hold your hand. We could face this together, instead of you going it alone."

You buried your face in his lapel. "I can not. I do not have the strength to pretend to be what I am not."

"What you are not?" A long finger tilted your head up. "You manage the state of this house with terrifying efficiency. You handle our staff with the correct blend of dignity and respect. You impressed my butler, a feat very hard to do."

"I just..." Biting your lip, you looked away. "As a maid, I can weather the insults because it is the station to which I was born. I am comfortable with myself in my own skin." A frustrated fist thumped lightly against his chest. "In pretty dresses, I feel like an imposter."

He snorted. "I assure you that you are more a 'real lady' than most of those bred to it."

As Sicarius stroked your hair, there was a knock on the door. You jolted bolt upright, wrenching out of his arms to smooth your skirt. Your husband chuckled and squeezed your shoulder.

"Well, since you are at your best when irritated, just think about scratching out my eyes, and I am sure you will find your courage," he teased, pulling open the study door.

From your hiding place, you could hear your husband's smooth greeting and a familiar male voice returning the niceties. A soft, feminine speaker issued her reply with polite poise. Footsteps traipsed to the front parlor. You pressed your head against the dark wood and took a few deep breaths. Then with a clench of your teeth and a whimpering groan, you darted out the door and bustled toward the kitchen.

By the time you retrieved the silver tea tray, Reeves and Ellsworth had taken their positions by the parlor door. The footman caught sight of your clenched jaw and furrowed brows. He flashed you a sympathetic smile.

"He's rather a foul creature, isn't he?" Reeves muttered as he took the handle in his grip. "Spent the whole trip telling his wife she was dressed like a slut. She's wearing one of Georgette's gowns too! Plenty tasteful."

You swallowed. "Lord Highton has always been obsessed with appearances. The name is old. They have a reputation to maintain."

"Still, that Mister Highton is a right pric—"

Ellsworth's hand shot out, reaching for Reeves's shoulder.

"Mister?" you asked.

Reeves's eyes popped open. He looked to you and cringed. "Oh…"

You froze, cranking your head around like a stiff mechanical doll. "Mr. Ellsworth, how old are our guests?"

Ellsworth pressed his thick lips together, his dark eyes raking over the footman like a tiger's claws over a fawn. Reeves sunk into his collar, taking a slow step back from the door.

"Mr. Ellsworth?"

As if some foul curse had seized his chest, Ellsworth developed the worst heaving cough you ever witnessed. "Forgive me, madam. It's my lung condition." Through the dry sputtering, he grabbed the footman's arm. "Mr. Reeves," Ellsworth rasped, hunched over like a man twice his age. His eyes flashed like a lightning storm. "Escort me to the kitchen."

"Huh?" Reeves paused, sweat beading down his furrowed brow. All at once, a spark of recognition flicked across his eyes. "Oh! Right! Lung condition." Reeves gave you an apologetic grin. "Rain season is a bear for him. You know. All that mold."

...and yet Alex told you this morning his mold allergies were doing just fine.

Ellsworth gasped before doubling over in another fit. The younger man wrapped his arms under Ellsworth's body. With an apologetic smile, Reeves shrugged and half-carried the still hacking butler down the hall. Dumbfounded, you stood outside the parlor door, clutching the tray. Dread warred with duty as your brain swirled with the new information.

If the guest was Mr. Highton, not Lord Highton, that meant he was one of the sons. When you considered that the eldest had yet to marry, that left only...

No.

There was no way.

After you had confessed how tormented you were by—

One alarming thought flashed across your mind. Sicarius and the professor shared an obnoxious hobby:

"You both enjoy baiting people."

It was in that moment that you realized he would. He *absolutely* would.

Hot rage flooded your blood. You held your breath and depressed the lever. The door slipped open on smooth, well-oiled hinges.

Inside the parlor were warm violet-brown walls surrounding sumptuous golden furniture. Draped across the long, rolled-arm sofa was a dazzling woman in a shimmering dress that looked like it was woven from starlight. The high front neckline stretched from one fluttering sleeve to the other, covering her clavicle enough to sate even the most prudish mother-in-law. However, as she turned, you caught sight of a low-slung cowl back draped just below her tail bone. A small, silver chain tipped with a pear-shaped diamond trailed from her choker necklace along the column of her spine. It drew the eye down toward her pert, peach shaped rump. Matching pins adorned a flawless nest of plaited blonde coils piled atop her dainty head. Sooty lashes hovered over jade green eyes. Laughing along with your husband's joke, Evangeline Calcraft had aged with the grace of a succubus.

However, as you came to realize "Calcraft" was no longer her name, you turned to the man sitting opposite your husband. When startled eyes met his disgusted sneer, your heart spasmed.

After all these years, Hunter Highton, your former master, was a guest in *your* home.

Chapter Twenty-One

Frozen by the door, it took everything you had not to drop the tray.

Hunter Highton stared at you like you had stepped on his tail. His square jaw clenched as he gnashed his polished teeth. The man's golden skin turned the color of sour milk. Broad shoulders tensed as he looked you dead in the face.

Sicarius's sly grin was smooth as silk. "Mr. Highton, whatever is the matter?"

Forget divorce. Mariticide was the only rational solution to this problem.

With a forced smile, you strolled to the master's side, setting the elegant silver tray upon the crystal and bronze coffee table. Steaming rose red tea filled the cups, hiding the frilly peonies on the bottom. You turned the delicate handles to face each of the occupants before placing a stirring spoon and a single, molded sugar cube on each saucer.

"Do be careful not to choke, Master," you stated in a saccharine sweet tone.

Your husband accepted the drink, chuckling as he took his first sip.

Mrs. Highton glanced back and forth between your stiff, venomous expression and the shaking shoulders of her host. "Have I missed something, Mr. Estrova?"

He shook his head. "No, just a joke between myself and my maid."

Hunter's eye twitched. "When did you acquire this maid?"

"Early snow season last year. She came highly recommended by a close personal friend." Sicarius turned to Evangeline. "Mrs. Highton, you are well-traveled. Did you ever meet Professor Campbell of Illestrad?"

Her button nose wrinkled. "Yes, a few times at my parents' dinner parties. My father was one of his early students at Carlsbridge."

"What was your impression of him?"

She pursed her pink, painted lips. "Not to speak ill of the dead, but churlish and biting. Rather like a disgruntled parrot."

Sicarius threw his head back and laughed. "A poetic summary of which he'd likely approve." Your husband cast his thumb towards you. "My maid was in his employ for about a decade and a half."

"A decade and a half?" Mrs. Highton looked like she might faint. "Good gods, how did she survive?"

Sicarius grinned. "She is a talented woman."

The word "talented" caused something dark to flash across Hunter's snidely curled face. "And what exactly are her *talents?*" he asked, as sour as a lemon.

His wife kicked the glossy toe of his patent leather shoe.

Sicarius leaned into the wide arms of his tufted, wingback chair. "Aside from a terrifying forte in polishing, transcription and taking dictation."

"Dictation?" The murky smile on Hunter's lips looked poisonous to the touch. He took the cup from your hand, his finger brushing against yours. "So she is literate now, is she?"

You recoiled, swallowing down a hiss.

"'Now,' darling?" Mrs. Highton glanced from your tempered discomfort to her husband's pointed stare. "Do you know her?"

Hunter folded his calloused hands under his cleft chin. The dimples in his cheeks looked like the venom pits on a viper. "She was my *personal* chambermaid growing up."

Sicarius lifted his cup to his lips. "What a coincidence," he murmured.

"She was not very good back then, and her manners were much coarser," Hunter continued, waving his arm. "I can only assume that the professor's *training* corrected that."

Mrs. Highton cringed before plastering on a polite smile. "Professor Campbell's standards were very exacting. I had two secretaries who worked for him once. They called him an ill-tempered tyrant."

Hunter sneered at your sober silence. "Well, she did always like men who knew how to handle snippy creatures." He took a swig of his teacup like he was slugging from a rum bottle. "She married our kennel master. What a strange match that was."

Hunter's words stabbed through your composure like hot iron pokers. Shaking hands clamped together at your waist. The taste of copper flooded your mouth as you bit your tongue *hard*. Your fingers tingled with icy cold. Prickling pain threaded up elbows.

Blue eyes rolled between you and the guest with glee. The clock in the hall chimed seven times. "Well," Sicarius set his cup upon the table. "Shall we move to the dining room? I am sure Mr. Ellsworth will be along with our dinner shortly."

Like a well-coordinated dance, the three stood in graceful synchrony. Turning your flaming cheeks away from Hunter's vile gaze, you gathered the tea set and hurried to place it on the tray. As your guests bustled out the door, Sicarius flashed you a wink and curled his hands into a cat's paws. When he pantomimed an air scratch, you snatched up a cup and jerked your hand over your shoulder. With a smug smile, he ducked out the door.

Over the past eight months, you realized that attending any of Sicarius Estrova's dinner parties was like watching a bridge collapse in slow motion. His habit of setting warring viewpoints across the table from each other was like mixing gunpowder and sparks. It no longer surprised you to see heated debates between "genteel" peoples. Despite tempers as ferocious as a barn fire, most guests managed to make their snide remarks in language fit for a charity ball. However, dinner with the Hightons was a true spectacle. Their fight was a slow waltz of domestic disquiet that threatened to swallow everything from dinner to the base of the hill under a smoldering flame.

"While it is sweet of you to cater to my wife's peculiarities, I do not know how you can stand this rabbit food," Hunter murmured, picking at the spinach and egg quiche like a child. As the jiggling filling plopped off his fork, he made a face like he had stepped into a bog.

Mrs. Highton, the vegetarian, chewed her meal before dabbing her lips with a dainty grace. "What my husband is trying to say, Mr. Estrova, is that he is unaccustomed to having such a gracious host." She glared at the brunet. "He rarely gets out in society these days."

Hunter's eyes narrowed. "My wife, by comparison, spends all her time at her father's company, playing at being a businesswoman." He sighed and shook his head. "Even when it makes her a laughing stock, Calcraft is compelled to indulge his precious princess."

Mrs. Highton's elegant fingers coiled around the stem of her crystal wine glass. Her palms were white from the pressure. "Father has always invited you to learn more about the business *you* will inherit, Hunter dearest. However, since you are disinclined to such visits, I must routinely send my regrets."

Hunter snatched up a bite of rosemary fried potato and chewed it like it was a bitter root. "Perhaps if *my wife* was around the house instead of at the dressmaker, *I* could afford to go out more."

"If *you* could find time to leave the track club and help father, *we* might afford a great deal of things, my love." She sipped her wine. "Another new maid, for instance? You do go through them quite frequently."

Hunter's face glowed red like a poker. Beside you, Reeves's teeth clamped down on his lip to keep in the laugh. It barely helped. His shoulders were still shaking.

Sicarius folded his hands in front of his face. "On that note, please convey my sincerest regards to your father for the new pistols. For such a large caliber bullet, the kickback is infinitesimal."

All at once, green eyes lit with excitement. "Do mention that to Her Highness when you next see her, Mr. Estrova. We are targeting that line to law enforcement, but the smoothness of the action should be very appealing to soldiers with scarred shoulders and women alike."

Her husband snorted, flashing his palms in the air. "I can see it now: '*Dainty weaponry for domestic ladies.*' Lord Dankworth and the Upper House will be in an uproar over your marketing tactics, sweetie."

Evangeline's eyes narrowed. "Perhaps they would not be if my darling husband were to show them the merits of such a weapon?"

"And turn myself into your father's little sales pitch?" Hunter rolled his eyes.

Your husband's smooth smile was placid as the moon. He nodded to Mr. Reeves. "Mrs. Highton, my footman is quite a weapons enthusiast as well. We both had a few questions about your new fast load magazines. Would you be so kind as to indulge us?"

Hunter sneered. "You need not be so polite about it. You can hardly stop her talking about her toys."

The dining chair screeched off the carpet and onto the wooden floor. Sicarius rose to his feet in perfect synchrony with the woman before him. Mr. Highton was two seconds behind. His wife's grin was all taut tension. "Anything for our most loyal customer." She held out both hands and gestured to the door. "Shall we have a look at it *now?*"

Sicarius nodded his head. "May I borrow your wife for a moment, Mr. Highton?"

"Everyone else has," Hunter murmured, taking a slug from his wine glass. "Where is the toilet, Estrova?"

Sicarius tilted his chin and flashed you a coy smile. "Just down the hall. Allow me to show you while my staff sets the table for dessert." He nodded at Reeves and jerked a thumb towards the exit.

As the four of them strolled out the door, you turned to Ellsworth with a mixture of raised brows and a horrified expression. When the dining room snapped shut, a polite cough huffed from the butler's teeth. "I shall go retrieve another bottle of wine," he declared.

"I doubt it will improve the civility of the conversation," you muttered.

Ellsworth sniffed. "Yes, but I suspect we will need some lubrication for the friction between them before the night is out."

"Then I shall handle the dessert." You nodded to the tray of flourless chocolate ganache cake. "I wish to remain as far from that bathroom as possible."

"Understood, Mrs. Estrova." Ellsworth turned on his heel and strolled out the room.

Shaking your head, you began to circle the long table, collecting dish after dish. While Mrs. Highton's plate was missing a bit of everything, Hunter's was only devoid of his ribeye and half the potatoes. The pile of tarragon butter mushrooms and his Gravelorne grown watercress salad remained untouched. Glazed sweet onions from the red wine sauce were piled to the side near the smashed quiche.

"So picky," you said, setting the plates upon the cart.

"Why bother with inferior things?"

You whipped around, only to find Hunter Highton's broad-shouldered frame filling the doorway. Despite the meal, his eyes were dark with hunger. It made your skin crawl. He crossed the room in a few strides. You backed away, hitting the wall beside the naked painting. His burning hand grabbed your wrist, and he hauled you to the door.

"We need to talk," he grunted.

You staggered forward, tripping over your own feet as he dragged you around the corner of the west hall. His bulky arms caged you between two china vases. As you opened your mouth to protest, meaty hands snatched up your shoulders.

"What are you doing?" you squeaked.

One muscular palm slammed into the wall, clipping the edge of your ear. "What am I doing!?" he demanded. "What are *you* doing?"

There, pinned under Hunter's furious gaze, the same terrifying paralysis that gripped you the night of his eighteenth birthday wrapped itself deep into your muscles. Your chest filled with ice as the nightmare from your younger days reared back to life. Despite all your years of practice, there was no snippy comeback, no violent curse, no raised palm that your panic-addled brain could muster. Everything you had learned, everything you promised yourself, lay forgotten as you curled away from his hot, garlic-butter breath. It was then that you realized how deep the trauma went.

No matter how far you ran or how high you climbed, Hunter Highton would always remain your boogeyman.

"So, letting the kennel dog breed you wasn't enough, was it? As soon as he croaked, that lying mouth of yours latches on to the first wrinkled cock that walks by?" Hunter sneered in your face as his hard grip ground your shoulder into the thick plaster. One hand came up to trace your lips. "I knew you were faking it that night. You're a slut, just like the rest of them."

Shallow, stilted breaths were your only reply.

"Do you know how much trouble you caused for me?" His fingers grabbed your scalp and yanked your hair from the root. The frilled headband hit the wood with a quiet clunk before bouncing down the hall. "While that brute of yours was strangling me, my prissy, perfect older brother sniveled off to tell father! Instead of going off to university like everyone else, I had to marry that daddy-complex Calcraft whore just to avoid being disowned." Hunter's face was the color of an eggplant. Hot, acrid spit splattered your cheeks. "You ruined my *life!*"

As he jerked your head back and forth, baby strands began to peel from your scalp. With trembling lips, you tried to talk. Just as you began to form the first word, Hunter slammed your head backward. Skin splitting pain blurred your vision. Something wet rolled across your scalp. You could taste iron.

"Don't speak!" Hunter snarled, wrenching your head up. "No more of your lies!"

While dizzy grey overtook the corners of your sight, he shoved his knee between your legs. Reeling from the head wound, you started to slide down the wall. A hard elbow hit your chest, knocking the wind from your lungs as it pinned you in place. One hand reached for the buttons of your dress.

"How is your new master going to like you when he learns his hussy maid runs around screwing the guests between courses?"

All at once, there was a wheezing gasp noise that sounded like an accordion being crushed. The hold on you loosened. Your body crumpled to the floor. The world spun around. Through your jumping vision, you could make out three things: Hunter Highton clutching his throat, your husband standing behind his guest, and a long stiletto knife gleaming in Sicarius's hand.

Sicarius smirked at the man before him, wagging the blade back and forth like the pendulum on a metronome. "I knew you were an impatient man from everything I was told but you really could not wait for dessert to be over?" The master of Gravelorne clicked his tongue. "Wherever did you learn your manners?"

Startled brown eyes looked from you to the scarred man and back again. A puff of air rasped between Hunter's fingers. He traced the front of his throat. Beneath flaps of loose flesh, you could see a black hole sputtering open and closed with each breath.

Your husband dragged your stunned attacker by his collar to the center of the hall. Sicarius stabbed a spot on the left side of Hunter's stomach, just below his ribs. When the nobleman doubled over, a flash of silver glinted in the lamplight. The blade dragged over Hunter's jugular, losing a burbling stream of crimson gore. Mr. Highton staggered away, gripping his oozing neck wound. Splatters of blood filled the air with each stumbling step. Large feet caught on the ruined carpet runner. Hunter slammed face-first into the floor. A boney crunch reached your ears.

As your horror-crippled brain began to process the events laying before you, a warm hand patted your head.

"Honestly, kitten, you will bite the man you *want* to have sex with, but not an attacker?" Sicarius scoffed. "I am glad to be the favorite but your tastes are almost as kinky as mine."

You stared at the grisly mess before you, mouth opening and closing like that of a fish flopping on dry land. As you watched, a long shadow appeared around the corner. Clutching a cigarette, Mrs. Evangeline Highton rounded the bend. Her green eyes took in the scene.

Hunter reached for his wife, a burbling explosion of breath and blood blasting out of the stab wound in his trachea.

The blonde's beautiful features gnarled in disgust. She tugged up her glittering hemline, wrapping it tightly around her calves. Fine silver slippers took a step back from the filthy sight. Her nose wrinkled, and she buried it in the back of her hand. With a voice as gentle as a blizzard, she said only one thing:

"I told you to stop chasing the maids, Hunter dear."

Mr. Highton's eyes darkened. His shaking hand dropped to the floor. The smell of copper hung heavy in the passage. Loud footsteps clattered up the front hall. Around the corner appeared Reeves, Lyle, and Ellsworth.

Lady Highton turned to your husband. "Well," she huffed, smearing on a polished smile. "Dinner was lovely, Mr. Estrova. When shall I learn what tragic accident befell my husband?"

Sicarius smirked, wiping some stray scarlet from his pale cheek. "It is very unfortunate, but it seems he woke in the middle of the night and, still quite drunk, wandered off into the forest. The ferals that live there are very vicious. I doubt the police will even find the bones."

"Poor Hunter. He always was a bit scared of dogs. It must have been terrible." She took a long drag of her cigarette before blowing a perfect ring of smoke from lush lips. "I will arrange a closed casket funeral."

Your husband bowed low. "I shall be sure to send flowers."

"Georgette was right, Mr. Estrova." She gave you a knowing smile. "You are ever so kind to widows."

As the blonde disappeared around the bend of the hall, Reeves let out a low whistle. He strolled to his master's side, keeping a wary watch on the corner. "Women are terrifying."

Your husband kneeled down beside you and nodded to the massive puddle of coagulating blood. It long overran the seams of the wool rug and spilled onto the polished hardwood floors. "Ellsworth, do you believe we can save the carpet?"

The butler raised a lone eyebrow.

His master chuckled, scooping your limp form into his chest. "Very well then, burn it and order new hall treatments to match."

"Of course, sir," Ellsworth replied with a stiff bow.

Lyle scratched his cheek, toeing the corpse. "So... since it's not a shooting accident anymore, what do you want me to do about the stiff?"

Cheerful wrinkles formed at the corner of icy eyes. "Have Mr. Norton use the hedge trimmers to remove one arm and toss it near a dog trail. I want the edges jagged, like they were shredded by teeth."

"And the bones go to Mrs. Norton, I presume?" Reeves asked, crossing his arms. "What do you want her to make this time?"

Sicarius pet your blood-matted scalp. "Perhaps a hair comb for my wife. If the china is not durable enough, then tell her to just make some small flowers and I will have Voskart and Bronsk put them on an ivory base. If she has enough left, I believe the garage needed a new washbasin."

Lyle giggled between gritted teeth. "Sorry about the last one."

Reeves groaned. "You broke Lord Eisenhall?"

The mechanic shrugged. "Dropped a wrench on him."

"Oh... so not that different from the first time around."

"Yeah, I had a good chuckle about it. Kinda poetic like." Lyle turned back to the silver-haired man. "Better give Mrs. Norton a third option, sir. You know how fussy she can be about her art."

Your husband cocked his head this way and that before a flash of inspiration lit his face. "A food bowl for Lemon."

Lyle clicked his tongue and gave his employer a thumbs up. "Got it!"

The footman peered at your vacant expression. He waved his hand back and forth, but there was no response from your dull eyes. "Brandy again?"

Sicarius's eyes narrowed. He curled protective arms around your cold body. "Tea, Garrick." Your husband pressed his forehead to yours. "The poor thing has head trauma. The last thing she needs is alcohol."

"On it," Reeves agreed, bustling off to the kitchen.

As your fuzzy mind reeled with horrifying pieces of new information, your demonic savior swept you up the stairs.

How much time passed between Sicarius setting you on the bed and someone pressing the teacup into your hand, you could not say. The dim splatter of the rainfall showerhead was hard to hear over the thoughts buzzing in your head.

Hunter Highton was dead. Your husband slaughtered him. Not killed him. Slaughtered him like an animal. No, not just slaughtered him. Slaughtered him and then told the staff of Gravelorne how to mutilate the corpse and divide up the evidence.

"Give the bones to Mrs. Norton."

"All the bone china in this house is her custom craft."

Your hands began to shake. Red liquid sloshed inside the delicate curves of the beautiful bone china. The saucer clattered against the painted rim. A wave of nausea bubbled up in your throat. The cup slipped from your fingers. Hot tea splattered onto your skirt. Your thighs burned. Copper pipes screeched as the steam-heated water came to a halt. You looked in the mirror. Your face was like a wax death mask. It was a perfect mimic of the expression Alex wore when he saw "Lady Milton's" lily-painted vase.

Every plate you had eaten off of.

The knobs of your dresser.

His pencil cups.

Each and every sink.

The tea sets.

Over fifty flower vases.

"Kitten, did you drink your tea?"

Horror glazed eyes lifted up to the source of the voice. Your husband's silver locks were plastered to his skull. With only a towel wrapped around his hips, he took a seat beside you on the bed. The back of Sicarius's hand pressed against your brow. He frowned before patting your face from cheek to cheek.

"You still feel cold," he murmured before looking down. The cup was sideways in your apron. Rosehip and hibiscus tea stained the white fabric a pale pink. Sicarius brushed a stray hair out of your face. "I suppose a bath ought to help."

The gaudy china bathtub.

"How many?" you whispered.

Sicarius pursed his lips and reached under your armpits. "We need to get you warmed up first."

You shook your head back and forth, sending reeling pain streaming across your body. As you burped bile, Sicarius sighed and rubbed your back.

"If I tell you, will you let me get you some aspirin?"

With a grimace, you nodded slowly.

"I lost the exact count a while ago." He tapped his chin. "Between all of us, we are nearing three hundred now."

Hollow eyes stared at the man before you. "All of us?" you croaked.

"Well, I do not know that you can count Alex. The boy has always been a conscientious objector," Sicarius wagged a finger. "...but very loyal. I think he understands what we do is for the best."

"You told me you worked in the shipping trade, not murder."

His fanged grin looked better fit for a Shadowhound than the master of some grand estate. He waved a flippant hand. "Oh, it is hardly work. Not really. Killing naughty nobles is more like a hobby."

A ***hobby!?***

"You see, even in our modern era, nobles are like little spiders. They build their webs wherever they like and live in their own little world outside petty rules." He shrugged. "I got sick of seeing them go unpunished just because they had influence and money. They needed to pay for their crimes just like anyone else."

Your teeth chattered. "What crimes?"

Blue eyes glowed like fae fire. "For example, beating their wheel-chair bound mechanic until his spleen ruptures because he asked for pay. Others might cut the ears off their butler because they think he took too long with their wine. Some even short the checks of their blind cook and threaten his family when he has the nerve to protest!" Sicarius laid one proud hand on his chest. "I fix that noble problem for no cost save a favor owed to me later."

Your mouth ran dry. "Just nobles?"

Sicarius gestured to the grand room. "Kitten, you are not naive. Do you honestly believe that I can run a business empire without handling people properly?"

Ice flooded your veins.

He sighed like he was in a stage tragedy. "I give the useful non-nobles a chance to comply, but there will always be a few stubborn ones who insist on getting between me and what I want. Their deaths are just a necessity, not a pleasure." He tapped the china cup. "I do not keep them."

"What do you mean, comply?" you whispered.

"Switch to my side and enjoy the perks." He chuckled. "Reeves, for example, was an excellent acquisition. In exchange for joining my household, he got to keep his life and use the knowledge acquired in his previous profession for better purposes." Sicarius sighed and pinched his nose. "He is rather unmotivated about being a footman though. It drives Ellsworth mad."

You swallowed to steady your voice. "What was his previous profession?"

Sicarius pressed his hand to the wound on his lower ribs. "Assassin."

"Assassin!?" you squeaked.

"And a rather good one too. He came the closest of all those my dear half-brother has sent so far." Sicarius grinned and shook his head. "Rather pathetic that he could be bought off though. The King of Gamoid should really be able to pay them more."

Your jaw hit the floor. "Your brother is the King of Gamoid!?"

Sicarius clicked his tongue. "Half-brother. Half," he emphasized, tapping your nose. "We may share the same father, but the 'common' Estella Estrova was much smarter than his noble-bred wife. Mother removed us from the country as the queen started eliminating any competition for the throne." He snorted. "I think she hated us in particular. You saw the painting. Estella *was* the prettiest of the mistresses."

Was he really bragging about his mother at a time like this?

"Still, I give His Highness some credit. After all these years of tit-for-tat, I have not been able to get close enough to collect my prize yet."

"Your prize?"

"His bones, of course." Sicarius grinned like a child clutching his favorite toy. "I plan to make him into a urinal."

Heart pounding in your chest, you looked up at the monster you married. His face was alight with unadulterated joy as he cheerfully chatted about murder, assassination attempts, foreign politics and his mother's beauty like every subject was equal. Slowly, the long clogged gears inside your head clinked into place.

"You kill people and make their bones into your furniture *for fun.*"

Sicarius kneeled before you, took your cold fingers in his, and puffed his warm breath on them. "We should really get you in that bath. That wound needs to be cleaned."

As you sat on his bed, wearing his ring and holding a serial killer's blood-stained hands, a feeling of heinous revulsion engulfed your body. Shaking, you reached for the buttons of your uniform. It was as if the little spiders speared your heart with their venomous pikes. Their icy poison was drifting through your veins, threatening to consume you. Before it paralyzed you whole, your dazed brain managed to come to one conclusion.

"You are evil."

Sicarius's comforting smile transformed into a villainous sneer. "Well, of course I am, kitten. I told you before: blood-borne nobles are evil without exception."

"So you admit it, just like that?"

He snapped his fingers. "Just like that," he agreed. Sicarius turned his back to you and strolled to the dresser. The towel hit the floor with a 'fwump.' Standing nude in the middle of the room, he cast his arms wide as his proud grin stretched from ear to ear. "I must admit this entire conversation is such a relief. I hated keeping secrets from the woman I love."

You choked. "L-love!?"

"Oh, dear. I think that blow to your head knocked your memory a bit loose. Do you not recall us having this discussion many times before?"

You gaped at him. "You can not be serious!"

He pointed at his nose. "Of course, I *can not* be Sirius. My name is Sicarius."

"That is not what I meant, and you know it!"

A short snicker flew from his lips. He stared straight at you, not even trying to conceal his shaking shoulders.

Your nails tore into the palms of your hands. Vitriolic rage bubbled up into your throat. An accusing finger jabbed at the silver-haired madman. "You are an unrepentant murderer, and you fully mean to keep on murdering!"

"So?"

"So!?" you demanded, stomping your foot. *"So,* I will not support this!"

A low, slow clapping filled the room. "Excellent! A little teasing, and she has found her claws again!" He pulled a pair of pants up hairy legs, tying them into place around his tapered waist. Tugging on his slippers, he grinned at you. "Though you must understand, whether you support me or not, you are still my lawful wedded wife until death does us part."

All rational thought screeched to a halt.

Sicarius stalked towards you, his eyes dark, and grin bright. You recoiled, but he snatched up your wrist and dragged you into his chest. A lone finger tapped the notch of your collar bone, right where his necklace sat. "And if you think I would let you go after all the effort I put into collaring you, then you are sorely mistaken, kitten."

With each beat of your racing heart, your pulse throbbed at the corners of your vision. Sicarius patted your shoulder. "Well, while you ponder that little complication, I shall go fetch you some aspirin."

Your husband strolled to the closet and wrapped himself in his dressing gown. Then he meandered to the door, humming a swinging tune. Terror overtook your brain. Blood rushed to your lungs. Your lips tingled cold. You lunged for the exit, but he was too quick. The latch snapped shut, locking from the outside. You reached for the key around your neck, only to find the double chain choker in its place. Patting down your uniform, you remembered a single fact:

There were no pockets in this dress.

Frantically, you tore at the handle, rattling the wood in its frame. **"Sicarius!"** Your fist banged on the door. **"Let me out!"** you shrieked.

A throaty cackle was followed by three, cheerful little words: "I *will not.*"

As the jaunty melody drifted further and further from the door, your hands clutched your skull. Panicked eyes darted back and forth, searching the room for a place where he might keep the key. When they settled upon the waterfall desk, you threw yourself at the drawers. Papers scattered everywhere as you ripped through the contents. Finding nothing, you tore through the room like a hurricane of hysteria.

No key.

No key.

Oh, stars above, there was *no key.*

You slumped onto the reading stool, clutching a hand to your painful, pounding heart. Hyperventilating, you gripped your apron to your chest and began to sob.

All at once, a night breeze rattled the window.

Burning eyes looked up. The full moon drifted from behind a cloud, scattering its light through the pane. Silver beams made the trails of snot smeared on your sleeve glitter. You reached for the window only to find it bolted shut from the outside. Just beyond your glass prison, thick old yew bushes stretched halfway to the second story. Their branches were strong.

If you hung from the ledge and dropped down, would they be enough to cushion the fall?

You looked back to the door from which Sicarius Estrova might soon return.

With one adrenaline-fueled heave, the heavy stool flew through the pane and into the night air.

EPILOGUE

"Sicarius! We have a problem!"

The master of Gravelorne manor stopped in the hall, holding a glass of water and two white pills. Lyle stood panting just outside the study door. His freckled face was as white as chalk. Babbling poured from the young man's mouth like water from a burst pipe.

"Norton and I were moving that noble guy into the shed when all of a sudden I heard something in the garage. By the time I got to the driveway, the Lacrima dang near ran me over!"

Reeves shouted from the top of the stairs: "She's gone! Busted the glass and jumped out into the hedges!"

Sicarius whistled, a smile on his lips. "Using the bushes to avoid injury? Not bad," he quipped.

"Not bad? Not *bad!?*" Lyle stomped his foot, thrusting his arm at the drive. "No! Very, *very* bad! It doesn't take a genius to guess where she's going. Straight to Marinar police headquarters to tell them what we did!" He moaned, sinking into a crouch. "Why didn't you talk to her about this before? You said you were going to tell her!"

Sicarius shrugged. "The Hightons only confirmed last night, and she was in a bad mood this morning. I thought it better to just see how things went."

"Oh, they went all right," Reeves scoffed. "Right out the literal window."

The master of Gravelorne made his way to his study door, using his elbow to open the way. "A small inconvenience but nothing I can not handle."

Lyle yanked at his hair. "Small inconvenience!?"

Reeves sighed. "Should I go after her, Sicarius?"

The silver-haired man nodded to the full moon outside. "We are already lucky she has light to navigate mountains. Stressing her with a tail will only make her drive recklessly. I have no intention of being a widower three months into my marriage." He turned to the mechanic. "Change of plans, Lyle. Tell Norton to put the body in a car and pour a pint of bourbon down his throat. Our guest decided to go drunk driving and must have missed a turn while he was chasing after his victim."

Lyle climbed to his feet on shaking legs. "W-what are you going to do in the meantime?"

"My wife was attacked by a madman and is now lost and suffering from a head injury. No doubt, she's in a state of confusion. So, I will do what any worried husband would." A vicious grin sliced across Sicarius's face as he flipped on the light in his office. "I shall call the police and ask for their help to find her."

Reeves scratched his cheek. "Ah… I think I get it." He patted the redhead on the back. "Come on Lyle, let's go find a cliff for Mr. Highton to have an *accident* on."

As the footman dragged the mechanic to the front door, Lyle's skin was still pale beneath the spattering of freckles. Each step was shaky as if he expected the hall floor to disappear from under him.

"Lyle?" Sicarius called.

The young man's head snapped around. "Y-yes?"

The master of Gravelorne set the water down and pressed the tiny button under his desk drawer. A concealed hatch popped open. He removed a small, leather bound notebook and wagged it at his employee. "Do not worry. There is always a contingency plan."

Lyle looked from Sicarius's terrifying smile to the notebook before gulping. "Yes, sir."

As the two servants rushed to find the gardener, Sicarius creased the small journal open to the ribbon bookmark. On the page was a long list of items marked "Grand Romantic Gestures." The first four ideas, *save from a runaway carriage*, *save from a fall*, *buy her pretty things*, and *teach her to dance*, all had checkmarks next to them. *Save from car troubles* had a large X through it. Sicarius ticked the box next to *save from a creepy man* before flipping through the next few pages. As his eyes rolled over the plethora of ideas, all stolen from his books, he smirked to himself and tucked it back into the drawer. With no haste, he reached for the phone.

"Operator."

"This is Sicarius Estrova. Please connect me to the Marinar police." Your husband slowly twirled the cord around his long finger. "And do hurry. I'm *very* concerned about my wife."

Afterword

For those of you that enjoyed this story, please spread the word by reviewing the book where you purchased it or telling your fellow deviants about this reader insert adventure. The more of us we can gather, the more fun we can have.

To find out when book two will be released, sign up for the mailing list at: https://afipiafelis.com/

For those of you who didn't enjoy this story, we recommend you pet a cat.

Author's Biography:

Afipia Felis is an irritable, foul-tempered feline who lives in a cold, dreary climate. Specializing in reader insert and second-person POV stories, she enjoys tormenting her main characters at every turn. Her hobbies include vomiting on white rugs and hissing at guests.

You can find Afipia Felis on the following websites:
Website: https://afipiafelis.com/
Twitter: @afeliswrites
Tumblr: afipiafelis.tumblr.com

CPSIA information can be obtained
at www.ICGtesting.com
Printed in the USA
LVHW100012210522
719350LV00004B/87